PLAYING WITH
FIRE

To Lizzy
Thank you for reading, I hope you enjoy it!
Happy reading!

1/6/19

What Reviewers Say About Lesley Davis's Work

Raging at the Stars

"*Raging at the Stars* is a very entertaining and engaging read. The alien invasion storyline—with a twist—is very original and the plot is very well developed. The two leads are very likeable and the supporting characters are equally interesting. The author's style of writing is very engaging, especially the witty dialogue."
—Melina Bickard, Librarian, Waterloo Library (London)

"A Sci Fi book with a side of romance and a hint of aliens (Or is there really a hint? What else could be going on?). Anyway, it's basically my perfect book, and I thought it was totally awesome."
—Danielle Kimerer, Librarian, Nevins Memorial Public Library (MA)

"I am 800% here for this book. It reminded me of a fun mashup of *X-Files* and *Independence Day*, with lesbians, and honestly, I can't think of anything cooler at this moment. ...I'll definitely track down more of Davis's titles. Definitely recommend."—*Kissing Backwards: Lesbian Book Reviews*

Playing in Shadow

"*Playing in Shadow* is different from my typical romance reading, but at the same time exactly the same. I loved the two main characters and the secondary characters. The issues they all face were realistic and handled really well. ...I do not often read LGBT romance, but thus far every time I have I have been thrilled with how fantastic the writing is. I guess I need to read more!"—Sharon Tyler, Librarian, Cheshire Public Library (CT)

"Overall this was an amazing read, great and engaging story, and as it progresses adding layers to the characters and the complexity of their struggles it starts to consume a little bit of your heart making you wish this was a Saga and not just one story."—*Collector of Book Boyfriends*

"The story is emotional and feels very honest. You won't miss out on the romance either, with equal parts of 'Awe, that's so sweet!' and 'Whoa, Steamy!'"—Katie Larson, Librarian, Tooele City Public Library (Utah)

Starstruck

"Both leads were well developed with believable backgrounds and Mischa was a delight. It was nice to 'run into' Trent and Elton from the author's previous book."—Melina Bickard, Librarian, Waterloo Library (London)

Truth Behind the Mask

"It is rare to find good lesbian science fantasy. It is also rare to have a deaf lesbian heroine. Davis has given readers both in *Truth Behind the Mask*. In her tightly wrapped novel, Davis vividly describes the feeling of the night wind and the heat of the fires. She is just as deft at describing the blossoming love between Pagan and Erith, two of her main characters. *Truth Behind the Mask* has enough intriguing twists and turns to keep the pages flying right to the exciting conclusion."—*Just About Write*

Playing Passion's Game

"*Playing Passion's Game* is a delightful read with lots of twists, turns, and good laughs. Davis has provided a varied and interesting supportive cast. Those who enjoy computer games will recognize some familiar scenes, and those new to the topic get to learn about a whole new world."—*Just About Write*

Pale Wings Protecting

"*Pale Wings Protecting* is a provocative paranormal mystery; it's an otherworldly thriller couched inside a tale of budding romance. The novel contains an absorbing narrative, full of thrilling revelations, that skillfully leads the reader into the uncanny dimensions of the supernatural."—*Lambda Literary*

"[*Pale Wings Protecting*] was just a delicious delight with so many levels of intrigue on the case level and the personal level. Plus, the celestial and diabolical beings were incredibly intriguing. …I was riveted from beginning to end and I certainly will look forward to additional books by Lesley Davis. By all means, give this story a total once-over!"—*Rainbow Book Reviews*

Lammy Finalist *Dark Wings Descending*

"[*Dark Wings Descending*] is an intriguing story that presents a vision of life after death many will find challenging. It also gives the reader some wonderful sex scenes, humor, and a great read!" —*Reviewer RLynne*

Visit us at www.boldstrokesbooks.com

By the Author

Truth Behind the Mask

Playing Passion's Game

Playing in Shadow

Starstruck

Raging at the Stars

Playing with Fire

The Wings Series

Dark Wings Descending

Pale Wings Protecting

White Wings Weeping

PLAYING WITH FIRE

by

Lesley Davis

2019

PLAYING WITH FIRE

ISBN 13: 978-1-63555-433-5

THIS TRADE PAPERBACK ORIGINAL IS PUBLISHED BY
BOLD STROKES BOOKS, INC.
P.O. BOX 249
VALLEY FALLS, NY 12185

FIRST EDITION: JUNE 2019

CREDITS
EDITOR: CINDY CRESAP
PRODUCTION DESIGN: SUSAN RAMUNDO
COVER DESIGN BY SHERI (HINDSIGHTGRAPHICS@GMAIL.COM)

Acknowledgments

Thank you so much, Radclyffe, for creating a publishing house I am so proud to be a part of.

Thanks to Sandy Lowe for letting me pepper you with questions and for the advice you impart.

A million and one thanks to Cindy Cresap for letting me constantly surprise you with new Britishisms in every manuscript you edit for me. You are patience personified, and I appreciate your hard work so very much in helping me bring these stories to life.

Thank you, Sheri, for a cover so vibrant I can almost taste it! You are awesome!!

As always, huge thanks and much love to my friends and readers whose generous support is truly mind blowing and greatly received:

Jane Morrison and Jacky Morrison Hart

Pam Goodwin and Gina Paroline,

Kim Palmer-Bell and Tracy Palmer-Bell

Cheryl Hunter and Anne Hunter

Annie Ellis and Julia Lowndes

Kerry Pfadenhauer (for always cheering me on!)

And to Cindy Pfannenstiel for all your much appreciated help, support, and enthusiasm for my stories. x

Dedication

For Annie Ellis

CHAPTER ONE

It was amazing how much the Columbia landscape had changed since the last time Dante Groves had been back to the place she considered home. New strip malls replaced her old familiar haunts. Apartment buildings were in place of the rest, or they were just completely gone. It was disconcerting how much of what she'd remembered had been erased from the area.

I really have been away far too long.

Nothing ever stayed the same, not even in Missouri. Dante turned off her GPS and let her memory of these roads take her to her chosen destination. Her stomach rumbled so forcefully it made her feel queasy. She checked the time on the dashboard clock. No wonder she was starving. She'd driven way past lunchtime and it was now bordering on dinner. Dante decided that appeasing her hunger was way more important than reminiscing over her lost youth. She had consigned that to the past long ago. At least the road she was on now was all too familiar. The Baydale Mall she was heading toward was looming in the distance. Even that looked larger than she remembered it. There'd obviously been a few structural additions since she'd last been there.

She prepared to switch lanes to head toward the mall, but a brand new building captured her attention. A restaurant lay just ahead with a bright orange awning that definitely hadn't been there before Dante left. Her stomach tightened at the thought of food. She'd had breakfast on the road, a hastily grabbed breakfast burrito from a drive-through, and now she desperately needed something more filling. She also needed to sit somewhere other than in her car. Decision made, Dante pulled off the road and into the parking lot of Takira's and managed to find the last space to park in. It was a relief for her to finally get out of the car and stretch her legs.

"I'm getting too old for cross-country driving," she grumbled, checking then double-checking that she'd locked the car securely as it held all her worldly possessions inside. *I'm forty-seven years old, and everything I own I can pack into the trunk of my car. How sad is that?* Dante smoothed down her shirt and hoped she looked less rumpled than she felt.

Ambient music greeted her, and the air conditioning was a relief after the heat of Missouri's temperatures beating down on her in the old secondhand car she'd picked up. The car's AC was hit or miss at best. Dante liked the fact the restaurant's music wasn't too loud to distract the customers from their conversations. *I sound like my mother.* She smiled as a greeter came straight for her and was soon directing her toward a table.

"Oh my God," someone said as Dante weaved her way through the tables. "*Dante?*"

Dante stopped in her tracks. She knew that voice. She turned around as someone behind her stood up from their seat. "*Trent?*" Dante tilted her head back a little to look up at Trent, grinning like a maniac at her. She welcomed the hug that enveloped her and returned it twice as hard.

"For God's sake, Trent, did you never stop growing?" Dante pulled back and stared at her. "What are you? Seven foot now?"

Trent laughed. "I peaked at six. Anyway, I'm not that tall; you're just economy sized."

Dante laughed at that old familiar retort. She'd last heard it from a much younger Trent Williams. She grasped Trent's arms and looked her over. "You've gotten even more handsome if that was possible. Look at you. You must be breaking hearts statewide."

Trent shook her head. "I gave that up some time ago." She pulled out a chair at her table for Dante to join her. "Man, it's so good to see you. How long has it been?"

"You were just a babe when I moved away." She thought a moment. "I'd just turned thirty-six so...my God, it was eleven years ago." She grimaced. "That time went fast. Feels even longer looking at how you've grown."

Trent got a faraway look in her eye. "I was twenty-three when you left. I still remember us meeting when I was just eighteen and new to the scene." Trent smiled at her across the table. "You were my hero and role model all rolled into one, Dante Groves. I hope you know how much you did for me back then."

Dante shook her head. "You'd have found your way, Trent. You just needed to be away from that damned family of yours to see your own strength and beauty in the world."

Trent picked up a menu. "You eating?"

Dante nodded. "Yes, I'm starving. I've been driving all day. I was heading for the mall but spotted this place first. And look who I find in here." She smiled. "So, how new is this place because I don't remember it ever being here before."

"It was built two years or so ago. We got this restaurant, a sporting goods store, and a comic book store out of it." Trent grinned. "The comic book store is a personal favorite." She beckoned over a server. "Can we order some drinks, please?" She looked back at Dante. "I'm waiting on someone before I order food, but if you want to go ahead don't let me stop you."

"I'll look at the menu in a minute but a light beer would be most welcome. I've still got to drive."

Trent put their drink orders in and then settled back in her chair. "So, what brings you back here? Didn't you move to Texas?"

Dante nodded. How did she even begin to explain what a debacle that had been? She'd thought it would be her happy ever after but instead had turned into her worse nightmare. She was still wondering where to start when her drink appeared before her, along with some appetizers.

Dante broke open one of the small samosas to get a taste of the spicy pea and potato filling crammed inside. She hummed at the burst of heat that tripped over her tongue from the mix of spices. She dipped her next one in the chutney, took a mouthful, and groaned in appreciation. "Wow, that is delicious." She went back for more. After another mouthful, she finally answered Trent's question. "Yeah...Texas. Turned out to be way too hot there for this soul. Also, not the smartest move I ever made."

"Didn't you move away to be with that nurse?"

"Counselor. Chloe was a counselor. Looking after the mental health of her patients tirelessly." Dante made a face. "Looking after them a little too much, to be honest. I caught her cheating on me a few years ago. Found out it wasn't the first time either. So I packed up my things and walked out."

"Fuck, I'm sorry to hear that."

"Yeah, well, it happens. Wish it hadn't happened in my bed with me catching her and another woman mid orgasm, but hey, shit happens." Dante held up her bottle to Trent in a toast. "Here's to my not being stupid enough to ever get burned again." They clinked their bottles together.

"You said a few years ago? What's taken you so long to come back home?"

"I decided to just shake loose and go places I'd never seen before. I'd played the dutiful partner long enough. It got me nowhere but homeless, woman-less, and eventually jobless. So I figured I'd go to all the places I'd always dreamed about but Chloe was too busy at work to have time for." Dante shrugged.

"Where did you go?"

"Universal Studios first, took myself to Disneyland too and rode every ride three or four times without hearing, 'Don't you think you're too old to be doing that?' in that disapproving voice Chloe always had when it was something I enjoyed doing. I bought myself a Mushu dragon there that has been my companion on the long journey that's finally led me back home."

Trent smiled. "I know Mushu very well. *Mulan* is a favorite movie in my house."

Dante took another bite off the plate. "Then where did I go? Oh, Germany, where I attempted to drown my sorrows in their very fine beers. But there's only so many hangovers you can wake up to before that gets old fast." Dante smiled as she remembered what came next. "And then I went to England. I stayed in London for about a year, found a job, and while there witnessed the glory of the Second Coming."

"Really? I think we missed that event over here somehow."

"I was incredibly lucky to score a ticket to see Kate Bush's Before the Dawn concert. It was only the second time in her career she performed a series of concerts, and I got to see her. It was the closest thing to a religious experience I have ever witnessed. I ripped up my bucket list there and then. That was the only thing I'd ever wanted to see, and nothing will ever come close to beating it in my lifetime."

Trent smiled at her. "I remember you'd have her playing in the car when you'd pick me and Elton up to go out with you. Every time I hear her I think of you." Trent eyed her over her bottle. "So, you played hooky and traveled the world, got to see your idol, and now you're back in Columbia. Are you here to stay or are you just passing through off onto your next adventure?"

Dante shook her head. "No, I'm hoping to stay put if I can find work. I've done a variety of managing jobs on my travels both here and abroad, but I'm looking for something more permanent. And I'm in need of a roof over my head. But I need to eat first and then I can sort out the details of what I have to do next." She took a long drink from her beer. "But enough about me and my failed love life, what about you, young Williams? How has life been treating you since I last saw you?"

Trent tapped at the badge fastened to her shirt. "I'm an assistant manager at Gamerz Paradise now."

Dante was proud of her. She remembered Trent starting at the job and how excited she'd been.

"Do they still appreciate your knowledge?"

"They do, and my staff are all gamers too so it's as good as it gets as a dream job for me."

"You still have that lanky long-haired guy by your side?" Elton and Trent were hard to forget, both for their heights and their looks.

"The one you use to call the String Bean Wookie? Yes, we're still BFFs, best friends forever."

"More like partners in crime," Dante said dryly.

"We were young and foolish. I forget you knew me way back when."

"So, my handsome butch, why no breaking young girls' hearts?" A big smile as gentle as she had ever seen broke out on Trent's face.

"Things changed, *I* changed, and life got a million times better." Her eyes lit up and sparkled.

"Mama!"

Dante startled at the high-pitched voice that sounded from behind her. Someone's child was obviously excited. What she didn't expect was to see the smile on Trent's face grow even brighter as she slipped from her seat to crouch beside the table.

"Mama!"

A little blond girl flung herself into Trent's arms. Her arms wrapped tightly around Trent's neck as they exchanged kisses.

"Mama, I missed you!"

"I missed you too, Harley." Trent stood back up and winked over Harley's head at someone.

Dante figured whoever it was must have sent the child after Trent. She didn't turn around to look; she was still reeling from the whole "Mama" business.

"Have you been a good girl for Mommy today?" Trent asked, settling back into her seat with Harley in her arms.

Harley nodded against Trent's neck. "Mommy said no eat worms. They not spaghetti."

Trent laughed and kissed Harley's head. "Good girl. No one wants worm breath." She nudged Harley gently. "Are you going to say hello to my friend Dante? She's going to be so happy to meet you."

Harley turned and smiled in Dante's direction, flashing a mouthful of little white baby teeth. "Hi," she said, burying her face back into Trent's neck shyly.

Dante had to admit this kid was incredibly cute. She had big blue eyes and a mass of blond hair tied up with a brightly colored scrunchie. She was dressed in a Wonder Woman T-shirt and a little pair of denim shorts. Tiny Wonder Woman sneakers adorned her feet. Dante reconsidered; the kid was certifiably adorable with a great taste in heroes.

"Hi, Harley."

Harley shifted to sit on Trent's lap and cuddled back against her to play with Trent's work tie.

"Did I hear right? I mean, I'm edging ever closer to fifty and the hearing isn't what it used to be." Dante still couldn't believe what she was seeing or what she'd heard. She watched as Trent gently rocked Harley back and forth in her arms while Harley swung on her tie.

"Harley, who am I?" Trent asked her.

Harley patted Trent's chest. "Is my mama!"

Dante's jaw dropped.

Things *had* changed.

Dante couldn't take her eyes off Trent with Harley sitting so peacefully in her arms. "Yeah," Trent said. "It was a big change for me too. But I wanted it." She kissed Harley's head tenderly. "I wanted it so bad. Look what I got blessed with, Dante. I have a daughter and she, like her mother, is everything to me. I got a family, Dante, one of my very own."

Dante recognized the disbelief that cast shadows across Trent's eyes for a moment before the sheer joy of being loved replaced it.

"I'm so happy for you," she said. "How old is Harley?"

Harley answered and held up two fingers and one slightly bent. "Two and a half," she answered seriously. "I go to school now."

"It's a mother and toddler meet-and-greet kind of thing," Trent said. "I guess it's to make sure that little kids are comfortable around other kids before they're thrown into a more structured school regimen. Harley's used to kids though because she's got cousins out the ass."

"Mama! Naughty word!" Harley looked aghast.

Trent grinned at her and kissed her head. "You are your mommy's daughter. I'll put a dollar in the jar when we get home."

Suitably mollified, Harley sat back to be cuddled a little more.

An incredibly pretty blonde navigating her way around the tables with a stroller caught Dante's attention. She was gorgeous, and Dante sat up straighter.

"What's just pinged on your radar?" Trent asked. "Or should I say *who*?"

Dante had forgotten Trent had learned all the right butch cues from her.

"A breathtakingly beautiful blonde is heading in this direction," Dante said, not taking her eyes off the woman.

"Is that so?" Trent said.

The blonde headed straight toward their table, and Dante stood up as she drew near.

"Well, aren't you sweet?" The blonde smiled at Dante and leaned down to kiss Trent's smiling lips. "Now why didn't you stand for me?"

"I have a lap full of baby," Trent said, stretching up for another kiss. "Hey, Juliet."

Dante sat back down as Juliet took the seat beside Trent's.

"Mommy!" Harley shouted.

Juliet held out a soft plush toy for Harley's grabby hands. "You left Yoshi in your stroller. He was getting lonely." She handed him over.

Harley kissed his soft fuzzy head and then walked him across the tabletop. "Yoshi wants ice cream," she said.

"Well, he'll have to wait until after you eat your meal and then he can share whatever flavor you pick out tonight," Juliet said.

Harley nodded and began chatting to Yoshi quietly, probably explaining the delay in dessert for little dinosaurs.

"Juliet, this is a very dear friend of mine. Dante, this is Juliet. My *wife*."

Dante tried not to look too stunned over that piece of information. She held out her hand to Juliet. "It's a pleasure to meet you, Juliet." She cast an eye at Trent. "You truly are the luckiest butch on the whole planet. You know that, right?"

Trent looked smug. "I'm well aware of how lucky I am, believe me. Jule, Dante is the one who taught me how to be the suave and sophisticated butch that swept you off your feet."

Juliet gave Trent a smoldering look that made Dante almost groan in frustrated arousal. God, Trent had snagged herself a looker. Lucky bastard.

"The Jedi Master to your Padawan, babe?"

Trent laughed. "Minus the lightsabers sadly, but pretty much yes. She got me out of some fixes when I first began negotiating the gay scene."

Juliet's full attention switched to Dante and all but seared her where she sat. "So you would be the one to know stories of a young Trent that maybe Elton wouldn't be a party to or unlikely to divulge?"

Dante shot Trent a less than innocent look. *Consider this payback for not warning me the gorgeous blonde I was eyeing was yours.* "I just might know a few tales best told out of earshot of your daughter and her mother."

"Is my mama," Harley suddenly piped up, patting Trent's arm. Then she leaned over to pat Juliet. "Is my mommy."

"You're a very lucky little girl," Dante told her. "She's the spitting image of you, Juliet." Dante had a feeling Trent loved that more than anything else.

"In looks, yes," Juliet said. "But she's her mama's child in temperament and likes."

"Mommy, my-pad, my-pad," Harley demanded as she pushed aside the menus on the table to clear space for her tablet. She took it from Juliet with a cheery "Thank you!" and switched it on.

"We had to get her a tablet of her own. She kept beating my Angry Birds scores." Trent's disgruntled face made Dante laugh. "It was demoralizing, and the sticky finger marks were getting harder to clean off. Plus it was prudent to get her one of her own so I didn't keep finding she'd deleted my games by accident."

"Naughty birdies, Mama." Harley pointed at the screen, and both her and Trent's attention fixated on the game for a moment.

"The gaming gene she definitely gets from Trent," Juliet said. She picked up the menu and scanned it. "Same as usual for you, babe?"

Trent nodded. "Yes, please." She looked over at Dante. "Order whatever you want. It's my treat."

"Trent—"

"No, Dante. You were there for me when I needed you as a young adult. I'm so glad to have you back here. Paying for your meal is the least I can do." Trent turned to Juliet. "We need to help her find a job and a place to stay. She's literally rolling in with just her wheels and nothing in place."

"What kind of work are you looking for?" Juliet asked.

"Anything that pays the bills. I helped manage a bar for a month or two in Kansas City to get the money together to come back here. I am a trained manager by profession, and that's come in handy in a lot of places. But I'll literally do anything as long as it pays." She wagged a finger at the managerial badge on Trent's chest. "Something I'm glad Trent didn't follow in my footsteps with. You stuck with it, just like I knew you would."

"I'm very dedicated to my job. It probably helps it's connected to something I'm passionate about."

"Well, when I get a job and someplace to live, then you can hook me up with a new console. Chloe wouldn't let me use mine, and I stupidly gave in to her." Dante shook her head at how gullible she'd been. "She didn't want me in the house 'rotting my brain with games.'" Dante air quoted. "Of course, now I know why she wanted me out of the house."

"When you're ready just come into the store and I'll do you a great deal," Trent said. She looked down at Harley in her lap. "You hungry, Harley Q?"

Harley nodded, her head bent over the pad in her little hands. "And juice please."

Juliet got up. "Darling, you know what I want. I'll go send Zenya over for our order. I can see she's on tonight." She pressed a quick kiss on Trent's temple as she slipped behind her. "I'm going to see if Takira is in." She smiled down at Harley. "Harley, you tell Mama what you want, okay?"

"Cheese," Harley drew out the word with a multitude of eee's.

Trent grinned and looked at Dante. "That's her favorite thing at the moment."

"And strawberries," Harley added.

"Just not on the same plate though, eh, baby?"

Harley laughed, muttered, "Silly Mama," and carried on with her game.

"You're happy, aren't you?" Dante asked. "And you're married. My God, dude, you're *married*!"

Trent held out her hand to show off her ring. A simple gold band sat on her finger. "I found me a keeper, and for reasons I will always thank God for, she wants to keep me too."

"Family life suits you. I've never seen you look so content. I just remember you downing shots and singing bad karaoke with Elton. Then I was having to carry you both home, and you still came back to the bar the next night raring to do it all over again."

"That was just existing. *This*," Trent nodded toward Harley, "this is living. Meeting Jule, us having Harley Quinn, it's everything my life should be."

Dante's lips quirked. "You really called your kid that?"

"It's Juliet's fault. There's a family thing where they use Grandma Sullivan's maiden name as a middle name for all the kids. We just carried that tradition forward, and there was no way in hell I was letting that opportunity pass me by."

"I've missed you, kid," Dante said.

"I missed you too. Wait until you see Elton."

"He still trying to grow that damn fool beard he was so desperate for?"

Trent laughed. "He got better at it. It's more than just peach fuzz now." She drew Harley's attention from her game. "Harley, Zenya's coming. Can you tell her what you want for your dinner, please?"

Harley scrambled up to stand on Trent's lap, balancing herself by gripping onto Trent's shirt collar. "Hi, Zenya, I want cheese!"

Zenya, an attractive dark skinned woman with dreadlocks tied back in a ponytail, laughed as she interacted with Harley. "Of course you do. One special order of mac and cheese for Harley Quinn coming right up." Zenya looked at Trent and Dante next and wrote down their orders.

Trent stopped her before she left. "Put this all on one bill, please. Dante's family and she's not spending a dime tonight no matter how much she asks for the bill, okay?"

Zenya nodded and winked at Dante. "Enjoy your meal."

Dante swallowed at the lump that had risen in her throat. Yes, she'd made the right move. She was back where she belonged. She was *home*.

CHAPTER TWO

Takira's head was lost in the endless stream of receipts and orders that she was scrolling through on her laptop. She berated herself for the millionth time for not realizing that her ex-manager's *little* habit of betting on every football game had grown into a full-blown addiction to gambling. She'd have been more than willing to get Claude any help he had needed. Instead, he had helped himself. Helped himself to thousands of Takira's restaurant takings and dragged her into a debt she didn't discover until it was nearly too late. Claude had been able to steal a huge chunk of money. Had he been less greedy or less in debt to the people he owed the money to, Takira might not have missed smaller amounts siphoning out of her bank account. But Claude had been desperate so he'd taken as much as he could get in one go.

The courts were now trying to recover Takira's losses. Her lawyer was in the process of chasing Claude from state to state as he fled from the promise of prison time for his crime. Also from the promise of having his knee caps shattered courtesy of the loan sharks he'd been supposed to pay off. So instead he had used the money to run.

Finding him was proving to be a challenge, and Takira was resigned to the fact the money was lost and she had to start from scratch to rebuild her safety net for the restaurant.

She lifted her head to stretch her neck a little to rid it of the tension that seemed to live there now. Takira's gaze fell upon the photograph that resided on her desk. It was a rare family shot. Her parents, Simone and Milton Lathan, stood behind Takira and her twin sister Latitia. Takira stared at her sister for a moment.

"I bet you're laughing your head off at my misfortune, aren't you? You never passed up an opportunity to celebrate any failure I suffered."

She couldn't believe how identical they were in looks but miles apart in personality. She knew Latitia had hated looking like her. "You might be happy looking like Viola Davis, but I'd have preferred a skin color like Beyoncé's." Takira ran a hand over her dark skin. She considered the actress a truly gorgeous individual so had taken it as a compliment. Latitia was never satisfied. She could have been the living embodiment of Rihanna, Beyoncé, and Janelle Monae, and she would have still found something to find fault with. Latitia had constantly complained about Takira's mass of natural brown curls that fell past her shoulders like a mane. Latitia had sat for hours in hairdresser chairs having hers cut, straightened, and dyed, anything to change her looks from Takira's. Anything to not be the person she was, to reinvent herself, to fit in with the *right* crowds, to be less *identical*. Takira understood the need to carve out her own sense of identity. But Latitia had inherited all of their mother's worse traits, including putting Takira down at every chance. They might have been twins, but their mother had pitted them against each other from birth. Over time, any bond they might have shared was shattered. Takira was destined to work hard and feel the need to prove herself constantly. Latitia grew up believing the world owed her a favor, and she wanted it paid in full.

Takira was so lost in the past that she barely registered the knock on her office door. She called out for whoever it was to come in, never taking her eyes off the photo. She waited for them to start reeling off something that was happening in the restaurant that only she could possibly deal with. At the silence that greeted her instead, Takira looked up and found Juliet Sullivan-Williams staring back at her, arms folded and foot tapping.

"Did I miss a meeting we had or something?" Takira searched her memory for an appointment that must have slipped her mind with Juliet who now took care of the restaurant's financial side for her. Never mix friendship with business, Takira had learned, but Juliet's financial wizardry had kept Takira's running and afloat once Claude had disappeared along with her money. Takira had never been more grateful to have someone she trusted watching over her business now.

"No, no meeting. But imagine my surprise when I'm informed by your staff that you're still ensconced in your office instead of braving the rush hour traffic with somewhere else you're supposed to be."

Takira checked the time, groaned, and put her head in her hands. "I lost track of the time. I've been sorting out the problem we had with our freshly sourced tomatoes."

"And then, no doubt, something else came up and your attention was diverted again."

Takira nodded. "The timing just couldn't be any worse. One of my servers quit yesterday because her boyfriend is moving out of town and asked her to go with him. And I still need a manager to replace the Claude-shaped hole in my team. But everyone I've interviewed just doesn't seem right to me. This restaurant is my baby. I want to work with people I know will take as much pride in it as I do. But then, I thought Claude was perfect for the job and look how wrong I was there."

"We'll find you someone. But you need a break from being all business, if only for an hour. And wow, isn't it a good thing that I'm eating here tonight with Trent and Harley as our usual Friday treat?" Juliet stared her down before Takira started to argue. "I've ordered you a meal. If I have to I will drag you out of here by your beautifully abundant hair and force you to eat something because I'm betting you haven't eaten all day either."

Takira realized her stomach was feeling decidedly hollow now that she'd stopped working. She smiled at Juliet's no-nonsense face. "Who knew I'd end up with such a wonderful friend from you being regular customers? And such an amazing accountant too."

"Flattery still won't get me to fudge your taxes, honey," Juliet said and gestured for Takira to leave her seat. "Come on. Come see my handsome wife and our gorgeous child and bask in our domesticity before Harley starts eating and we all end up wearing it."

"My staff loves that child." Takira began powering down her laptop. She wouldn't be working anymore today. "I swear they fight over who gets to serve her dessert just to see her smile."

"Harley does love her sweet treats. It's a good thing she's so active otherwise she'd be a little baby butterball. Zenya has our orders tonight, and I've given her yours too." Juliet reached out to catch Takira's arm gently. "How are you doing today? Honestly now, no bullshit, because I can spot that a mile off."

"I'm resigned."

"And procrastinating," Juliet added gently. "You have to go to your mother's eventually today. You know that, right?"

Takira nodded. "I'm just working more on it being later rather than sooner."

"Come with me. You can eat, have a coffee to fortify yourself to face your mother, then you can leave. My offer still stands if you want me to go with you."

Takira shook her head. "No, no, I'll be fine, I promise. I just wish things were different."

Juliet pulled her in for a hug. "I know. I wish things were different for you too. But you know you have Trent and me ready to help you every way we can. You're not alone, Takira. We're here for you. Don't be too proud to ask." She guided Takira out of the office and waited while she locked it up. "I just wish you'd let me find you a good woman, get you all settled down and not doing everything by yourself."

Takira snorted. "I have more than enough on my plate, thank you very much. I don't have time for any woman. She'd come second to the restaurant, and no woman in her right mind would settle for that."

Juliet squeezed her arm in sympathy as they wandered out into the bustling restaurant. Takira put on her bravest face and waved and greeted her regular customers warmly. She was proud of what she had accomplished with her restaurant and how well received it was in the community. She'd worked tirelessly to achieve her goal of being a restaurateur. This was the fruition of years of hard work. This was her life.

Juliet's voice pulled her from her musings.

"You know, I get to see Trent every day, but she still makes my heart skip a beat."

Trent looked up and locked eyes with Juliet. "Look at how she looks at you," Takira said. "How do you ever keep your hands off her?"

"We have a two-and-a-half-year-old," Juliet said. She slipped her arm out of Takira's to retake her seat, leaving the last empty seat for Takira.

Trent smiled at Takira. "Did Juliet drag you kicking and screaming from your office like usual?"

"She did, but it was worth it to see you all." Takira planted a kiss on Trent's cheek.

Harley held her arms out. "'Kira, up, up!"

Takira gathered Harley in her arms and cuddled her close. "Hey, baby. Are you being a good girl for your mommies?"

Harley nodded seriously, her attention distracted by Takira's hair which she started playing with.

"Takira," Trent said, "I'd like you to meet a very dear friend of mine."

Takira turned, embarrassed she hadn't realized there had been a fourth person at the table.

Dante stood and held out her hand. "Dante Groves. You have a beautiful restaurant. I'm looking forward to eating here."

Takira's breath caught in her chest. Dante was like an older version of Trent. A more mature butch, the kind of woman Takira found unashamedly sexy. She had a weakness for androgyny. For her, the butcher, the better. There was just something about a woman comfortable in her body that displayed a more masculine air.

Dante might be as butch as Trent, but she was nowhere near as tall. She was pleased to note that in her heels she was just that bit taller than Dante too. Dante was solid in stature, not slender or curvy, but broad. She was rounder in the face than Trent was; her obvious maturity had softened some of the sterner lines. Dante's gray hair was shaved on the sides with the top left a little longer in an artfully disheveled quiff. The severe cut suited her.

Takira took in Dante's dress. She tried not to swoon over the rolled up sleeves of a black denim shirt that displayed toned arms. There was even a hint of a tattoo. She couldn't quite make out the design from where it peeked out under the precise folds that creased the shirt just so. Dante wore black jeans with a rolled up cuff, and Takira could see a pair of well-worn but shiny black leather boots. Takira realized she'd been silent just that little too long and that she was still holding Dante's firm hand in her own.

"Any friend of Trent's," she said huskily, sitting down as carefully as she could with Harley still in her hold. "I hope you enjoy your meal with us tonight."

Dante sat down too. "I'm sure I will."

"I'm having cheese!" Harley announced to pretty much the whole room.

Takira laughed at her. "That's because you have my head chef wrapped around your baby fingers, and he won't let anyone else make your mac and cheese but him."

Harley giggled and reached back for Trent and her game.

Their food soon arrived, and Takira dug in, trying hard not to critique the taste of her meal seeing as it wasn't something she had made herself. She still liked to make time to cook in her restaurant. That was where she truly belonged.

Trent was managing to eat her meal and help Harley with hers. Juliet leaned over from time to time to wipe food from Harley's face and from off Trent's once-clean white shirt. Takira took a moment to just enjoy the company and the food and let her mind drift to the woman next to her who was eating like she hadn't had a meal in days.

"How are you enjoying the lasagna?" Takira asked, trying not to laugh at Dante having to slow down in order to answer her.

"I am so glad I was driving past this evening. I found the most excellent company, and everything else…" Dante looked up from her plate directly into Takira's eyes, "is beautiful."

Takira smiled and hoped her blush wasn't too noticeable. For a moment she let herself bask in the ambiance of the room and tried to push everything else from her head aside. She existed only in this moment, and nothing was going to change.

She knew she was lying but continued to pacify herself with those thoughts before she had to face reality's harsh truths. Her future plans were about to be taken out of her hands. Not even the welcome distraction of this woman was going to save her.

Another coffee, beer, and juice arrived at the table, and the empty plates were whisked away. Takira smiled at how efficiently her staff performed. She laughed at Harley's excitement when her strawberries arrived, topped with soft ice cream and covered in sprinkles. If only life were that simple. Trent wrangled Harley closer to the table so she could eat her treat. She made it look so easy. Takira looked away and caught Dante looking at her.

"You appear to have the weight of the world on your shoulders."

Takira shook her head trying to summarize her feelings that were making themselves known even to complete strangers. "No, I'm just…it's been a stressful few weeks and I've lost a few staff members, which hasn't helped." She tried to shrug it off. "But that's the nature of business I guess."

Trent wiped some sticky juice off Harley's chin. "Dante's a manager by trade," she said. Takira stared at her. "Just putting it out there. You need a manager. Dante needs a job to help get herself settled back at home here in Columbia. It would kill two birds with one stone." She smiled at Takira's frown. "I can vouch for her. You won't find a harder worker. She managed the bar where we first met and then took on the restaurant next to it when they joined forces. They were devastated when she left. Said they'd never find better, and they didn't. They went out of business within two years after their new manager mishandled the books."

Takira adored Trent but wasn't just going to take her word for it that this Dante was suitable material to take a role in her business. She eyed Dante speculatively. Dante looked as surprised as she was by Trent's recommendation. "I'd have to see your résumé before any decision could be made."

Dante nodded. "I have all my paperwork in my car. I can give you a copy."

"Let me finish my coffee, then you and I will go talk." She looked up at Juliet's pointed cough of disapproval. "I can manage an interview before I have to leave. I know exactly what I'm looking for in a manager. It won't take long."

"Thank you," Dante said sincerely. "I appreciate you even giving me an interview on such short notice."

"It's hard work," Takira warned her. Dante just smiled.

"I never shy away from that."

"Then we'll talk." Takira refused to talk business on the restaurant floor, but she had to admit to being curious about just who this Dante Groves was. She did need a manager though and quickly, thanks to Claude's disappearance. Everything had happened so fast and she'd been so stunned that she hadn't had time to put out any feelers to see if anyone at another restaurant wanted to change locations. If Dante had the right credentials, Takira wasn't going to knock fate bringing Trent's old friend home and delivering her right on her door step.

Fate owed her something good to balance all the bad she'd had to suffer through lately.

Takira's office was a stark contrast to the rest of the restaurant. It had less of the bright oranges and yellows that was the restaurant's theme. The office was a calmer mix of creams and lavender. Dante spotted a small figurine on Takira's desk. It was Olaf from *Frozen*. His presence made her feel more at ease. She couldn't help herself; she grinned.

Takira looked up from reading Dante's résumé.

"What?"

"You have an Olaf on your desk."

Takira looked over at the happy snowman then back at Dante. "He makes me smile," she said.

"It's one of my favorite movies." Dante leaned over the desk a little. "I have a huge collection of Disney movies in the trunk of my car. Those and my portable DVD player have kept me sane in many a motel room."

"You're a Disney fan?" Takira looked surprised.

"From the classics to the new stuff with Pixar. Every time I visit Disneyland it's like the first time all over again. I usually go on my own though because not everyone appreciates the House of Mouse."

"The last time I went was with my sister and my nephew. He was barely three months old, which was way too young to appreciate it, but Latitia had insisted on going. She soon left me pushing the stroller while she took herself on all the rides and then wandered off ahead of me doing her own thing while I tagged behind. It wasn't much of a trip for me, and she still complained she'd had to deal with the baby." Takira frowned.

"Well, if you ever want to go again with someone who will drag you on and off every ride and in and out of every store, then count me in. I would make sure you enjoyed your trip and had a blast. I'm going to live there once the Star Wars theme park is open."

That made Takira laugh. "*Now* there's no doubt you're a friend of Trent's. She and Elton can prattle on about those movies for hours if you let them."

"I can't believe I literally just stepped foot back in Columbia and there she was. Now I know I'm home."

Takira riffled through the papers in her hand. "You worked at the Albion in London. That's a highly renowned restaurant. Even I've heard about it over here. You had a year managing there, correct?"

Dante nodded. "I applied for a work visa to stay there and run it for a while. That was a great place to look after, always very busy. The clients were so friendly and London is an amazing mix of cultures. The whole world passes through there. I got that job through a friend of a friend. It pays to make contacts in this business. You never know where it might take you."

Takira handed Dante back her paperwork. Dante smothered her disappointment and struggled not to let it show.

"You've done a wide and varied selection of jobs and quite some traveling in the past four years. How likely are you to actually stay in a job before the wanderlust has you wanting to roam again?"

"I'm ready to put down roots. I've been gone too long as it is. The traveling was great at the time and fulfilled its purpose, but there was only so long I could afford it, and I eventually got tired of not having my own bed to sleep in at night."

"Where are you staying now?"

Dante looked sheepishly at her. "That's next on my list of things to sort out. I'll probably find a cheap hotel tonight to stay in while I find a place to rent. I'm tired of living out of my suitcase too."

Takira looked thoughtful for a long moment.

"Your credentials are exemplary and your references are full of praise. For that reason, I'm prepared to offer you a probationary period here at Takira's. After which you may decide that you don't want to work here or I might decide you're not suitable for the role I need." She stared Dante down. "I hear the boss is a bit of a ball-breaker."

"Good thing I don't happen to possess a pair then, isn't it?"

Takira's laugh warmed Dante as she felt a weight lift from her shoulders. For now, she had work with the promise of something more permanent if she did a good job. She wasn't going to turn the opportunity down.

"The job also comes with a place to stay if you want it."

"You're kidding."

"There's an apartment above the restaurant where I live. It has an extra bedroom with its own bathroom attached. You'd be sharing the living room space and the small kitchen that's up there with me. But I'm rarely in residence as the restaurant takes up most of my time. Being here would save you worrying for the probationary period and give you more time to look for a place of your own without feeling rushed into settling for the first thing you saw."

Dante let the words sink in as she realized how lucky she was. She'd only been back in Columbia three hours. She couldn't help but wonder what she'd done to deserve the abundance of opportunities being gifted her.

"The room is free, but you'd be expected to contribute to groceries and do your share of the cleaning," Takira said in the silence. "The room's not exactly big, and it's just temporary until we decide if this is going to work out."

"Yes," Dante blurted out. "Yes to it all, please. Thank you!" She hadn't relished the idea of having to live in yet another impersonal hotel room.

Takira smiled. "Something tells me you're not rendered speechless often."

"Hardly ever, but then I'm never given all I could wish for in one go. It's overwhelming. I'm waiting for the other shoe to drop. Things don't usually just fall in my lap this easily."

"Well, you've yet to experience working and living with me. Reserve your judgment until then." Takira's eyes fell to the clock on the wall. "I really need to go. I recommend you go get yourself settled in upstairs. Your room is the one to the left of the living room. I'll have a word with Eric on the way out. He's been temporary manager since Claude...left. He'll be glad for you to take the job off his hands. He can go through the job with you tomorrow…unless you don't work weekends?" Takira cocked an eyebrow at her.

Dante wondered if this was a test. "Just tell me what time he wants me and I'll be there."

Takira nodded as she stood up. "Familiarize yourself with the restaurant. If you want any food everything you eat here is now free."

Dante stood up too. "Free?"

"You'll be working here. The food is excellent, if I do say so myself. You might as well enjoy it."

"Damn, I'm beginning to wish I'd come home sooner."

"But then the job wouldn't have been available and you might not have run into Trent who kindly steered you in my direction."

"Everything for a reason and a time for it all," Dante said.

"Is that one of those Yoda quotes?" Takira asked.

"I can see we're going to have to work on your knowledge of *Star Wars*. It's severely lacking."

Takira looked like she was about to argue when her phone rang. She looked at the screen and grimaced. She cut the call off abruptly. "I have to go." She slipped a key off her key ring and handed it over to Dante.

"Here's the key to the apartment. Make yourself at home, and I'll be back some time later tonight. If there is anything you need, Eric is in charge so just seek him out. I'll warn him who you are on my way out." She stuffed her phone in a pocket and then held out a hand to shake Dante's. "I'll sort all the paperwork out for you tomorrow, and we'll discuss your salary and benefits before you sign. For now, welcome to Takira's. How are you with children?"

Dante's eyebrows raised at the non sequitur. "Okay, I guess? Kids, animals, and oddly enough, little old ladies seem to be drawn to me."

"Good to know," Takira muttered. Her phone rang again and her face fell. She looked unhappy.

"Are you all right?" Dante asked, feeling the need to reach out and touch Takira because she just looked so…lost. She wisely kept her hands to herself. It didn't pay to get touchy-feely with an employer no matter how upset they seemed.

"Family," Takira said bluntly.

Dante nodded. "Enough said. Go." She opened the door for Takira to precede her out of the office.

Takira stayed where she was. "I'd better tell you before you hear it via staff gossip. My last manager left taking a great deal of money that he'd stolen from the restaurant. I trusted him and he let me down..."

"I won't let you down. Just give me the chance to prove it."

Takira hesitated like she still didn't want to leave, and Dante knew she couldn't exactly ask. She was almost in two minds whether to offer to go with her, but Takira nodded at Dante sharply, took a deep breath, tightened her jacket around her, and strode down the hallway like a woman on a mission.

Dante looked at the key in her hand. It had been a long time since she'd been in possession of one. It had mostly been key cards for the last few years. She shot another look after the disappearing figure of Takira and then up at the stairs that led to her new home.

Time to settle in before she did anything else. She headed back out into the parking lot to gather up as many of her belongings as she could carry. She balanced some clothing bags on top of her precious box of DVDs. She wasn't leaving them out in the heat any longer. They had a shelf in their future, and Dante hoped she had as secure a place for herself to rest as well.

She stopped for a moment and took time to look over the restaurant's handsome architecture. She would have hugged herself if her hands weren't so full. Welcome to Takira's indeed.

CHAPTER THREE

Takira didn't hurry walking up the path to her mother's door. Had she not felt so terrible she might have managed to conjure up a smile at her reluctance.

You'd think I was preparing to face a firing squad.

She rang the doorbell and for a brief moment considered just turning tail and running back to her car. She wondered if she had the time to manage it and if her heels would hinder her.

The door opened.

Too late.

"Hi, Mother," Takira said, noting the defeated tone in her voice and hoping her mother didn't pick up on it.

"I thought you were supposed to be coming earlier. I've been waiting for hours on you."

"I'm sorry. I had to interview a new manager. Remember, I told you Claude had left and I need to get someone in to take his place?" Takira wondered how much longer her mother was going to keep her waiting on the doorstep while she explained her tardiness. *God, it's like being a teenager all over again and having Mother yell at me over something so all the neighbors could hear.* "I had someone literally walk through my door today with the right qualifications. I couldn't let the chance of her being perfect for the job pass me by."

"So, now you have someone to take that job off your shoulders? Because you know you're going to have to cut down on your work." Her mother ushered Takira into the house, talking a mile a minute the whole time.

Takira followed behind trying not to let the chastisement send her spiraling back to when she was younger, back when she could do nothing right and her mother took great delight in pointing that out to her. She tuned her mother out by habit and walked into the living room. The TV was on showing the bright and colorful characters from a new cartoon featuring dogs in hats. The reason why Takira was there sat right in front of it, his attention rapt by the story unfolding.

"Hey, Finn," Takira called, and he scrambled to his feet to fling himself at her and wrap himself around her legs.

"Auntie Kira," he squealed, lifting his arms for Takira to pick him up and kiss him.

"Hi, sweetheart. Have you been a good boy for Grandma?" He nodded solemnly, his hand already occupied with the necklace Takira wore. His mother had worn one exactly like it. Takira tried not to think about that too much and let him play. She looked at her mother. "Did you pack everything or do I need to…"

"He's ready. He was ready hours ago." The sharpness of her mother's voice pricked at Takira's skin as it always did. "You just need to put everything in your car. Have you been so busy that you forgot to buy a car seat? He has to have one, but I never got one because you know full well I don't drive at my age now."

Takira nodded. "My friends helped me pick one out. They have a child the same age as Finn."

Her mother huffed. "His name is Phineas. You know Latitia named him after Phineas Newborn Jr. because of your daddy."

Takira steeled herself for the rest of the speech that she knew verbatim. She had to hear it every single time she shortened *Finn's* name.

Her mother continued. "Because he was your daddy's favorite jazz pianist and you know what a good girl Latitia was. She wanted to honor that when her baby was born."

Takira wisely kept her mouth shut and schooled her features not to give away what she was thinking. Latitia hadn't named her child in memory of the musician they'd grown up listening to back when their father would hold them in his arms and dance them around the kitchen. No, Latitia had named her baby boy some ridiculous name that was sure to get him beat up at school by some crazy kid called Denzel or Dwayne. All because Latitia had counted on showing her father what a good and dutiful daughter she was, providing him with a grandchild when his *lesbian* daughter wouldn't. Then she could ask him for anything and he would give her all the money she wanted because no grandchild of his would ever go without.

Finn's own father hadn't stuck around once Latitia had told him she was pregnant. He'd run back to his wife and kids and paid Latitia enough money to keep quiet. But there was no way Latitia would have ever kept her mouth shut once the money ran out. Sadly, their father had died before Finn reached six months old. With him gone, Latitia could only rely on their mother, and she wasn't as easy to con out of money as Father was.

And now your mommy is gone too.

"I hope you didn't just buy the first car seat some other person showed you. It has to be just right for him."

Takira's wandering attention came back to the room to find her mother still prattling on about the car seat.

"Juliet came with me to find the one she has for her daughter. She wouldn't let me buy any old thing. She helped me find the right sized bed for him too. She's been invaluable." *After all, it's not like you gave me much time to prepare, is it? One phone call telling me to come take him off your hands because you just couldn't cope with him.* Takira bit her tongue. Nothing she would say could change anything. She looked at Finn in her arms. He looked so much like Latitia, which meant he resembled Takira too. Takira had been the first born, meaning her sister was designated the baby of the family forever just for being born five minutes after her. *Yet I came in second to her all my life.* She shook those feelings off; she had more important things to do than wallow in self-pity.

"Did Grandma tell you what we're doing today?" she asked Finn. He bobbled his head. Takira had a feeling her mother hadn't prepared Finn for yet another upheaval in his life. She looked at her mother, but she studiously looked away. Takira faked an excited tone. "You're coming to live with me at my home now."

Finn looked at her, then over at his grandma who was pretending to move an ornament on a shelf. "With you?" he asked.

Takira nodded. "Yes, all your toys are coming with us in my car, and we're going on a little trip back to my restaurant where I live and work. You're going to have a new room to sleep in." Takira prepared herself for her next words. She'd never expected to have to say them. "I'm going to look after you now."

"Grandma?"

"She'll still see you, but you and I are going to look after each other. Do you think you'll like that?"

Finn pondered this silently for a moment then nodded. "Go play with you now."

Takira released a shaky breath. Okay, this was really happening. "Shall we go home?"

Finn looked again at his grandma who had been his constant companion for the past two weeks. Takira wondered what was going through his little head as her mother refused to look at him.

"We get ice cream, Kira?"

That's who she was. She was the cool aunt who took him out for an hour and they had ice cream at the park and played on the swings. "Yeah, we can have ice cream before you go to bed." Her mother made a grumbly noise that made Takira want to roll her eyes. "Just this once as a 'welcome to your new home' treat."

Finn was just happy at the mention of ice cream. He let Takira put him back down in front of the TV while she gathered the pitiful array of possessions that had made it to her mother's home with him. She couldn't believe how little he had to show for the time he'd been with her mother. Takira seemed to remember packing way more toys than what were now stowed in the plastic bags in the trunk of her car. She had a feeling her mother had deliberately gotten rid of most of them so that they didn't take up too much room in her own house.

Just like Finn had, apparently.

Her mother had been adamant that she would take Finn in, raise him like she had her two daughters. But she was so much older now and didn't have either the patience or the energy to run around after a child. Finn's father was out of the picture so Takira had to face her nephew going into foster care if she didn't step up and step in.

I'm all he has left and I won't let him down by refusing to raise him.

She leaned back against her car and looked up at the sky, searching it for an answer to whether she was doing the right thing in taking on a child. The restaurant was her baby. It was the most important thing in her life and would always come first. She heard a noise from the direction of the house and found Finn at the door, hopping in his little socked feet, mindful of the fact he wasn't allowed outside without his shoes on.

"You ready to go on an adventure with me, Finn?" Takira clapped her hands at him to make him smile. She was just thankful he was too young to realize what exactly was happening. That his grandma was making her take him off her hands because she can't cope with him. For all her big talk and assurances that she'd already raised two girls so what was another child to raise?

Obviously, one too many.

Takira hated how that sounded and how she felt concerning it. She hadn't had a great deal of choice in it all. Her mother just assumed she'd put everything she had worked for in her life on hold and take care of a child for the next however many years. Takira was angry at her sister for dying while Finn was still so tiny. She was furious at her mother for telling everyone she was going to be the best grandma and raise her grandson right. She'd gotten a great deal of sympathy and attention for that pronouncement at her canasta group. Her mother and Latitia had always shared the same selfish genes. They both talked big, but when it came down to doing something, it usually had fallen to Takira or her father to actually see it through.

Some things never changed.

Takira picked Finn up, and it tore at her heart how he cuddled into her. He was hers now, as close to a son she'd never expected to have. The weight of him in her arms was nothing compared to the crushing responsibility she felt pressing down on her shoulders.

"Let's go, Finn."

"Grandma coming?"

Takira found her mother sitting on her sofa pouring herself a drink. She'd already changed the TV channel over to something she wanted to watch. Takira recognized a dismissal when she saw it.

"No, Finn, it's just going to be you and me now."

For a moment, Dante had hesitated putting the key in the door. After so long living out of a suitcase and just sleeping wherever she found a room with a mattress, this was an awfully big step. A place to stay, a promise of a job to go with it, it all spoke of a permanency she hadn't adhered to in years. And living with someone else? She'd been single, celibate, and relying on her own company for the past four years. Sharing with someone was going to be challenging after so long living a solitary life. She'd gotten used to being alone; there was less chance of being hurt again that way.

The first thing that struck her was how large the upstairs apartment was. It was basically a huge living area with a small kitchen to the right and two hallways down either side leading toward the bedrooms. Dante felt comfortable in it. Takira's choice of furnishings was tasteful yet functional. She hastened to find her room. She stood in the doorway of it and just grinned.

"Perfect," she muttered. It was big for a bedroom, spacious enough she could live in it should she feel anti-social. She scrutinized the layout and decided where a TV could go so she could get back to her gaming. She blamed Trent and Elton for that. They'd pestered her into joining them on a game night on more than one occasion when they had been teenagers, and Dante had caught the gaming bug and gotten one of her own. Consoles had changed, but the thrill of the game hadn't. She was looking forward to buying a new console with her first paycheck.

For now, she busied herself sorting out her DVDs and putting them on a wooden bookcase that seemed placed in the room for entirely that purpose. She'd left the house she'd shared with Chloe pretty much empty-handed. Maybe this time she'd feel more at home. She could stay in this apartment for a while, and if things worked out, find a little place of her own to settle down in.

She placed Mushu on top of the bookcase, turning him this way and that until she had him positioned just right. She could hear Chloe's mocking voice in her head. "You're butch, for God's sake. It's embarrassing having to explain to my friends that the Disney prints on my walls are yours. You're supposed to be able to talk about sports or cars with their husbands. No one wants to talk about your silly cartoons."

My friends, *my* walls. Dante should have known there and then how it was going to be. Chloe had been adamant she favored a minimalistic look. Dante soon came to realize that meant only when it came to *her* stuff being under consideration for a place in a room. The priceless original artwork Dante had was stored in the trunk of her car like everything else she'd retrieved from a storage locker. She reminded herself to ask Takira if she minded her hanging them in her room. She was long overdue getting some pleasure from them.

Dante dropped her suitcase and backpack by the bed and then spread out on the mattress to stare up at the ceiling. "Best day in ages," she said with a smile.

Her thoughts drifted to Takira. She was beautiful. From the riot of curls framing her face to her no-nonsense attitude. Trent's kid obviously liked her too, and weren't kids supposed to be great judges of character? Dante berated herself. There'd be no lingering thoughts about how pretty her new boss was. But it was nice to know she could still find someone attractive enough that they stole her breath away when they smiled.

She'd thought she'd lost that rush to lust thanks to Chloe and her tricks. Getting the hots for her new boss was not the smartest move she could ever make though. Especially seeing as Takira was highly successful, unashamedly beautiful, way too young for an old dog like Dante, and probably hooking up with some young stud who had less gray hair, muscles in all the right places, and way more stamina. Dante had learned her lesson well; she knew better than to risk playing with fire. And that woman would burn her alive in a heartbeat.

Dante closed her eyes and groaned. Takira had the most soulful eyes she had ever seen.

Deciding to just not go there, Dante picked herself up off the bed to go clear out the rest of her car. She had a job to do, and that didn't entail daydreaming about her new boss.

CHAPTER FOUR

Dante managed to fit in a very quick meet and greet with Eric to sort out a time and place for them to get better acquainted. She decided she'd be best to leave him to the organized chaos of the restaurant running in peak business. At least she knew what to expect. She hadn't missed his curious and less than subtle shift of his gaze to stare at her chest. She'd resisted the urge to acknowledge that, yes, she did indeed have breasts and therefore was female despite how she appeared. Her unusual name didn't help to clue people into her gender. But she'd rather be a Dante than a Davina. Anything too overtly feminine just didn't sit well with her at all.

She retired to her room to unpack the rest of her belongings. She was meeting Eric the following morning and needed to press a shirt to look professional and presentable. She tried not to dwell on the double-take he made when she mentioned she was living upstairs now.

Dante sniffed at the plate covered in small coconut cakes that Zenya had handed her with a cheery "Welcome to the madness." One bite and the cake melted in her mouth, leaving her with the taste of coconut and a rich raspberry jelly tang heavy on her tongue. They were heavenly. It was a white cake rolled in raspberry jam and covered in coconut sprinkles. It was exactly like the English madeleines she'd eaten in London. Dante savored them one by one, chilling in her room and enjoying the view. From her bedroom window, she could see beyond the rear of the restaurant and out to where a small forest of trees grew en masse. It was relaxing and made such a welcome change from her usual "room without a view" living accommodations.

A noise coming from the living room distracted her. Dante wandered out expecting to see Takira, only to stop dead in her tracks. There was a small boy puttering around the room. He held onto a toy rabbit that was nearly as big as he was, and his thumb was firmly stuck in his mouth. He stopped the second he caught sight of Dante. His dark brown eyes widened and he stared at her.

Dante wondered if some family from the restaurant below had turned their back for a second and he'd toddled off. They both kept staring at each other. Dante didn't have that much experience with children, and she wasn't sure that if she made a move he would start crying and she didn't want to risk it.

Takira walked in as they were both standing still in the middle of the living room in some kind of strange standoff. Dante couldn't have been more relieved to see her.

"I think he's lost," she whispered.

"No, he's with me. Dante, meet your other roommate. Finn, say hi to Dante. She lives here too."

Finn looked from Takira to Dante and then back to Takira again. Dante looked between Finn and Takira.

"He yours?" Dante could see a strong resemblance to Takira around his eyes.

"He is now. Long story short, he's my sister's kid, but she died three weeks ago. His grandma made a big deal of looking after him but found he cut into her church events and canasta nights, so now he's all mine."

The lack of emotion in Takira's voice surprised Dante. "I'm sorry for your loss."

"Yeah, well, even in death my sister managed to leave me with her responsibilities." She scooped Finn up and held him close.

Takira looked decidedly frazzled. "There was no one else to take him?"

"No. His father has a family of his own and a wife who has no idea Finn exists. He paid out quite a tidy sum of money to make sure it stayed that way. Daddy dearest cut and ran the second the check was signed." Takira rested her chin on Finn's short buzzed hair. "It was just my twin and Mom and me. And now it's just me, I guess."

Dante couldn't miss the nerves that shook in Takira's voice. "You can do this," she said, not knowing whether Takira could or not but feeling the need to encourage her.

"Let's hope I can because it rests on my shoulders whether I like it or not." Takira carried him off toward her room. "I'm informed he takes a bath before bedtime. I'd better get into that routine now."

Finn's little face peered at her from over Takira's shoulder as she left the room. He was very quiet for a little child. Weren't they usually testing the limits of people's eardrums at that age? She didn't think he looked much older than Harley. Harley was way more talkative and wriggly than this Finn appeared to be. He hadn't spoken at all.

Dante wandered back to her own room. She hadn't expected to be sharing with a child. She thought about the look of loss and resignation that colored Takira's face. Dante wasn't going to make this any harder for her. If the job panned out she'd be able to move out anyway and get her own place. It wasn't like Dante was going to have to live with them forever. She sat on the bed and looked at her newly arranged shelves. If nothing else, she and the kid could watch movies together. Might as well start him off in the right direction when it came to superior animation and storytelling.

Dante was up bright and early the next morning. She'd slept well in her new bed and had enjoyed a quiet night just watching a DVD in her new room. Once Takira had put Finn to bed, she'd headed back down to her office armed with a baby monitor set up on a tablet. Dante hadn't expected to spend the evening in Takira's company, but she couldn't recall hearing her come back to the apartment any time before Dante turned her light out and went to sleep.

She walked out into the kitchen and listened for any sound of movement from the rest of the apartment. All was quiet. Her roomies must have already gotten up and were gone. Dante wondered where Takira would be taking Finn while she ran the restaurant. *God, how do single mothers juggle everything all at once?* She spared a thought for Trent and Juliet. At least there were two of them to look after Harley. Dante determined to make the most of her time before she had to meet back up with Eric.

She hurried back to her room and brought out a small speaker. She attached her MP3 to it and was soon listening to the melodious voice of Kate Bush surrounded by birdsong from *A Sky of Honey.* Dante busied herself looking through the cabinets and helped herself to eggs and a pancake mix. She'd be sure to replace it all and made a mental note as to what she was using. Soon she was scrambling eggs and flipping pancakes and swaying to her favorite song, "Sunset." She was quietly singing along when something caught the corner of her eye. Finn was standing watching her. He was still in his Spiderman pajamas.

"Hey, Finn. Did I wake you up? If so, I'm sorry." She noted that her music wasn't loud enough to have blasted through the apartment. She might have lived alone for the past few years, but she was still mindful what was too loud when appreciating quality music.

Finn shook his head and padded over toward the kitchen table. He scrambled to drag himself up onto a chair and then situated himself so he could lean his elbows on the tabletop. He looked up at her expectantly.

"You want some breakfast?" Dante guessed, bowled over by his radiant smile as an answer. She smiled back at him. "Okay, kid. Do you want pancakes? Or maybe some eggs? What do little kids like you eat?"

He didn't say a word but just nodded so Dante took that to mean yes to both. "I get it." Dante turned back to the stove. "You're one of those strong, silent types in the morning. I can totally dig that." She hoped he wasn't allergic to anything. She flipped out a small stack of pancakes onto a plate and set to making some more. Her favorite part in the song came on, and Dante put down the spatula and began to join in along with the flamenco-like clapping that energized the melody...much to the amusement of Finn.

"You have to clap to that piece, Finn. It's the best part. It gets you ready for the day ahead no matter what you face." She slipped a few pancakes onto a plate and put them in front of him along with a small dish of scrambled eggs. She caught him eyeing the syrup bottle that was just out of his reach so she poured some onto his pancakes for him. He still didn't eat so Dante began cutting them up for him into bite-sized pieces and held out the fork for him to take. He grinned at her and began to feed himself with enthusiasm.

"You're easy to cater for, thank goodness." She grabbed up her plate and stacked her own breakfast on it. They ate in silence, he somewhat more messily, but Dante just placed any escaping pieces of pancake back onto his plate where he quickly grabbed them up to eat. Dante cringed at how much syrup was running down his pajamas. "Dude, next time, BYOB, bring your own bib." She wiped at his sticky chin with a piece of paper towel. "What you lack in table manners you make up with in appreciation though." She got up and was thankful to see a small sippy cup left out on the sink. She poured some milk into it and put it beside him. "Here, wash it all down a bit. I swear, if you're allergic to milk or pancake batter I'm going to be out of a job before I even work my first hour."

"He doesn't have any allergies so you're safe."

Dante jumped at Takira's voice coming from her bedroom doorway. She was wearing a silk dressing gown that clung in all the right places, accentuating Takira's generous curves. She looked rested but still had the faint remnant of shadows under her eyes. Dante nudged out a chair with her foot.

"Finn thinks I make a mean pancake judging by how fast he scarfed his down, so please, come join us. I have plenty of pancakes left over and a pot of coffee brewing as we speak."

The groan of appreciation Takira made sent shivers racing along Dante's skin. She couldn't look away as Takira joined them. She took a mug of coffee gratefully from Dante and sighed over the first taste.

"Who's this singing?" Takira nodded toward the speaker still pouring out its music.

"The sweetest voice ever to exist. It's Kate Bush and, just to warn you, my appreciation of music begins and ends with her."

"Biased much?" Takira said over the rim of her mug.

"With good reason," Dante replied with a smile. "No one else has ever come close enough to her in my estimation."

"What, not even Whitney? Beyoncé? Gaga? Pink?"

Dante laughed. "Nope, not even close."

"Wow, that's some serious dedication."

Dante just shrugged. "I know what I like and what makes me *feel*, and her music does all that and more for me. And it's the perfect way to start my morning with her singing." Dante pointed toward Takira's plate. "Eat up before they go cold."

Takira took a mouthful of pancake and hummed her approval. "Finn is right, you do make a mean pancake. Thank you for this. I had no idea what I was going to do to feed him this morning."

Finn was guzzling down the last of his milk. A dribble ran down his chin and soaked through his pajamas. Dante cast Takira a look.

"I'm adept at loading a washing machine too."

"You're going to be a godsend. Do you have much experience with kids? Because, to be honest, I have zip to zero except for auntie duties."

Dante shook her head. "No. I was an only child so only saw babies when my cousins started to breed."

Takira smiled at her blunt choice of words. "I know that feeling. It was a shock when Latitia announced she was pregnant.

I couldn't ever see her putting someone else first." Her laugh held little humor. "And I wasn't wrong there."

Dante spared a glance at Finn who was running his fork around in a puddle of syrup on his plate before switching his attention to his eggs. "Is he always this quiet?"

"He's not a great talker. My mother had no clue what to do about that so mostly ignored it." The *and him* went unsaid but rang loud and clear in the room. "I guess it's up to me to try to get him to speak. He starts at a toddler group on Monday. Juliet takes Harley to it, just a small kind of thing for playtime and interaction, she says. Maybe he'll come more out of his shell there."

"He's got time. He's just learning his way, and this upheaval the past few weeks has got to be upsetting for him. He's been through a lot of changes in such a short space of time." Dante topped up Takira's coffee and poured some more for herself. Dante didn't fail to miss how Takira liked her coffee with just a splash of milk and two sugars. She filed that away for the next time. "You've been through a lot too. You need to remember that."

Takira finished off her plate and picked up her coffee. "Can I possibly bother you for one more thing?"

"Anything."

"Can you watch him while I take a quick shower, then I can get him dressed. He's spending the day in the office with me until I can work out proper childcare arrangements. My mother kind of dropped all this on me at a minute's notice. Trent and Juliet got me his bed, God bless them. I wouldn't have had a clue where to start if not for them."

"You didn't help your sister prepare for his birth?"

"No. I had the restaurant to run, and we didn't exactly always see eye to eye with one another. She thought I was a workaholic with a God complex, and I thought she was a gold digger who tried to catch herself a rich man by getting pregnant by him. We may have shared a womb, but we were nothing like each other. Her death was a tragic accident, and I got thrown into the deep end with Finn once my mother decided she wasn't as prepared as she thought for *her* life to be disrupted." Takira stood and moved to kneel by Finn who was playing with his cup. "But we're going to be okay, aren't we, Finn?"

"Okay," Finn repeated and held out his hand to her. Takira grimaced as her hand touched his.

"Oh, we have to work on your table manners. I can't let you loose in the restaurant with sticky fingers." She kissed his hand anyway. "Please be a good boy for Dante a minute. I'll go shower really fast, and then we'll tackle getting all that syrup off you." She looked up at Dante. "You're meeting Eric at eight and shadowing him when we open for the brunch crowd, yes?"

Dante nodded. She still had an hour and a half to get ready.

"We'll go through your contract when there's a lull in customers." She pressed a kiss to Finn's head and then gathered up her coffee mug and hastened to the bathroom. "I won't be long, I promise."

Finn looked up at Dante and held up a sticky, eggy hand.

"How about I just stick you in the sink and wash you up with the breakfast things?" Dante reached for a cloth and tried to clean Finn off as best she could. "This isn't exactly how I expected to start my first day of work, but you're entertaining, Finn. So thank you for keeping me company."

She had to grin when Finn beamed at her praise...and then knocked his cup over. The last remnants of milk dripped down off the table and puddled on the floor.

Finn sat quietly for a moment and just watched it. "Oh-oh."

Dante sighed. "Good thing I'm the patient sort, isn't it?" She reached for the paper towels. "You're going to be a handful once you're all settled in. I can see it now."

She hoped she would get to see him flourish under Takira's care. She also hoped they both found what they needed out of their being pushed together by an unforgiving fate.

CHAPTER FIVE

The restaurant's kitchen was a carefully choreographed dance between those armed with cooking utensils and the wait staff bustling about with loaded plates. Dante made sure to stay out of everyone's way as they prepped for the brunch customers. She was impressed with how orderly everything ran. Everyone knew their places. Dante just had to learn hers.

Eric called for the staff's attention. "Everyone, this is Dante Groves. *She's* here to take the manager's job off my unworthy hands."

There was a smattering of "thank God" comments and laughter, and more than a few people eyed Dante up and down when Eric emphasized the pronoun. Dante was dressed for business in a dark blue suit teamed with a matching blue shirt and a lighter patterned tie. She knew her style of clothing only served to confuse people even more to her gender. Her voice held a deeper register too. She had long since resigned herself to the fact she'd never look feminine. That just wasn't who she was.

"Good grief, you look like that woman from *Game of Thrones*," a man said, looking around at everyone else for agreement. "Brienne, that's the one. Brienne of Tarth."

A woman chuckled. "Jake, she's about a foot short of being that warrior woman." She gave Dante a considering look. "But she's handsome enough."

Dante tried not to react to the ribbing the woman got for speaking her mind. She wasn't going to argue if anyone wanted to compare her to one of her favorite characters. She was just relieved they'd commented on her looks in a favorable manner. Previous jobs hadn't always been so polite. She'd had one old man call her an ugly bull dyke at one interview. He apparently saw his masculinity under threat by hers. He didn't want "her sort" around his pretty young wife. Dante told herself she should be used to it. She never was though, no matter how thick her skin had grown. Every rude jibe left a barb under her skin to fester and sting.

Dante greeted everyone as Eric called them out. She would make it a point to learn everyone's name as soon as she could. After all, she was going to be managing them and needed to be aware of their individual needs and personalities to keep the business running smoothly.

Takira's staff was a colorful crew. There were people of all races and a healthy mix of genders too. And sexualities, judging by the young Asian woman Eric introduced as Kae. She was a baby butch with numerous tattoos and her Takira's tee sleeves rolled up to the shoulders to show them off. Dante nodded in Kae's direction and got one back. Eric began telling her about the day-to-day management needed to run a restaurant of this size and popularity. They walked and talked while he welcomed the customers coming in for brunch. When there was a lull in the serving and seating, Eric and Dante stepped back, and Eric gave her some of the background of Takira's. While he was talking, Dante felt something brush against her leg. She looked down and found Finn hiding behind her, her pant leg clutched in his hand.

"Hey, Finn. What are you doing in here? I thought you were helping Auntie Takira today?"

Finn wouldn't let go of her and hid his head farther in the back of her leg. "Okay, little man, I guess you just wanted to learn how to help run your auntie's restaurant so let's get you started." Dante managed to detach him and lifted him up easily. "Everyone, this is Finn. He's a new guy here like me, but I can already tell he's going to be a hard worker." She hitched him higher in her arms. "Finn, say hi to everyone."

He stared at her and hid his head in her neck. "First thing we need to work on are his interpersonal skills. Excuse me for just a moment, please." Dante stepped out of the kitchen to stand on the sidelines while everyone did their jobs. She felt Finn's body lose some of its rigidity. *Not used to being the center of a lot of attention are you, Finn?*

Eric gave her a look. "Takira's got her work cut out for her running this place and looking after him now."

Dante didn't comment. It wasn't her place to gossip about whether or not her new boss could cope having her nephew foisted on her. She just smiled at Finn who was playing with her tie. "We're going to see how much I can help to take some of that workload off her shoulders. Family comes first, or so I'm told by people who had decent ones." She looked up to see Eric sporting a small smile. "What?"

"You're going to fit in here just fine." He tickled Finn's arm, but Finn didn't look very impressed by the friendly overture. He moved his arm away and leaned more into Dante. "He seems to have taken a liking to you."

"I only met him last night and then only briefly before he was put to bed."

Finn patted her cheek and said, "Pancakes."

Eric looked surprised that Finn had spoken.

"That's right, I made you pancakes for breakfast and you ate every bite."

Finn smacked his lips. "Yummy."

"Thank you, Finn." Dante looked over his head and saw a frantic Takira running into the restaurant. She called over to her. "Takira, he's here." She shifted Finn in her arms so that Takira could see him.

Takira hurried over. "I swear I just turned my back for one second and he was gone."

"He didn't go far," Dante said, handing Finn over to her.

Takira looked shaken having Finn escape on her watch. She hugged him close.

Dante pulled her gently aside, away from the prying eyes of the staff. "Takira, kids do this. They are mini masters of escape. But he's safe. He was in the restaurant with us."

"Actually," Eric interjected, "he came straight to you."

"Well, I'm no baby expert, but he'll always be safe with me. I can promise you that." Dante held up her hand, and Finn grinned and high-fived her. "Awesome, little man, now quit terrifying your aunt and stay where she can see you, okay?"

Finn nodded. "Okay." He flung his arms around Takira's neck and squeezed her.

Takira sighed. "It's impossible trying to work and keep an eye on him at the same time."

"You'll get into a routine together, a rhythm. It's going to get easier."

"He's been with me one day and I've already lost him."

"He was in the restaurant. That's not lost that's just… displaced."

Takira stared at Dante for a moment then smiled reluctantly. "Really? That's what you're going with to calm me down?"

"He didn't run off and join the circus. He was just in here with me. He knows me. I make yummy pancakes."

Finn nodded against Takira's neck. "Yummy."

"You've got this, Takira. You run a successful business, and from what Eric has been telling me you did that all on your own. That's no small accomplishment. Bringing up a baby? That's going to be no problem for a woman like you." Dante caught Takira's unsure gaze. "Cut yourself some slack. You've only just started the job. You've still got your training wheels on. He's safe, he's okay. He was exploring his new home because that's what this is now. He's bound to be curious."

"God, what am I taking on?" Takira said. "Running a business and keeping it afloat is so much easier. At least with the right manager." Her eyes held a gentle humor that Dante was grateful to see.

"It's nearly time to set up for lunch. How about grabbing a quick bite for yourself?" Dante asked.

"I don't really have time," Takira said.

"Finn needs feeding. If you're not hungry, that's no problem, but he's a growing boy. He needs regular meal times and snacks."

"How do you know all this?"

"I had a dog once." Dante grinned at the startled look Takira gave her. "I'm joking. A couple of the places I managed had children, and you get to recognize the routines the parents had to abide by."

Takira caught Finn's attention away from where he was curling some of her hair through his fingers. "Are you hungry, Finn? Is that why you wandered off?"

He nodded. "Hungry now."

Takira gave Dante a chagrined look. Dante just shrugged at her. "You'll start picking up the cues and signals he gives for what he needs. And once he gets his talking going you'll wish he'd shut up telling you what he wants."

"I should have asked him if he wanted anything."

"You'll get into that routine too."

"Guess I'd better feed him, then I can get back to my work."

Dante could see Eric standing back a little, watching them both with interest. "Eric, what's on the menu today for growing little boys and their overworked aunts?"

"For the discerning youngsters among us, we have the finest selection of finger foods starting with sweet potato fries, our own homemade fish sticks, a small salad on the side, and a choice of ketchup. This can be followed by fruit and a small serving of ice cream."

Finn's eyes lit up at the mention of dessert. "You've got to eat all your fries first before you get to the ice cream," Dante told him, giving him an exaggerated frown. He stared at her then laughed. The sound coming from him astonished Dante. Judging by the surprise on Takira's face, it did her too.

Yeah, you're going to be just fine. Dante followed Takira to a table set up with a child seat. She watched Finn settle in and Takira move her chair closer to be by his side. *Your aunt's going to be just fine too.*

"What would you like, Takira?"

"You don't have to wait on me, Dante. You're here for the managerial position, not serving."

"I tend to work all the positions so as to manage them correctly. I'm not the kind of manager who sits back and directs from the sidelines. I'm very hands-on."

Takira looked impressed. "Then I'll take one of Zenya's salads. She always surprises me with what she prepares."

"Let's get those orders in." Dante took a step away then paused. "Finn?" He looked up at her. "No more running away, okay?" His nod was so somber and penitent Dante had to bite her cheek to stop herself from laughing at him.

Eric was waiting for her in the kitchen. "I'm so glad you're here. No one has ever gotten the boss to take a break before. She needs your kind of stability and calm right now."

Zenya passed over a colorful salad that made Dante's mouth water. Zenya started putting together another. "I figure you could eat something too, right, Boss-In-Training?" Zenya gave Dante a wink.

Dante thanked her. "Eric, please join us. I think Takira could do with all our support for a while."

Eric grabbed Finn's meal and snagged a burger for himself. Zenya pushed a large bowl of fries and some extra fish sticks in Dante's direction. They traipsed back to the table where Finn was occupied playing with the straw in his juice. Dante was pleased to see Takira looked like she was finally breathing easier and was a little more relaxed. Dante's chest tightened at the small smile Takira directed at her.

Dante tried not to get caught staring at just how captivating Takira was. Even when visibly out of her depth worrying about her nephew, she was still beautiful. Dante tried to shove such thoughts to the back of her mind, locked and bolted behind a huge sign that said "Keep out, fraternization is frowned upon in the work place." Takira Lathan was just too appealing though. Dante's gaze fell to Takira's lips. She couldn't help but wonder how they would taste.

"Dante?"

She jumped at the sound of Eric's voice. "Sorry, I was miles away." She started eating her food to cover up her mind wandering in places it had no right to tread. "What did you ask me?"

"I was asking if you still have family here in Columbia."

Dante shook her head. "Not that I'd know of." She caught Takira's look. "I was estranged from my family very early on."

"I'm sorry," Takira said.

Dante just shrugged. "It happens sometimes."

The family Dante dreamed she could have with Chloe one day died when she'd caught her fucking one of her patients in their bed. She just couldn't seem to make relationships stick. She wondered if someone was trying to tell her something where family and she were concerned.

Maybe I'm just meant to always be on the outside, looking in.

Chapter Six

After Dante finished meeting the staff, she had her meeting with Takira to get everything between them signed off and official. She then sat at a computer for hours to familiarize herself with the technical side of running the restaurant. Now she was tired and hungry and surprised at how late it was. Eric had been meticulous in showing her every spreadsheet and client list that she would need. She'd seen enough for today. She took her reading glasses off and slipped them into the breast pocket of her shirt. Carefully, she undid her cufflinks and rolled her shirtsleeves up above her elbows. That was her signal that the day was over and she could relax. Dante looked up as the door to the office opened just wide enough for Finn to squeeze through.

"Finn, I told you to wait..."

Dante could hear the exasperation in Takira's voice, but it wasn't as strained as it had been.

Finn bounded over to the desk and stood waiting for Dante to acknowledge him. It tore a giant hole in Dante's heart at how he waited silently instead of barreling forward demanding to be seen and heard like any other child would.

"Hello, Finn. How can I help you?"

"Come eat, please." Finn reached out for her hand to try to pull her out from behind the desk. Dante went willingly enough. She was surprised that he kept a firm grip on her much larger hand in his own very tiny one. She swung their hands a little. Takira was waiting at the door for them.

"He was supposed to knock first before entering," she said, and Finn looked up guiltily at Dante.

"You'll knock next time, won't you, Finn?"

"Yes. Come now, Auntie Kira cook."

Dante followed along dutifully as Takira ushered them through the restaurant and into the kitchen. She made straight for one of the preparation areas and began to hold out various vegetables for Finn to peruse. He wrinkled his nose at a particular one, and Takira began explaining to him how delicious it was going to be cooked a certain way.

Dante became enraptured watching Takira in what was undoubtedly her element. This was a woman not meant to be stuck behind a computer dealing with deliveries. Takira's heart belonged in the kitchen, and she put on a show for Finn to teach him how much fun it was to cook. Finn tugged on Dante's hand signaling he wanted her to pick him up so he could get a better view.

"First, the gathering of the ingredients." Takira swept around the kitchen picking out every condiment she needed and utensil she would use. "Then the preparation." She reached into her pocket and pulled out a hair band to tie her hair back.

Dante's gaze fell to the soft curve of Takira's neck now visible without her long hair falling around it. She surprised herself imagining kissing just above the pulse point, feeling the beat of Takira's heart beneath her lips. Of nibbling along that fine neck line, dragging her tongue up and under Takira's ear to whisper what she intended to do to her next.

"Dante?"

Dante jerked so violently Finn stared at her in surprise. Takira laughed at her.

"Where was your mind? You were miles away."

Dante couldn't help but wish things were different for them. If she wasn't reliant on Takira for her job, she'd be tempted to ask her out in a heartbeat. But she probably wasn't the kind of woman

Takira would want by her side. Dante was no longer sure she was the kind of woman anyone would want. Break-up baggage still weighed heavily on her back. She dismissed the traitorous thoughts that lead her in a direction she wasn't even sure she wanted to venture. Takira was all business and Dante had already had one woman put her business and pleasure before her. She needed to keep this strictly professional. Dante was nowhere near the league Takira was a part of.

"I was just...watching you. You seem very at home here."

"It's my favorite place in the whole world." Takira chopped up the vegetables and set some rice to cook. Every move she made was measured and exact and totally natural. She was a dancer and this was her stage. She commanded it.

Dante breathed in deep the delicious aroma that began to lift from the giant pan Takira was mixing everything in. Takira didn't work from a recipe; every measurement she apparently knew by heart and added with a flourish. Takira dripped a splash of alcohol over the pan's lip to catch on the gas flame. A burst of flame ignited in the pan to sauté the vegetables. Finn squealed a little then leaned forward even more to watch the food being prepared.

"It's nice to have an appreciative audience," Takira said, bowing playfully at Finn.

"Do you always cook for your managers-in-training?" Dante asked.

"Only the ones who can corral my nephew with more baby wrangling skills than I possess. You've been working hard all day, Dante. Don't think it's gone unnoticed. I may not hover over my staff, but I see all."

"Well, from what I've been seeing and hearing today, this restaurant is a credit to you."

"Having my own restaurant was my dream ever since I was a little girl. My grandmother taught me how to cook. I'd spend hours in her kitchen by her side, watching everything she did and made. My sister couldn't stand to be around her. She wasn't interested in what she was giving us. Latitia held Grandma's money and jewelry of higher value than the time we spent with her. Grandma was sharing her life with us, her experiences. And now," Takira stirred the pan again and gave it a little flick that tossed the veggies inside, "I'm telling her story in every meal I prepare and adding my own to the pot."

Takira laid out some rice on each plate then layered the vegetables on top. The contrast of colors from the brown of the rice to the vibrant vegetables leapt out from the white plates. Takira whipped up a sauce that she drizzled over the food. She stepped back and looked at both Dante and Finn. Finn just stared at her blankly so Takira let out a playful, "Ta-da!" which made him giggle and clap his hands. "Let's go eat," Takira said, gathering all three plates and carrying them to a free table.

When everyone was settled, Dante took a mouthful of her food and couldn't suppress the moan that was borderline pornographic in her appreciation.

"Oh my God," she said, taking another mouthful and sitting back in her seat to just enjoy the explosion of tastes on her tongue. "What you can do with basic foods is downright criminal. I promise that I will do everything in my power to make sure you have all the time you need in that kitchen to work your magic. This is amazing."

Finn was less expressive but was putting as much rice as he could into his mouth and chewing with great enthusiasm.

"You enjoying that, Finn?" Dante asked. He nodded and spooned in more.

"Can I ask you something, Dante?"

Dante looked up from her plate. "Ask away."

"Why are you so kind to Finn?" Takira made a face at how silly that probably sounded, but she obviously felt the need to ask.

"You mean, am I being nice to the kid because he's your nephew and I might gain something work-wise if I pretend to get along with him?" She saw something flash across Takira's face that told Dante her flippant comment had been pretty close to the mark. "I'm not that kind of person, Takira."

She looked over at Finn who was concentrating on chasing a piece of rice around his plate. "Where this little guy is concerned, he's a sweetheart. Sure, he's quiet and kind of shy, and that's okay. He's just a baby and no one in their right mind should be mean to a little kid."

She took a drink from her water glass, weighing her next words. "He's learning something new every day. I don't ever want him to feel he's in the way." Dante looked over at Takira. "I may be speaking way out of line here, but I recognize the 'be seen and not heard' signs. I had them drummed into me as a child. Forgive me if I'm wrong, but I lived with a mental health counselor for years and learned to recognize certain patterns and behaviors from things she talked about. At his age, he should be demanding stuff. He doesn't. He waits for acknowledgment. That's unusual for such a little kid."

Takira wouldn't meet Dante's gaze. "I can't say because I wasn't in his life day after day. I saw him maybe once a month, twice if I could get away from the restaurant. That wasn't very often, to be honest. Latitia and I led very separate lives. We weren't a very close family. We were twins with wildly contrasting views on the world and our places in it. There was very little love between us. I do know she would palm Finn off onto anyone who would take him off her hands. My mother helped her when he was first born, but the bigger he got the less she was bothered. Latitia got a lot of her selfish ways from her, so poor Finn probably didn't receive the undivided attention he should have gotten from an attentive mother or doting grandmother." She puffed out a breath. "And now he's stuck with me, the workaholic aunt who never expected to be tied down by a child in her lifetime."

"But you already include him. He's got a play space in your office. You've just had him watch you cook. You both end up with a bubble bath at bedtime."

Takira laughed. "I was hoping you hadn't spotted that last night."

"You came out of the bathroom with bubbles all down your front and in your hair. It was kind of hard to miss. What I'm saying is, you're already including him in your world. I know it's hard because it's not what you signed up for, but you're doing it. As for me, I'd like to think that my showing him I am listening, one day he'll pass that forward onto others he meets. A child who is dismissive of others or too timid to interact isn't going to find a kind world to grow up in."

"So you're not only a manager in business but you're going to help me manage my life too?" Takira said.

"I'll help any way I can. Just warn me if I overstep."

"Well, he and I have that mother and toddler group with Juliet, and she's fixing me up with her sister who has said she'll babysit."

"Juliet has a sister?"

"Kayleigh. She's a teenager, and once school is out she's going to be Finn's best buddy for the summer. Apparently, I am helping contribute to her college fund with the money she'll be making, but I'm happy to do it for the peace of mind that he's looked after while I can get back to my work. This restaurant won't run itself and it's my responsibility."

"True, but don't forget you have people like me and your staff to lean on when it gets sticky, and you need to take time off because Finn needs you more."

"I'm not used to putting something else before the restaurant."

"Not even yourself, I'll bet."

Takira narrowed her eyes at Dante. "It's barely been a day and you already think you know me?"

"I recognize the type. Hard working, high achiever, mistress of all you do. You've just got to add full-time auntie to your list."

Takira's gaze shifted to Finn who had cleared his plate while also managing to cover a lot of the tablecloth surrounding him.

"He's going to be a handful," Takira said.

"When he's older, get him working in the kitchen. Make him think it's playtime. If nothing else, when he's big enough, he can clean the tables."

"He's just two and a half years old. It might be a while before I can put him on the payroll."

Dante shook her head. "I'm going to manage this place soon. I'll just sneak his name on the schedule, set him up a piggy bank for his wages, and have him bring me those little coconut cakes that I tried last night. Zenya gave me some when I was saying hi to Eric. They were to die for."

"I make those," Takira said. "Am I going to have to worry about my staff slipping you nothing but sweet treats to keep you going during the day?"

"No, I aim on having a proper lunch served every day with my boss and her cute nephew because I need to make sure both eat properly."

"You're here to manage the restaurant. I don't remember managing *me* being part of the contract."

"It's a new clause. I added it in myself. Got to keep the place running to its maximum efficiency. You eating regularly is part of that. Finn eating and keeping us entertained with his table etiquette is another."

"My mother would be furious at the mess he makes."

"Your mother isn't the one looking after him. *You* are. And he's still small. He'll work out the rice to spoon ratio one day. He has time. We all have to learn."

Takira stared at her then gaped. "Oh my God, I can totally hear Trent in your voice. She has this strange calming vibe she puts out that makes you believe she can fix anything and everything. You have it too."

Dante just gave her a little smile. "It's totally a butch thing. Only a few of us ever truly master it."

"Well, you two have it in spades." She gave Dante a sassy look. "Both the vibe and the butch thing."

"Well, speaking for myself, it's something I've never been able to hide, especially looking the way I do."

"I think you look gorgeous," Takira said and then blushed. "God, that was totally inappropriate. I apologize."

Dante's heart sped up a beat, both at the unexpected compliment and at Takira's utterly mortified reaction to letting it slip from her lips. "Please don't take it back. It's rare for me to get compliments, so thank you."

Takira took a while getting her composure back and her heated cheeks under control. She took a healthy swig from her water glass. "You can't tell me you don't have women fawning all over you. Look at you, you're…"

"The living embodiment of an old-fashioned butch that would be more at home in the nineteen sixties than today? I'm aware I out-butch most of the wannabes I see nowadays with their tattooed arm sleeves and their trousers hanging down, exposing their asses." She winced at the slip but was grateful to notice that Finn wasn't paying attention to their conversation. He was too busy watching Zenya waiting on the tables and taking orders.

"There's room for handsome women like you and Trent on the wide and varied spectrum that's the gay community. I've known Trent a while now. I know she is as beautiful inside as she is on the outside, and Juliet is so in love with her it's almost painful to see. I also know Trent still gets the side looks and name calls. Especially as she's married to Juliet who is very femme and could easily pass for straight. Trent usually has Harley in her arms so people can be even crueler when they can't see past her masculine features to see the mama who loves that child with all her heart."

Dante's chest grew painfully tight at the thought of Trent still having to put up with people's ignorance and bigotry, even when she was with her family and being the happiest Dante had ever seen her.

"My parents stopped talking to me years ago. They died without us ever getting the chance to reconcile," Dante said. "I was the daughter they had prayed for, the apple of my father's eye. But when I started to look exactly like him, they couldn't cope with it. I was their daughter, the product of their love they told me, yet because I followed in my father's looks and not my mother's they felt betrayed. When they realized I might be gay as well, I ended up ostracized in my own home. I left as soon as I could and worked in any job I could get to make sure I only had myself to rely on ever again. Years later, when I was an adult and more hardened to the stares I got from people, I met Trent. She was another young butch taking on her power. Just finding her feet in a world that will always judge her for her looks. Because she's not feminine, because she can easily be mistaken for a man. Because she loved women. I'd walked that path alone long enough. I made damned sure she knew what to expect and how to rise above it."

"You were her mentor."

"And a friend. Something we all need when we don't fit in with what is deemed *normal*."

Takira ran a hand over her own cheek. "Oh, you're preaching to the choir here."

"I'm sure. So, you need to arm this little guy with all he needs to go out into the world so he doesn't get trodden down by it."

"Is it wrong of me to admit I hate my sister for dying and leaving all this on me?"

"It's understandable. You couldn't prepare for this. But you have friends willing to help you, a staff ready to support you. And a new manager ready to keep Finn's sticky hands off your clean blouses and him otherwise occupied when you're tearing your hair out over him."

Takira brushed a hand through her hair and released it from its band. "Good thing I have a lot of hair," she said, fluffing it back out into its natural shape.

"You'll probably have less by the time he hits his teens." Dante laughed as Takira dramatically put her head in her hands. "If I'm still here managing by the time he's a teen I might be a little too old to help him blow off steam on a basketball court or on a football field. You might have to trade me in for a younger model to keep up with him by then."

"You're not old," Takira said.

"I bet I have a few years on you. I'm forty-seven and you're what, barely thirty?"

Takira smiled. "I'm thirty-five."

Dante counted their difference in years. "Well, by the time Finn here is a teenager I'll probably be needing *him* to feed *me*!"

Takira laughed at her. "I never saw you as someone prone to exaggerate, but listen to you, playing the age card."

"I can see it now. I'll be old and grayer and consigned to the kitchen. I'll be the one left sitting on a high stool, eating nothing but those little coconut cakes."

"Will I be paying you for sitting around all day eating cake?"

"I hope so because it will be the best job I ever had."

Takira ran her hand over Finn's hair and drew his attention back to the table. "I'm glad you're here, Dante."

"And I'm glad you're willing to give me a chance. I won't let you down."

"No, I don't believe you will."

Takira sat in her office, head resting on her hand as she scrolled through the endless pages on a baby site Juliet had recommended. Her eyes were hurting from having the desk lamp on and from the brightness of the screen. She had a list that Juliet had written for her, all the things that Finn needed that were considered essential. Takira checked the list again. He was missing a lot of the things her mother had supposedly gathered from Latitia's house while Takira had been speaking with the police about the accident.

She tried not to scoff out loud. *Accident.* Her mother could tell her friends that it had been a terrible freak accident that had taken Latitia's life, but Takira had seen the reports. The driver and his passengers had all been intoxicated. One of the women had received a raise, and a group of them had gone out to celebrate her success and party until dawn. Four of them had staggered out of a bar and gone to a club until four a.m. They'd piled into a car and started to drive to someone's house where their drinking would continue. Four had left the bar. Only one survived the journey home. He was only alive because of the machines keeping him breathing. The police had told Takira it was only a matter of time before he died too.

The fact her sister had been drunk didn't surprise Takira. She loved to party. Their mother always excused it as her being "free-spirited." Takira called it irresponsible because Latitia still kept her crazy lifestyle going when she had Finn at home in the care of yet another babysitter.

To make matters worse, the car they'd been in had nearly wiped out another vehicle before it ran off the road and smashed down an embankment. Latitia had gone through the windshield. Takira had seen the photos. There was something eerie about seeing what looked like her own face battered and bloodied hanging over the hood of the wrecked car. She'd had nightmares about it for a week.

Takira had spoken to her mother earlier that day. She'd called to ask if she wanted to see Finn over the weekend, but her mother had somewhere else to be. Takira didn't push, and her mother wasn't about to change her plans to see her grandson, so all that was left was their usual stilted conversation until one of them made an excuse to end the call. Takira was very aware her mother hadn't once asked if Finn was settling in with her.

She rubbed at her eyes and clicked off her laptop. She'd go through the list again tomorrow. She stood and stretched. Her gaze shifted to the scene on the baby monitor she now carried everywhere with her. When Finn was napping or asleep at night, Takira had a camera on him. That way she could get back in the kitchen to cook or sit in her office until she'd finished her paperwork and not have to worry he'd gotten out of bed and was looking for her. It had a motion detector too so it only had to beep and Takira could go back to him and soothe him. Or Dante could.

Dante.

Takira smiled at the thought of her. There was nothing Dante wouldn't try her hand at, and she had such an easygoing manner that was great for hospitality. But she also brooked no arguments so if they ever had trouble in the restaurant, Takira had no worries that Dante wouldn't be able to sort it. She knew Dante had done bouncer work in some places. She still looked to be in great shape to step in should the need arise. Takira hoped that part of her résumé would never have to be tested.

The fact that Dante had stepped up and helped Takira with Finn straight away was something else she admired. And she seemed really attuned to Finn's needs. Takira wondered if Dante was right about him. *He waited.* Once Dante pointed it out to her, she couldn't *un-see* it. But she'd never spent much time with children, not even Finn, and didn't have a clue what was normal or not for a child to do, to express, or not to express.

If Latitia was alive…Takira wondered what she'd do or say to her after seeing how repressed Finn was. He could just be shy, or slower to learn, or he could be the result of what Dante suspected. *Neglect.* Just the thought of it made Takira livid. Latitia had deliberately brought him into the world and then not looked after him.

And I never saw it. I was too busy working to pay attention to my nephew while he was just a baby and needed my help.

She stood with her hands in her hair and heard those words echo in her mind. *He needed me…like he needs me now.* She lowered her hands and touched the screen on the monitor at the little lump curled up in his big boy bed.

"I let you down before, Finn. But I promise I'll try so hard to do right by you now. But you'll have to be patient with me because the only baby in my life has been this restaurant and it's so hard to take on another child. And I hate to say it out loud, but there's a part of me that resents you having to be here." She trembled with the myriad of emotions running through her. "God, I'm a terrible aunt."

She turned everything off in her office and made her way back upstairs. Dante was nowhere to be seen. Takira wondered what she was doing in her room, if she was making plans with anyone now that she was back on familiar turf. She admitted to herself she wanted to know more about Dante. She was sharing her home with her. It would be nice to get to know her better, find what made her tick. There was something about Dante that just made Takira stop and look. She knew that Dante was older than the women she usually dated…Takira stopped herself right there. *Dating? I have two other lesbians in my restaurant, and not once did my head go to wanting to date them.*

But Dante was different. She was the epitome of butch, and there was just something about her that inexplicably drew Takira to her like a moth to a flickering flame.

"Okay, I really need to go get some sleep if I am considering trying to date a woman I've only just met who is on probation for a job here. I must be crazy. This is what I get for not dating in months. The first handsome butch that crosses my path and I get ready to throw my heart at her? I'm not like that. "

Yet Dante is like no one I have ever met before. She calls *to* me.

She reached into her fridge, pulled out a bottle of wine, and grabbed a half-eaten bag of M&M's off the counter. She picked up her biggest glass and filled it. She put the bottle away before she was tempted to fill it up even more.

"Two people come into my life on the exact same day and I have no idea what to do with either of them. No wonder I'd rather stay in the kitchen. Life is so much easier when you have a recipe to follow."

CHAPTER SEVEN

Dante had never been one to subscribe to Sunday being a day of rest. Today was her first day taking over for Eric. Dante rolled out of bed bright and early, showered, then dressed in a loose T-shirt and a worn old pair of sweat pants. She picked up her MP3 player and its speaker and padded barefoot through the apartment. She stepped out onto the balcony that ran the length of the rear of the restaurant, mindful to close the door behind her so as not to disturb anyone else. Dante set up her music and took a deep breath as the soothing sound of pipes and strings played her go-to starter in her practice of tai chi.

Dante lifted her face to the sky and began her warm-up with a sun salutation. She ran through a series of stretches then, as the music changed, she began her regular routine. The slow, measured pace of each deliberate movement grounded her. It calmed her racing mind for the day ahead. She moved her body through the forms, sweeping, stepping, and molding the air in her hands. Dante welcomed the sun's light touching her skin, heralding the start of a new day. She could hear movement below as the morning staff prepared the kitchen. Dante tuned it out, concentrating only on the sound of the strings and pipes as the music guided her through the patterns that gave her peace.

She heard the sound of the door behind her opening but paid it no heed. She continued with her exercises until they reached their conclusion. Then she felt a tug on her pants leg.

"Whatcha doin'?"

"Good morning, Finn. I am waking up my mind and body." She looked down at him. "Do you want to try?" She got a thrill at seeing the big smile that broke out on his face. She turned to face him so he could see her better. She dropped her hands by her side and settled her stance. "Okay, follow what I do. First we say good morning to the sun."

Finn squinted as he looked into the sky. He waved a hand at the sun shining above them and shouted, "Hi!"

Dante laughed at him. "That's very good, but how about we try doing it in a way where you'll be less likely to burn your retinas out?" She carefully showed him some easy movements. He copied her well. "Good boy, you did that perfectly. You ready for some more, then we'll go make you some breakfast?"

He nodded eagerly. Dante guided him through it all and was pleased how well he picked it up. When she figured he'd had enough, she bowed to him. "You are on your way to becoming a master, young Finn. Next time you join me out here I'll try to remember to wear my Batman pj's too so we can match." She turned off her music and gathered everything. "Now, what do you want for breakfast seeing as you've said hello to the day so well?"

"Pancakes!"

"I'm sensing a theme here. Pancakes it is." She ushered him back into the living room and switched the music on her MP3. Finn clapped as he recognized the voice that came out from the speakers.

"I'm not sure Ms. Bush wrote this song to accompany the making of pancakes, but it's one of my favorites of hers and what better way to start your morning than with your favorite song?"

"Pretty," Finn said, giving his approval.

"Well, it's safe to say she's the only woman who's never let me down," Dante said, letting the music flow over her as she whipped up the batter. "Finn, how many pancakes do you want?"

He held his arms out as wide as he could. "This many!"

Dante pretended to be shocked. "How about we start with two and see how many you can keep down after that?"

He nodded and scrambled into his chair. "Ready!"

Dante served Finn his and flipped the top of the syrup open for him to try to pour for himself. She took it back from him before he drowned the whole plate in syrup.

"Note to self, old enough to appreciate Kate Bush, not old enough to know when to stop pouring," Dante muttered, moving the bottle well out of Finn's reach.

"Yes, that's something I learned the hard way too, only with Mr. Bubble." Takira wandered into the kitchen and planted a kiss on Finn's head. She laughed at his sticky face. "I need to start taking photos of you like this to use as blackmail material for when you start dating."

Dante held out a plate laden for Takira.

"You do know you don't have to make breakfast for us both, don't you? That's not why I hired you."

Dante shrugged. "I'm up early and Finn doesn't seem to mind how I make them. As long as you give me a heads-up when you get tired of them and would rather eat cereal, then I'm more than happy to usurp your status as head chef in the apartment." She slid Takira a sly look and smiled when Takira playfully narrowed her eyes back at her.

"Don't even think you're going to stage a coup to try to get my restaurant away from me to turn it into an IHOP."

"I wouldn't dream of it. Who'd make the coconut cakes I love so much?"

"You're in charge today."

Dante nodded.

"Nervous?"

"Yes. I'd be a fool not to be. But I know my job and take pride in the fact I do it well. I'm worried about letting you down more than anything. This restaurant is more than just a place you work in; it's *yours*, heart and soul."

"Well, if you promise not to growl at the customers or seat them at the wrong tables today, then I might be feeling generous enough to show you how I make those coconut cakes you enjoy so much."

Dante rubbed her hands together. "Challenge accepted."

"Finn will be with me again today. Hopefully, he won't end up with you in the dining area this time."

"It's no problem if he does. Sooner or later he'll have to learn his boundaries here. You might want to start that sooner given his habit of toddling off." Dante began eating her own breakfast. "That way the staff can get used to his presence too. I'd rather they learn to work around him than him being consigned to just one area of the whole place. That wouldn't be good for him, and he needs to be a part of this restaurant." Dante looked up at Takira. "Because maybe one day he'll take it on and tell *his* stories in the food *he* serves."

Takira stared at her, then looked over at Finn who was cramming a much too large piece of pancake into his mouth with glee.

"I never considered that."

"He may not be your son, but he's a part of you. Your legacy here could pass down to him, if that's the road he wants to take."

Takira let out a breath. "I need to change my will and everything, don't I? There's so much paperwork to mess with when someone dies. I'm still having to take care of Latitia's estate because my mother couldn't cope dealing with the lawyers. Now I realize I need to change some of my own papers. He's mine now. I'm just waiting on the papers to finalize that. Good thing I have a lawyer who can get things moving when he needs to."

Takira's gaze softened as she watched Finn. Dante could see she loved Finn immensely, even if the task of doing so was daunting.

"I never got as far as thinking that maybe he could follow in *my* footsteps."

"Either that or he opens a pancake joint right next door in competition." Dante laughed as Takira glared at her. She held her hands up in surrender. "I take it back. He's going to learn from the master and become as big a success as his aunt." She caught Finn's attention. "Hey, Finn? What do you want to be when you grow up?"

Finn licked at the syrup plastered on his lips. "A train!"

Dante and Takira shared a look between them.

"I think it's safe to say your business is still in your hands for a while longer."

CHAPTER EIGHT

The Baydale Babies mother and toddler play area was teeming with children all with one volume—loud, and set to squealing. Takira's jaw hurt from fighting back a grimace at just how loud a group of toddlers could be.

Beside her, Juliet laughed at her discomfort. "Believe me, you get used to the noise. You'll learn how to differentiate the 'I'm happy and expressing it' screams from the 'I've fallen and think I'm dying' ones."

Takira glanced around the playground where the "baby wranglers," as Juliet called them, were keeping the youngsters corralled. To Takira it looked as easy a job as herding cats.

"I can't believe you actually chose to have a child and subject yourself to this madness."

Juliet bumped her shoulder into Takira's and directed her attention to where Harley was playing. "Just look at her. She's the best thing I have ever done, that and falling for Trent."

"I get it. She's cute and all, and watching Trent melt around her is sweet to see, but all of this," Takira gestured around her, "this was never on any of my to-do lists." She knew the responsibility of Finn's welfare rested on her shoulders, but it didn't fit well there at all. "I know I'm going to have to get used to this, but I was never cut out to be mommy material."

"He doesn't need you to be his mommy. For now he needs you to be the aunt you've always been."

Takira watched as Harley broke out into a spirited run for no reason. Then she stopped, turned around, and realized Finn wasn't with her. She ran back to his side, took his hand, and tugged him along. "Your baby daughter handles him better than I can."

"I told you they'd get on."

"She thinks he's a character from *Star Wars.*"

"He shares a name with one of the heroes from the latest trilogy. Of course she thinks he's super cool. She just hasn't worked out why he's her size yet."

"She'll be disappointed when she finds out he doesn't have one of those light sword things."

Juliet grinned. "She already has a lightsaber of her own at home. Uncle Elton bought it for her so they could duel."

"Why am I not surprised?"

"It was all fun and games until Harley channeled her inner Sith Lord and sabered Elton right in the baby maker. He fell to the ground quicker than Obi-Wan did in his death scene."

Takira laughed. "What did Trent say?"

"Something along the lines of he should be thankful it hadn't been a real one seeing as Vader had cut Luke's hand off with his." Juliet's gaze never wandered far from the children as they played. "You've got this, Takira, and you have all of us to help you too."

"That's exactly what Dante said, and she's known me for less time than you have." Takira shook her head. "I never expected that when you all came into my restaurant that I'd gain such a colorful array of people in my life. Even now, with the advent of Dante just walking through my door."

"The gamers, the goths." Juliet paused deliberately. "*Bryce.*"

"Yes, she is oddly *normal* to everyone else. I just love how she looks at Scarlet though when Scarlet is decked out in all her finery and those crazy high heels."

"Like she won the girlfriend lottery," Juliet said. "I've seen that same lovestruck look on Scarlet's face too so it evens out."

"Scarlet's photography really helped me with my marketing." She conceded a nod to Juliet's smug look. "I know, I know. You told me so. You do realize you could be making a fortune if you had your own big business going instead of helping others run theirs?"

"I probably could, but I'd rather spend time with Harley as she grows and with Trent when work allows. I've got my part in the landscaping business with Monica and my bookkeeping. That's more than enough to keep me busy."

"The mural Scarlet painted in the restaurant was money well spent too. I can't believe it's only been two years since I got the place up and running. It feels like I've been working there forever. I moved in and Harley was just a tiny babe in arms. Mostly Trent's arms."

"That's because she can control her better when she's out in public." Juliet nodded over to where Harley was showing Finn how to do something and patting him on the back when he did it. "Look at her. She's got Trent's people skills. She'll be running this group before long."

Takira could see Finn following Harley's lead, his little face too serious for his age. "He's so damn quiet."

"He's been through a lot. He'll start getting more confident once he's settled. And he'll be with Harley. She'll help him see he can be a happy little boy now."

"God, it's so much for me to have to live up to." Takira felt the pressure weigh down on her once more. She smiled weakly at Juliet's reassuring hand on her arm.

Juliet's head lifted. She looked around and smiled. Takira knew *that* look. She turned to see who Juliet was beaming at. She didn't need to say anything. Harley's loud squeal broke through the excited chatter of all the other children.

"*Mama!*"

Trent wandered into the play area not far from where Takira and Juliet were standing. She didn't get a chance to see them before she sank to her knees to catch Harley as she ran and flung herself into Trent's arms.

"Mama! You here!"

"I told you I would be." Trent kissed Harley's smiling face. "Are you having fun?"

Harley nodded enthusiastically. "I gots a new friend." She shifted onto Trent's lap and pointed at Finn who had followed at a more leisurely pace.

"Who's this then?"

"Is Finn, Mama, like Rey's Finn. But he doesn't have BB-8 yet and he's little like me."

Trent managed to keep a straight face. "Hi, Finn."

Finn stared at her, then looked at Harley, then back at Trent again. Takira could see his little mind working overtime.

"Harley's daddy?" he asked.

Takira cringed.

Harley shook her head at him. "Is my mama, not a daddy," she told him.

Finn stayed silent and just stared at Trent a little more. "Not a daddy?"

"I know I look like a daddy, but I'm a mama. I'm Harley's mama."

Finn digested this and then looked over at Juliet. "Harley's mommy there."

Trent caught Juliet's eye and winked at her. "Yes. Harley has two mommies," Trent explained. "A mommy *and* a mama."

Finn's quiet contemplation of this made Takira nervous. Her sister hadn't been the most welcoming to Takira's coming out when she'd been a teenager. She'd made a comment about being thankful she hadn't been the twin with the queer gene. Takira hoped Latitia's barely disguised bigotry hadn't rubbed off on Finn. Takira had never had a girlfriend around him for him to see her in a partnership like the one Trent and Juliet shared. How Trent looked, though, had to give Finn something else to consider. Takira wondered if he'd start to realize that Dante was the same too.

"Not a daddy," Finn said finally.

"Is my mama," Harley said and beckoned him over. "Mama, Finn fell down." She motioned for him to roll his pant leg up which he did dutifully without a word. A large Star Wars Band-Aid was stuck haphazardly across his knee.

"Did you give Finn one of your special Band-Aids, baby?" Trent asked.

Harley nodded. "He only bleeded a little, but it's an owie and Finn feels all better now."

Trent squeezed her. "Good girl. You always look after your friends."

Finn edged closer to Harley, bringing him nearer to Trent. Tentatively, he got closer still and leaned ever so slightly against Trent's leg.

"I swear that wife of yours is a child magnet," Takira muttered loud enough for Juliet to hear.

"Finn's my friend now. He come feed the ducks with us?" Harley laid a hand on Finn's shoulder, and they both looked at Trent expectantly.

Trent looked over at Takira and Juliet and gave them a hopeful look. "How about we ask Finn's auntie if they can join us?"

"And he can have ice cream," Harley stated.

"Have you asked him if he likes ice cream?" Trent asked. Finn was already nodding his head firmly.

"See, he likes ice cream, Mama. It's okay."

"Then I think once you're all played out here and it's time to go we'll all go feed the ducks and get a treat." Trent gently put Harley back down. "Go finish playing, Harley. You too, Finn. You've got five minutes left so make the most of them." Trent shooed them off and got up to join Takira and Juliet. Trent gave Juliet a swift kiss and she smiled at Takira. "Hey, you two. Takira, he's gorgeous."

"He looks just like his mother which must mean he looks like me too. It's both comforting and upsetting all at the same time."

"Well, Harley isn't going to let him be lonely. He's going to have to find his voice soon though because Harley will talk enough for the both of them if he's not careful."

"She's surrounded by adults unless we visit with Elton's family," Juliet said. "She's used to being with bigger kids. It will help her to have someone her own age to hang out with."

"How did Finn get hurt?" Trent asked.

Juliet answered. "He got caught in a mass toddler pile and a smaller boy knocked him over by accident. He wasn't really hurt, but Harley got her Band-Aids out because he'd been startled and looked like he was about to cry. He didn't though because *your* daughter fussed over him and made him feel better. Especially after she'd turned to the kid who'd bumped into Finn and told him to 'play fair'!"

Trent had the grace to look chagrined.

"Oh, there has to be a story behind that," Takira said.

"That's what Trent always tells Elton off with when they are playing online and he's haranguing his cousin to put him off his game. Since she was a baby, Harley has sat in her mama's lap watching her play and has obviously picked up on that particular phrase."

"We're going to be in so much trouble the bigger she gets," Trent said.

"I'm her mother and probably biased, but I think she's going to be awesome." Juliet's eyes softened as she shared a loving look with Trent. "Just like her mama."

"Who's not a daddy," Trent added. "Takira, can you face another hour or so to take the terrible twosome for a quick visit to the park next door and to the ice cream truck?"

Takira was fretting about the time she'd already lost from the restaurant, but she nodded. "I can. I warned Dante they'd probably have to do the brunch crowd without me today."

"So how's Dante working out for you?" Trent stuffed her hands in her pockets and rocked on her heels, looking immensely proud of herself.

"She's doing better than I expected for someone who just walked in off the street and wowed me with her stellar references. And had you to sing her praises as well."

"Fate is a curious thing, Takira. You never know what it's going to bring to your door when you need something so bad."

A bell rang and the children either ran to their mothers or were complaining about having to leave the sandpit. Harley tore across the grass with a wicked gleam in her eye.

"Incoming!" Juliet said as Harley jumped. Trent caught her effortlessly and swung her around. Harley settled herself on Trent's hip, talking a mile a minute.

Finn ambled up to stop by Takira's side. He looked up at Trent.

Takira remembered what Dante had said about Finn always waiting for acknowledgement before he did anything. She was at a loss what to do for him.

"Hey, Finn, do you want a ride too? I've got room for another one up here with Harley." Trent held her arm out.

"Up, Finn! Up!" Harley called, looking down at him.

Finn stepped forward slowly then held his arms up. Trent picked him up and settled him on her hip.

"Okay, kids, your mission, should you choose to accept it, is to feed the ducks and to make sure they don't peck at Mommy like they tried to do the last time."

Finn looked over Trent's shoulder at Juliet.

"I held onto the bag of seed too long," Juliet explained. "They took that as a sign I was holding out on them. I don't know which was worse, my backing up nervously under the onslaught of a multitude of duck beaks or the fact I had to be rescued by Harley who ran through them, arms swinging, yelling at the top of her lungs with her newly acquired warrior cry."

Takira laughed at Juliet's embarrassment. She was watching Finn who had made himself at home in Trent's hold. His head was bobbing back and forth between listening to whatever Harley was babbling about and looking down at how far from the ground he was. He leaned into Trent and she instinctively kissed him on his head like she usually did with Harley. He didn't shy away but instead leaned in closer.

Takira's sigh caught Juliet's attention. "What's wrong?"

"Your Trent is a natural with children. How does she make it look so easy?"

Juliet shrugged. "Damned if I know. She's a baby whisperer."

"Dante's really good with him too. She talks to him as if she's known him since birth. And he follows her around like a little duckling."

"Something tells me Dante is made of the same unflappable stuff Trent is. I think those three are ready to skip school and get out of here. Stop thinking about how much you're missing work and instead think of the quality time you're going to have watching the children, including the big one I married, play."

"I heard that," Trent called without turning around.

Takira let Juliet lead the way as they left the play group and headed toward the park. It seemed so natural and easy and... Takira's thoughts ground to a halt. This wasn't her dream though. She wanted a chain of restaurants, to build up a brand and make a name for herself. It came before everything, before family, before lovers, before herself.

"I'm going to have to devise a new schedule with him included," she said.

"That's a good idea. A routine that works for you both. Kayleigh will help you with all that as soon as school is finished. I wouldn't say the offer of food from your restaurant swayed her decision, but I think it helped. She's fantastic with Harley so Finn will be no problem."

"You've got such a supportive family. My sister was a pain in my ass from the moment we stepped out of the womb."

"I didn't spend as much time as I should with Kayleigh when she was growing up, but she's becoming a wonderful young woman. I love being with her now."

"And it's obvious she worships Trent."

Juliet grinned. "Who doesn't? She's a total babe. Besides, she and Kayleigh are two peas from the same pod. It's all about the games when those two get together."

Takira envied Juliet her life. She was successful in her chosen career, head over heels in love, and had the family she'd dreamed of. Takira had no idea what she needed to do now. Her sister's death had derailed all her carefully laid out plans.

"When will the feeling go away that I'm just babysitting him and that someone will be coming to take him back?" she asked quietly.

Juliet wrapped an arm around Takira's shoulders and pulled her in close. "When you've had more time together. Things like this can't be rushed, Takira. It's not all going to sort itself out in a few days and your life will go back to what it was. He's yours now and he needs you. But remember, you built your own restaurant from scratch. There isn't anything you can't do once you put your heart in it."

"Thank you for being here for me." Takira leaned in and rested her head against Juliet's.

Juliet pressed a kiss to her temple. "That's what friends are for."

❖

Dante had dressed to impress. She didn't subscribe to dressing casual for work and she was firmly of the belief a manager should look professional at all times. She'd pressed a pale blue shirt and teamed it with a dark blue vest. A chain hung across the vest's front attached to a pocket watch left to her by her grandfather which now sat snuggly in her pocket. She had a dark pair of chinos on and a comfortable pair of black Doc Martens that she'd polished to perfection.

She opened the front doors for her first time to let in the diners. Some of them stared at her with critical eyes, others just walked right by, and some greeted her and congratulated her on her new job on spotting her name tag. Dante was courteous to all. She found tables for them, called on the waiting staff, and then went behind the bar to help sort out teas and coffees. This was the part she enjoyed the most, mixing with the diners and getting conversation flowing and food served.

Dante checked the time on her watch. She wondered how Takira was getting on with Finn's first day at the toddler group and if Finn and Harley had hit it off. She knew getting invested in their lives was foolhardy, but she cared about them. She couldn't explain why, but from the second she'd met Takira she'd felt something tangible. It was a feeling she couldn't explain and one she berated herself for because, for all she found Takira fascinating, Dante wouldn't do anything to jeopardize her working relationship with her. And that meant no matter how much she'd like to get to know Takira on a more personal level, it couldn't happen. Dante's last partner had always put her job first, and Dante didn't want that kind of relationship again. Keeping it strictly business was the key. And her own crippling anxiety about being with someone again only increased the need to keep it friendly, nothing more.

She spent the rest of the morning dealing with customers, talking with the staff, and trying not to keep checking the time when she knew the toddler group was over and Takira still wasn't back. Dante was getting anxious until, finally, Takira came through the doors with Finn sprawled out fast asleep in her arms.

"Who knew a mother and toddler group could be so exhausting?" Takira spoke quietly above a softly snoring Finn. "Harley wore him out. He barely lasted past his ice cream in the park before he was sitting in my lap and drooling on my shirt."

"This little dude parties hard. Did he at least cut loose a little?"

"Trent and Harley were making him laugh. It was wonderful to hear. And Harley was full of questions for him that he couldn't just answer with a nod or shake of his head so I actually got to hear him say more than a few words. I think going out with other children is going to help him tremendously."

"Excellent. Are you going to let him nap while you take your place in the kitchen? I'm told you're cooking something special today."

"I'll go get him settled, grab the baby monitor, and then come and get back to work. After all, it's my name over the door. I need to keep it that way." She took a step but then turned back, her eyes lingering over Dante's attire. "God, you look good. I wish Eric had taken lessons from you in how to look professional. I got tired of telling him that however hot it was, sandals were *not* proper foot attire in the kitchen. One slip of a carving knife and he'd have been minus a few toes."

"He wears shoes now."

"Yes, there was an incident with a can of tomatoes. To this day I can't work out if Zenya did it deliberately or not. Eric had a bruised foot for ages and learned the hard way to listen to his boss."

"I'll be sure to remember that too." Dante felt like her heart skipped a beat at the smile Takira gave her before carrying Finn upstairs. Dante rushed ahead of her, opening the door to the apartment so Takira didn't have to juggle for her keys.

"Are you sure what I'm wearing isn't *too* much?"

Takira looked her over with a small smile. "I love how you dress, Dante. It's professional and very you. Don't ever think you can't be yourself here. I hired *you*."

"I've had comments before about not exactly helping myself with how I look." Chloe had led that charge after a few years of them being together. Dante was at a loss as to when it suddenly became abhorrent.

"People come here for the food. If they have a problem with you being yourself, me being black, my servers being out and proud, or the fact my head chef is a drag queen on his nights off and sometimes can be heard belting out show tunes from the kitchen, then they can take their business elsewhere. I think you look fantastic. Don't change just to fit in, Dante. You are a perfect fit here already."

Dante smoothed a hand down her vest, adjusting its fit. She felt more at ease and confident than she had in ages. She couldn't change who or what she was. It was nice to be told she didn't have to.

"Before you head back to the restaurant, we've been invited to a 'welcome home' party Trent and her friends are holding in honor of your return."

"They don't have to do anything special for me."

"Well, there's a barbecue being set up and, take it from me, I have eaten from it before and it's to die for. I have considered everything short of sleeping with Zoe's dad to get him to part with the recipe for his barbecue sauce. I'm joking, but the food is really amazing so it's worth going for that alone. I think they're going to combine it with a baby shower thing for Monica so the spotlight won't all be on you."

"Thank God for small mercies," Dante muttered.

Takira settled Finn on his bed and removed his shoes without disturbing him. She turned on the baby cam and pulled the door ajar. "Okay, he's set. I just need the monitor now and I'm good to go." She carried it across the room to Dante. "So, seeing as you are sorting the scheduling out now, I need you to make sure both of us are free and clear for your party on Saturday evening."

"Isn't that an abuse of my power?" Dante asked.

"If anyone questions it tell them the boss agreed to it because I am not missing out on trying to work out what that man puts in his hot sauce. I'm so close to cracking his recipe."

"It will be nice to see Trent again, and Elton, I hope."

"He'll be there. Those two are very close."

"They always were." Dante held out a hand for the tablet. "I'm due for a break soon. Let me keep an eye on the monitor while you get to work in the kitchen. Someone ate all the coconut cakes last night. I think you should be aware of this discrepancy and, as the new manager of this establishment, I'd recommend you rectify it."

Takira laughed at her. "Now *that's* definitely an abuse of your power."

"Which part? The requesting of coconut cakes to be made or the fact I'm the one who ate the last of them?"

"I've never had my coconut cakes praised so highly."

"Well, I've heard rumors that you also make a mean blackberry cheesecake that melts on your tongue."

"Have you been talking to Zenya again? Don't think I don't see you two colluding every chance you get."

"I love blackberries, and I love cheesecake. Almost as much as I love coconut cakes. As your new manager—"

Takira clasped her hand over Dante's mouth. "I'm going to cordon off the dessert area in the kitchen so you can't set foot in it without alarm bells ringing."

Dante grinned at her when she finally moved her hand away. "I have access to *all* areas, *and* I get to order the inventory. I'm seeing blackberries arriving in your future, Ms. Lathan. Mark my words."

Dante was still grinning at the sound of Takira's laughter as she headed to the restaurant with Dante trailing behind. She could still feel the touch of Takira's hand where it had touched her lips. She tried not to dwell on it and forced herself to go back to work and do the job she was here for. Not to lose herself in the delicate fragrance of apples she could detect in Takira's shampoo or the softness of her skin that her lips were so close to being able to kiss.

Do your job, Dante, she berated herself. That's what she was being paid to do. Not fantasizing for the first time in years about a woman she could never have.

CHAPTER NINE

The first week of Dante's new job sped past. Before she knew it, it was Saturday. Dante couldn't help but feel trepidation at the thought of the party she was going to. She hadn't had a party in her honor since she'd been a child. Chloe had never been one for making a fuss on birthdays so this party thrown by Trent was making her unusually nervous and strangely tense. Surrounded by unfamiliar faces at work was one thing, socializing with old friends who had grown and changed was something else. She felt old and out of place. You couldn't always go back. Things changed, people changed. *I've changed.*

"You really need to stop looking like you're facing a firing squad instead of going to a party," Takira said, walking into the living room while fixing her earrings.

Takira looked amazing. The summer dress she wore was a deep rich red decorated with tiny flecks of white. It fell just above her knees. She'd chosen a pair of white strappy sandals to complement it.

Takira held her arms out and spun around at Dante's attention. "What do you think? Do you think it's dark enough to hide any of the many spills Finn is likely to make on me?"

"I think it's perfect, and we'll make sure Finn is surrounded by napkins so you stay that way." Dante tugged at her sleeve. She'd already rolled it up twice, but it just wouldn't lay right and her nerves weren't helping her get it any straighter.

Takira brushed Dante's hand away. She smoothed the shirt down and then folded it back just so.

"There, now it matches the other one. I've never seen you so nervous."

"It's just I haven't hung out with them in so long. Trent's all grown up with a family. And the last time I saw Elton he was a gangly guy with way too long hair. Will I even recognize him now?"

"You'll have no trouble at all, believe me." Takira's hands rested on Dante's arm. "I have to ask. You have a tattoo hidden even when you roll up your sleeves. My curiosity is killing me. May I?" She lifted the cuff up just a fraction, waiting for Dante's permission. Dante nodded and Takira uncovered the small colored tattoo. A perfect rendition of Mickey Mouse, circa 1970s, rode high on her bicep. His face was rounder than his earlier incarnations, and he was wearing his recognizable red shorts, big yellow shoes, and a wide, cheery smile. "That's awfully cute," Takira said, desperately trying to suppress a smile. "He looks almost real."

"Disney has been my favorite thing since I was a child, but I'd advise you never get drunk in Germany and wander into a tattoo parlor talking about Disneyland. I remember going in, don't remember quite how I got out, but know I somehow got back to my hotel room with a friend and when we woke up the next morning we both had tattoos. I got the better end of the deal. At least I got something I like and in a place where I can hide it. She ended up with a humanized hot dog in a bun. Remember the commercials for hot dogs that used to run at the drive-in? One just like that. Neither of us could remember what the hell she'd been talking about to end up with it, but I have a horrible feeling she'd been describing her boyfriend in great detail and so the tattooist got a little creative."

Takira ran her fingertip across the tattoo. Dante swallowed hard at the gentle touch and the sparks of electricity it left in its wake.

"Was hers as easy to hide?"

"It was on her ankle of all places. Beer had a lot to answer for that night."

"You ever think of adding to it?"

"No. The only reason why I got through this one being done was because I was three sheets to the wind and never felt a thing."

"Do I need to keep an eye on you tonight in case you suddenly want a matching pair?"

"No, I just stick to light beer now. I'm older, wiser, and not as self-destructive as I was a couple of years back."

"You have a Mickey Mouse tattoo." Takira grinned at her. "It makes me see you in a whole new light."

Dante huffed at her and pulled her shirtsleeve down to cover it up. "Do *you* have any tattoos?"

Takira looked horrified. "Hell no. My mother would have killed me. I got the silent frosty glare of disapproval for a month when I dared to get my ears pierced. Of course, once Latitia got hers done it suddenly didn't matter anymore."

Takira called for Finn and he came running out of his room in little shorts and a Mickey Mouse T-shirt. Takira coughed to hide her laughter. "I swear I didn't do it on purpose. He picked out what he was wearing today, not me."

Dante smiled down at an excited Finn. "Are you ready to see Harley?"

He nodded and reached for Takira's hand. She looked startled for a moment but quickly hid it. She held out her car keys to Dante once they were out of the apartment.

"We'll take my car because it's already fitted with Finn's child seat. If you can get him strapped in I just need to go get some things to take with us. I can't show up to this shindig empty-handed. My reputation would be in tatters."

Dante took a hold of Finn and walked with him to the parking area. Dante made sure Finn was secure in his seat and waited for Takira to join them. She came out the back door carrying a large box. Dante opened the trunk so Takira could set it inside. She lifted the lid of the box just enough so Dante could peer inside. Four smaller boxes were stacked inside, all labeled.

"An apple pie, a salted caramel cheesecake, a strawberry tart, and a blackberry cheesecake made especially for one of the guests of honor," she announced.

"Thank you. You didn't have to do that though." Dante leaned in closer and lifted the lid to check the cheesecake out. "God, you've marbled the top too. It looks fantastic."

"You deserve something special. This past week you have taken on the restaurant *and* gone above and beyond for Finn and me. That was more than you signed on for. I think you deserve more than a cheesecake for what you're about to undertake." Takira replaced the lid and closed the trunk. "Now, is the promise of a slice of your favorite dessert enough to stop you from wigging out about this party?"

"No, but maybe by my third slice I'll be too blissed out to care."

Elton and Monica's house was an older home, painted white with black trimmings. Wind chimes hung from the porch's wooden beams. Dante looked closer and realized they were witches flying on their brooms amid metallic stars and moons. There was a Halloween themed doormat by the front door and a small skeleton sitting on the porch swing.

Takira helped Finn out of the car and onto the driveway. "In case you're wondering, it's Halloween all year round in that house."

The gate at the side of the house was wide open, and Dante could see there were already a lot of people inside. Dante shifted the box of cakes in her grasp, making sure not to jostle it.

Finn was holding onto Takira's hand tightly. He looked as nervous as Dante was, but she was hiding hers better. She smiled at him to let him see this was all right. It was a party; parties were fun. Dante drew in a deep breath and tried to calm herself. She was back with the people that knew her before Chloe. They'd remember her as the solid butch who bounced people out of the bar when they got rowdy. The one who knew exactly who she was and was unashamed in her butch persona. She owned it. She embraced it.

She'd lost so much of that strength in the breakup.

Her confidence had been shattered, her belief in herself torn to pieces, her trust abused, and her heart split wide open. She wasn't the woman they once knew. She didn't even recognize herself sometimes.

"Come on, you two. Let's get this party started." Takira led the way up the drive and through the gate.

The smell from the barbecue assailed Dante's nostrils. Takira sniffed at the air and let out an appreciative moan.

"My God, that smell is divine, isn't it?" She sniffed again and licked her lips.

"It smells amazing." Dante tried not to get caught staring at Takira's lips while she was in rapture over the smoky, oddly tangy air that permeated the backyard. "Between the barbecue and the cake I'm probably going to regret not wearing stretchy pants."

Takira looked her up and down. "You look perfect to me. If you overindulge you'll just have to pop your top button and untuck your shirt to hide it. You're not going to want to miss out on that meat."

Takira guided them straight to the kitchen where Dante was able to place the box on a table. Monica greeted Takira with as big a hug as she could manage given her pregnancy bump. Dante was surprised to see there were such things as Goth maternity dresses. Monica was beautiful, with her long black hair and her dramatic black makeup accentuating her eyes. She looked like she'd stepped out of a Hammer Horror movie with the flowing sleeves of her dress and its plunging neckline. A silver ankh hung around her neck, falling just above her cleavage.

"Hey you! What have you brought?" Monica didn't pull away from the hug; she just lifted the box lid one-handed and looked inside. "Apple pie!" She hugged Takira even harder, making her laugh. "Baby's favorite dessert. You are a darling. Thank you." Monica spotted Finn next. "And you have to be Finn because Trent said you were a handsome boy and she was right. Hi, sweetheart."

Finn smiled sweetly at her. "Vampirina," he whispered. Monica heard him and winked at him.

Monica's attention shifted to Dante.

"You have to be Dante." Monica stepped closer. "I'm not usually so huggy, but we're blaming everything on my crazy hormones." She embraced Dante in a welcoming hug. "It is fantastic to finally put a face to that name. Durante degli Alighieri, author of *The Divine Comedy*. Dante's *Inferno*, then *Purgatorio*, and *Paradiso*! Magnificent works! Who wouldn't be inspired by a poem about someone who travels the nine circles of hell to find their love?" Monica's eyes sparkled as she became almost rhapsodic in her enthusiasm. "Please tell me you were named from this master?"

Dante nodded. "My mother taught languages, Latin especially, at a private school. The poems were part of her curriculum. Considering how strict she was on gender roles, for some reason she picked Dante for a baby girl. I do remember hearing her say to someone that my birth had 'put her through hell' so maybe my mother had a sense of humor that I never got to see growing up."

"Elton speaks very fondly of you."

"You're his wife."

"Yes, I'm Monica, and I hear that you had a hand in helping him get his act together when he was a teenager."

Dante shrugged that off. "Kids act out. They drink, test boundaries. I just watched over him and Trent when they drank too much at the bar and needed to be taken home."

"His version of that puts you in a much more heroic role, but either way, thank you for watching out for those two."

"Yes, thank you, Dante."

Dante turned around at Elton's voice. She stared at him, taking in the features of a young man now grown. She tugged at his long beard, fashioned into two Viking braids.

"Elton Simons, you finally got the hang of growing a beard!" Dante ran her palm along the length of the braids that fell almost to his chest, holding them out and marveling at the length.

Elton wrapped his arms about her. He rested his head on top of hers. "You were away from us for way too long, Dante. We missed you."

"I missed you too. But I'm back now. I came home." She hugged him back just as tightly.

"Trent's out in the yard with Juliet. You got to see their Harley, didn't you?" Elton pulled back and reached to tug Monica into his side. "You're in time to see our baby being born. Well, not being *born* born, not unless you're actually there in the birthing room to make sure I don't pass out."

"Which he nearly did when we got shown a video of a birth at the birthing class," Monica said sourly.

"In my defense, there were extenuating circumstances. It was unbearably hot in that room. I told you they needed better air conditioning in there."

"And I've told you, you faint on me, Elton Simons, and you'll be on diaper duty until the kid is out of Huggies." Monica poked him in his side making him squirm.

"You haven't changed one bit. You're still tall, gangly, hairy." Dante tugged at his beard again.

"A String Bean Wookie?" Monica added.

"Who grew up into a handsome man with a beautiful wife and a child who will be the best of both of you."

Elton looked down at Finn. "Little dude! You're Harley's new buddy, aren't you?"

Finn stared at Elton who was even taller than Trent and cut quite the imposing figure in his all black clothing and wearing a belt buckle shaped like a skull. He snapped out of it at the mention of his friend's name. "Harley here?"

"She sure is. I can take you to her." He held out his hand and, for a moment, Finn looked hesitant. He looked at Dante for assurance. She nodded at him.

"Elton's a good man, Finn. You're safe with him."

Finn held up his hand for Elton to hold and let him lead him out into the yard.

"He's either an old soul or that baby's been through something." Monica stood by the window to watch the two walk across the yard. "I can see shadows of it in his eyes."

"I don't think I'll ever know the full extent of Latitia's neglect of him." Takira crowded into Monica's side and slipped an arm around her shoulder.

Finn pulled free from Elton's hand to run to join Harley. Monica laughed at the squeals. "I can't wait for my kid to join in that puppy pile."

"That's not the same little boy I brought back with me last week."

"He's got a friend now and adults around him who care." Dante stepped out the door to go find Trent. "He can have fun now. He's earned it." She took a few steps then turned, aware that Takira's eyes had been on her. "And so have you. So enjoy the party. Just save me some cheesecake please."

"You and your sweet things," Takira said.

"Thank God she didn't mention the apple pie." Monica dove back into the box and muttered something Dante was sure was, "Come to mama!"

"I'll hide your cheesecake," Takira promised her.

"I appreciate that."

Dante heard her name called and then Trent was bounding over to her, Elton right by her side. For a moment, Dante was shot back in time and it was like she'd never left. Trent and Elton crowded around her, pulling her forward to meet all their friends.

Trent finally found her family, Dante thought. No one had deserved their happy ending more.

Dante had long given up on finding her own.

❖

As the evening wore on, the attendees thinned out until just eight stayed behind. Finn and Harley had been carried inside an hour ago when they fell asleep. They'd worn each other out playing. Takira was heartened at how Finn's personality had started to show itself when he was allowed to just *be*. They were the only children at the party and had provided more than enough entertainment for everyone until they finally got cranky and began rubbing at their eyes.

Takira watched them for a moment as they slept. Both of them were cozy in little sleeping bags that Trent had brought especially for them for their sleepover, even though neither would actually be staying the night at Elton and Monica's home. A baby monitor stood beside them and its partner sat on the table outside.

She stepped out the back door to rejoin the stragglers, armed with the toffee cheesecake she'd hidden so that they could share it. Dante was talking to Scarlet Tweedy and Bryce Donovan. Takira couldn't help but notice how Scarlet's hair glowed in the dying light of the day. Bryce had her hand on Scarlet's back, absently running her fingers through a lock of Scarlet's long hair. Elton sat on Dante's left side, with Monica leaning into him as she listened to Scarlet explain how she'd come up with the design for Takira's mural. Trent was on Dante's right with Juliet beside her. Juliet was holding Trent's hand, and every now and then, rubbing her thumb over Trent's wedding ring.

Takira placed the cake on the table and began cutting it into generous slices for everyone.

"Where did you hide that?" Monica asked.

"I'm not telling you in case I have to use the place again." Takira doled out a piece for everyone and handed out forks. "This is a new recipe, a salted caramel one. Let me know what you think, please."

Juliet pulled her plate close. "I love it when we get to be guinea pigs for you. It's a chore, but someone has to do it."

"Might as well be us," Trent said, cutting into the dessert and humming loudly on her first mouthful. "Fuck me, that's amazing."

Everyone tucked in and expanded on Trent's sounds of enjoyment.

"Elton said you used to live in Texas, Dante. How long were you there?" Bryce asked.

"Seven years."

"What made you leave?" Scarlet asked.

"I found out that my girlfriend had been cheating on me pretty steadily throughout our whole relationship. I figured it was time to move on."

Takira heard the nonchalance in Dante's tone but saw the tense line around her mouth and noticed she never looked up at anyone. Who would be stupid enough to cheat on someone like Dante? Her ire rose just thinking about this mystery girlfriend who couldn't see a good thing when she had it.

"Oh shit, I'm sorry, Dante. I didn't mean to pry." Scarlet grimaced. "My bad."

Dante brushed it off. "It's in the past now. One good thing came out of it. I realized I'd outstayed my welcome there and packed and saw the world. It was quite the experience and opened my eyes to all I'd been missing. Life is to be experienced, right? We only travel this way once."

"Unless you believe in reincarnation," Monica said around a mouthful of cheesecake. She waved her fork in the air for emphasis. "Then you get to screw up multiple times and keep hoping that the next life's the charmed one." She leaned into Elton. "I think this is mine."

Everyone "awwed" at her and then burst out laughing.

"So of all the places in the world you could go, you came back to Missouri?" Bryce said. "Your memories of here had to be fond ones."

"I grew up here. It's always been home. When the need to come home outweighed my need to stay away, I booked a ticket back. I took the long way home and then I crossed from Kansas City into Columbia and stumbled upon Trent. It was like I'd never been away."

Takira wondered what it would have been like to have traveled by her side and seen all she'd seen. Especially Disneyland. She would wager that Disneyland with Dante would be quite the experience. She wondered if the others would come with them and make it one big holiday. Takira figured Finn would be able to enjoy it better now than he did as an infant. She would look into it once the finances of the restaurant were back in a better state. It would be fun and she hadn't had a vacation in ages.

Dante pushed aside her plate and groaned. "That's it. I need to stop eating right now, otherwise you guys will have to roll me like a boulder back to the car." She squeezed Trent's hand. "I've had a wonderful visit with you all. Thank you for this. Your family is amazing, the close ones you have here at this table, and the others that you've brought into your life." She tugged on one of Elton's braids. "And especially this crazy dude you just can't seem to leave behind."

"He's a keeper," Trent said, grinning over at him.

"Sooo," Dante drawled, "I've met everyone, talked to everyone, shared my blackberry cheesecake with Monica..."

"Crazy baby hormones," Monica complained. "I'm going to be the size of a whale."

"But there are things I need to know."

Trent nodded. "Ask us anything."

"It's not you I want to ask, darlin'." Dante looked directly at Juliet.

Trent started to fidget nervously.

"Miss Juliet, I can see *why* she did it, but I'd really like to know *how*. How did my girl Trent ask you to marry her?"

Everyone burst into laughter at the embarrassed look that Trent now wore. Even in the evening's fading light, her blush was unmissable. She groaned and put her head in her hands.

"We could tell you how Katy Perry's 'Teenage Dream' became the lip sync proposal to end all proposals," Elton said, reaching for his phone and swiping through a few screens. "But you really have to see Trent's inspired dancing to truly appreciate it." He passed the phone to Dante. "Please note Kayleigh and I were her back up dancers."

Dante hovered her finger over the play button, eyeing Trent who was shooting daggers at an unrepentant Elton. "*You* danced?"

"I wanted it to be memorable," Trent said. The look she and Juliet shared showed it had been all that and more.

Everyone crowded around Dante as she touched the screen and the video began to play.

Takira loved how the women around the table, and Elton, all interacted. They were a formidable team. Dante fit right in with them. She hoped Dante could feel how much Trent and Elton loved her, and how the others were welcoming her into their fold too. They might not be family by blood but their bonds were stronger. They were a family by choice and Takira was realizing that, sometimes, that was the best family to have.

CHAPTER TEN

It was late when Dante and Takira got back to the restaurant. Dante had carried Finn inside still wrapped like a burrito in his sleeping bag and laid him on his bed. She wandered back into the kitchen to grab a glass of milk and groaned when she found an empty carton. Dante headed downstairs to raid the restaurant's fridge. She grabbed a fresh carton, picked up a glass out of the rack, and sat at a table to just wind down after a very active day.

Takira wandered in behind her, saw what she was doing, and got a glass of her own.

"Finn drinks all the milk," she said, pouring out a small measure. "I forgot to replace it this afternoon. I'm sorry."

"He's a growing boy." Dante stretched and grunted. "And I'm going to be growing in all the wrong places if I keep eating as much as I did today. But you were right. The barbecue sauce on the spareribs was to die for." She cast a look in Takira's direction. "Even *I* was tempted to sleep with the guy to get the recipe for you." She grinned as Takira nearly spat out her milk.

Takira mopped at her mouth with a napkin. "One day I'll have to ask him what he does. As it stands now, it's great incentive to keep eating it to try to find his secrets in the sauce."

Dante swirled the milk around in her glass. "They all looked happy, didn't they?"

"Yes, they did. That's not to say they haven't had their trials. You saw Bryce's scar?" Takira gestured on her own forehead where Bryce's scar cut through her skin. "She still battles with nightmares from the car crash she was in. It's terrifying to realize how close she was to dying and we'd have never known her."

"She's got a level head on her shoulders. I liked her. The others though." Dante smiled. "Elton found himself a looker, and a Goth too. Finn's little face when he saw her. I swear he was so close to fanboying all over her."

"He thinks she's a vampire like in the Disney cartoon he watches." Takira smirked. "Monica will *love* that. She makes all her own clothes, makes costumes for Harley too. And she and Juliet run a landscaping firm together. Monica has had to let someone else do all the hard work she usually does because of her being pregnant."

"I can't believe Scarlet painted this mural." It was a striking feature for the restaurant and quite the focal point. She walked over to the wall. "I hadn't noticed this bit before." On the wall was a history of the local area and also some of Takira's own story. There was an homage to North Carolina. A trailing corsage of flowering dogwoods hid a family of bright red cardinals inside.

"My father was born and raised in North Carolina. I was born there too. My grandma refused to come with us when he relocated us to Kansas City because of his work and then again here to Columbia. I lived for my holidays with her. I never wanted to come home. She was the sweetest woman to me."

Painted on the wall was a Polaroid picture of an old woman smiling next to her stove. "Is this your grandma?"

Takira came to join her. "Yes, it is. It seemed only fitting that she should have a place on the wall of my restaurant. She made the best sweet potato pie you could ever taste. I learned at her side how to make it. It's still one of my most popular dishes here. A taste of Grandma's heavenly soul food."

"You look a little like her. The shape of your nose and your chin."

"Thank you. I'll take that as a huge compliment. She was the only one in my family who showed me any love and respect for what I wanted to do with my life. I miss her every day."

"I didn't do all that well in the family stakes. My grandparents died before I was born, and you know what my parents were like. I got respect through my jobs and the hard work I put in, but it would have been nice to have it from someone who cared for me too."

"Surely you've had partners who—" Takira hushed at Dante shaking her head.

"I've never done the multiple lover thing. I like to get to know someone first before I commit. I couldn't just pick a woman up, sleep with her, leave in the morning, and then move on to the next. I can't get my head around it. Where's the intimacy? Where's the love?" She felt Takira go still beside her. "Sorry. I know not everyone is like that. Each to their own. I just…can't. So I haven't really had a great deal of women in my life, and the ones I did? Let's just say they weren't as committed as I thought."

"You left Texas because of the last one."

Dante nodded and sat back down. "Yeah. I thought she was the one. I'd known her for a while, liked her, it turned to love…at least on my side. When she asked me to move away for her, I did without hesitation. I found a job, I settled down, and I let myself be blinded by what I thought love should be." Dante took a gulp from her glass. "Forgive me. You don't want to hear me crying into my milk."

"Have you ever talked about how it all ended?"

"No, because it was the worst thing I've ever felt. And that's over my own parents shutting me out of their lives because I was gay. But Chloe? I thought Chloe loved me. It was one hell of a betrayal."

"I'm sorry you had to go through that. But is it wrong of me to say that I'm kind of glad that in the end it brought you back here to m—my restaurant?"

Dante wondered at the slightest hesitation. "Well, the traveling was kind of cool, the throwing up foreign beer not so much. The incessant rain in England? Also a bummer. But being back here, meeting you and Finn, and seeing Trent and Elton all grown up? Those have been the highlights of my returning home."

"Do you think you'll ever date again?"

Dante was tired of being hurt, of always having her heart handed back to her, or having it trampled so hard that she didn't know if there was anything left to give to someone again. She didn't dare look up. She could feel Takira looking at her, but Dante couldn't return the gaze. She was starting to care for Takira quicker than she'd ever done for anyone else so early in a relationship. But this wasn't that kind of relationship.

"Dante?"

Dante startled at the sound of Takira's voice.

"I'm sorry. What did you ask me again?"

"Do you think you'll ever date again?"

"No, I don't think so." Dante said. Something that looked like disappointment flickered in Takira's eyes. She had to be mistaken. She was projecting her feelings onto Takira and seeing things that she wished were there but couldn't be. "Maybe I'll take a page out of your book. Devote myself to my job and put that first. It hasn't seemed to do you any harm."

"Business partners all the way," Takira said a little too brightly. "It's been a busy day. I'm going to bed. Good night, Dante."

Dante wanted to ask what was wrong, but Takira was taking the milk back to their apartment before she even managed to open her mouth.

And this is why I don't date. I just don't have a way with the ladies.

❖

The next morning, Takira sat looking out Juliet's living room window at the children playing outside. There was a large part of the backyard designated as a play area, and she could see Finn and Harley painting while Kayleigh supervised.

"Your sister has a remarkable amount of patience for a teenager."

Juliet nodded. "I think she got out most of her rebellious phase before she hit puberty. She had a thing for storming out the house and just walking for hours. That was how she met Trent so I'm not going to complain. I just hope Harley doesn't follow that path. She's got so much energy she'd be in another state before we realized she was gone."

"Finn seems to like her too. But I think he's just happy he's with Harley. He needed a friend."

"How's he settling in?"

Takira shrugged. "It's hard to tell. I mean, he's sleeping, eating, and doing early morning tai chi with Dante every other day."

"Really? Well, that goes a long way to explaining her calm demeanor."

"I think if I left him with Dante all the time he'd be content. I can't help but wonder though if he thinks she's a man and he's latched on to a father figure."

"You refer to her as a she so I doubt it. And once he knew Trent wasn't a man I don't think he'd still mistake Dante for one. Besides," Juliet leaned forward a little, "she's definitely got boobs."

Takira sighed. "I know. I get to see her in the morning when she's in just her workout tee and sweats. She's as handsome in that as she is all buttoned up and smart in her pressed shirts with that perfectly knotted tie and vest."

Juliet looked at her with an eyebrow raised. Takira rolled her eyes at her.

"She's the kind of woman I fantasize about, okay? You know what it's like. You have Trent after all."

Juliet nodded. "I always did gravitate toward the butches, but Trent is in a league of her own. None of the others even began to measure up to what I found in her."

"I've dated my fair share of women. I found some of them sweet, a few more were bitchy, so those dates were cut short before we even got to dessert. But to be on the arm of a handsome woman just feels right to me. And I'm not looking for a substitute man, I'm looking for that something that makes a butch woman exciting and intriguing. The trouble is, I attract those that don't want a relationship, and those that do always seem to end with them eyeing my restaurant as a cash cow. And I am no one's sugar mama."

Juliet laughed at Takira's exasperation.

"Or I get the ones who start off sweet and courteous, but then start getting a little too demanding, or get off on telling me what to do. No one, not even my mother, tells me what to do. I am my own woman and that restaurant is mine, and if I want to work all the days God sends me in it, then I will do so."

"So, Dante's caught your eye?"

"From the moment I laid eyes on her there's just been this spark, you know? This frisson of energy that makes my skin itch when I'm near her. And she's lovely. I mean, I thought Trent was a drop-dead gorgeous lean, mean, butch machine when I first saw her. But get her around you and that baby and she's just so sweet she should come labeled with a cavity warning."

Juliet laughed at her. "She's just full of love. I'm eternally thankful I get to receive so much of it."

"Dante is so good with Finn. I mean, right from the very start, once she realized he wasn't wandering around the apartment lost. She talks *to* him, not down to him, and he just laps that up. She thinks Latitia and my mother might have starved him of attention. Once my eyes were opened to that thought, I hate to admit that I can see it in him too. It breaks my heart and makes me think ill of the dead."

She took a deep breath to calm herself down. "Do you know Dante's made Finn his breakfast every single morning he's been with me? She doesn't have to do that. And she looks after him when I'm working. That's not her job, but she took it on, without my even asking her, once it was clear he was happy being with her. He has a play area in her office when she's in there. They are starting to watch her humungous collection of Disney movies when she's got the time and he's not napping. You should see them, cuddled together on the sofa, eyes glued to the screen. He loves her already. She's his buddy."

"She's a Disney fan? Remind me to give her Harley because if I have to sit through *Tangled* one more time I will rip my own hair out."

"We talked, after the party. I mean, I didn't know about her ex and the cheating before that night. It's not like that was part of her references when I read them. So I thought, I'm free, she's free, maybe if she was interested we could hang out more."

"You make it sound like you're teenagers getting a milkshake to share through one straw." Juliet's smile was kind.

"We were just chatting, and I might have slipped into the conversation a question about dating. Not directly. I mean, I didn't ask her out but, you know, was she open to dating should the chance arise?"

"And?"

"No," Takira said bluntly. "She doesn't see herself dating anywhere in the foreseeable future. I mean, that door is closed, barred, and bolted, no entry allowed, no dating, period."

Juliet hummed quietly. "So whatever that ex did, she did an excellent job of it."

"I want to go find that bitch and slap her through a month of Sundays." Takira had never felt so much animosity toward someone she'd never met before.

"When I asked Trent about it, she said she didn't remember much about the woman Dante gave up everything for. She only remembered seeing her once or twice in the bar and that she was nothing special, but Dante was head over heels for her. She'd always told Trent that when she found the love of her life to treat her special because she was a gift to be treasured."

"I'd say, looking at you, Trent learned that lesson well. And you'd better tone down that look right this second. Your girl's out working all day. You'd better save those big romantic heart eyes for when she walks through that door tonight."

"So, what are you going to do about Dante? I mean, can you even ask her out? You being her boss and all that."

"I have three couples in my restaurant. That damn staff of mine keeps pairing up, so even if I wanted to be strict about fraternization in the workplace they'd laugh me out of my own kitchen. As long as they don't bring any arguments to work where they handle sharp knives all day, then I am fine with it." Takira reflected for a moment. "I've never had anyone I've worked with before that I have been attracted to. I'm usually too busy cooking to pay attention."

"Maybe having Finn around is making you have to stop and take a breather for a while."

"Or maybe it's just Dante," Takira said, knowing that was closer to the truth. "But then I get to thinking, maybe I'm not her type."

"You're smart, accomplished, and gorgeous. And you have curls to die for. Who wouldn't want to date you? Trent told me Dante doesn't have a racist bone in her body. She used to throw bigots out of the bar by the scruff of their neck if they even dared to mouth off to anyone. So I don't think that's a problem."

Takira looked at her watch and was surprised she felt disappointment at the time. "I've got to go. My shift starts soon. I think it's safe for me to leave him here now, don't you? He's with Harley and he's painting…" She stood to go look out the window more closely. "Well, he's kind of painting, and I thank you for the little coverall you got for him. Judging by the colors covering it already I'd say his painting leans more toward abstract than old master."

Takira stepped outside to tell Finn she was leaving and that she'd see him later when Kayleigh brought him back home. He looked a little unsure at first, but Harley and Kayleigh distracted him so he kissed her good-bye and went back to splashing red anywhere he could.

"He'll be fine," Juliet said. "Kayleigh has this, and I'm working from here today if there's any problem."

"Do you think it's silly of me to be so disappointed that I might not get a chance with Dante? It's just she's the first woman I've taken notice of in ages."

"Not since that Janet woman got more than one date out of you."

"Oh my God, the woman who was dating me literally just for my cooking! I'd forgotten her." She made a face as the details flooded back. "She was definitely odd. Pleasant enough but a little off and spent as much time in my kitchen as I did. Why do I always attract the strange ones?"

"Because you're not willing to put the time and effort into really dating someone that could become important to you."

Takira felt the weight behind those words. She knew them to be true. She tried to ignore Juliet's all too knowing look. "With that dig still stinging like a bitch, I'm leaving before you start weighing in on my relationship with my mother next."

"Sweetie, there aren't enough hours in the day for me to lay that whole mess out." Juliet kissed Takira on the cheek. "Go back to your restaurant, cook my sister that pasta thing she loves so much that only you can do. She'll bring Finn back in plenty of time for his dinner. She's excited she gets to have hers in the restaurant with you like a grown-up. All her friends are jealous that your meals get to be part of the deal with her babysitting."

"It's the least I can do. Thank you for doing his lunch for him."

"It's no problem."

"And thank you for listening."

"Don't lose all hope. Maybe Dante will come to realize what a catch she has right before her."

"I don't know. She sounded awfully set in her decision."

"Then maybe it's time you put yourself out into the dating arena again. Find someone who is perfect just for you and who'll love Finn as their own."

"You're not asking for much. It was hard enough me dating being single and always working. Now I come with a kid attached. I'm narrowing my target audience here."

"But if you find that special someone who'll take it all, then it will be worth it. Trust me. You need to leave that kitchen once in a while and start living a little. You have Dante now. Let her do her job and leave you time to do yours and other things too."

Takira hugged her again. "I'll consider it." She waved her farewells and headed for her car. For now, Takira's was calling to her, and that call was always going to come first above everything else vying for her attention.

CHAPTER ELEVEN

Dante couldn't believe her third week at Takira's was already here. She was also surprised to realize it was *only* three weeks because she felt like she'd always been there.

Working alongside Takira was a pleasure. Dante loved getting up in the morning and spending time with Takira and Finn over breakfast. Finn was starting to be a bit more animated and she loved seeing his little personality shine through.

Dante couldn't help it. Her eyes shifted to the kitchen where she could just make out Takira hard at work. She'd been putting in extra hours the last week, both in the kitchen and in her office once Finn was asleep.

I miss her.

"That was a rather heartfelt sigh, my friend."

Dante hadn't realized she'd made a noise. She shook her head and shifted her gaze back to Trent who was watching her closely. "I'm fine. Don't worry about me."

Trent looked past her into the kitchen then back again. "Well, I know you're not watching Joe in there so that only leaves…"

"The one person in the whole of the restaurant that I'd be crazy to even begin to have catch my eye." Dante felt stupid. "Besides, I'm way older than her. I've literally just walked in off the streets and started working for her. I'm sleeping for free under the same roof as her."

"And you *like* her. Maybe more than like? Like, *like like* her?"

Dante elbowed Trent in her side. "You are such a smartass. That never changed, did it?"

"So, what's holding you back? Nothing you've just listed holds up as a decent excuse."

"She's my boss. Would *you* date your boss?"

"My boss is Elton. Dating I could do, but he'd never get to first base with me." Trent skipped back out of the way before another well aimed dig hit its mark. "You're worried about someone crying sexual harassment in the workplace? Have you even asked her first to see if she frowns on fraternization?"

Dante shook her head. "I'm not asking anyone out any time soon."

"*Ever*?"

"Not after what Chloe did."

Trent's eyes widened. "You haven't had sex—" Dante clamped her hand over Trent's mouth to stifle the remainder of that question. Trent mumbled against Dante's palm, and she reluctantly removed it. "Not even once?"

Dante hissed at her. "No." She hoped her embarrassment wasn't on display for anyone to witness.

"Wow. I was climbing the walls during Juliet's pregnancy when she wasn't in the mood, and that was hard enough."

Dante stared at her. "You didn't…"

"Cheat on her? Fuck, no! She's my one and only, and I'd kill myself before she had the chance to do it for me. I'd never even entertain that idea. Nonononono."

Trent's emphatic denials amused Dante.

"No, I didn't look elsewhere." Trent gave her a sly smile. "Juliet always made sure I got attention, if you know what I mean."

"Thank you for sharing that," Dante said dryly.

"But you've really not been with anyone since Chloe?"

"We hadn't exactly been together properly for years before I caught her getting it from someone else. She was always working.

Her clients came first, and how true *that* turned out to be. Her clients, her work, and the overnight trips she *had* to make. It was always her job first and me fitting around her time, on her schedule. *If* she could bear to tear herself away. I came somewhere way down the bottom on her to-do list."

"So since you left, there hasn't been even one woman who caught your eye in all your travels?"

Dante's attention drifted back to the kitchen where Takira was now talking with Kae. "No. You know I don't sleep around. It's not in my nature. I'm someone who is particular who they get intimate with."

"But Takira has caught your attention."

Dante groaned. "Yes," she gritted out. "But that doesn't mean I have to do something about it." She waved a hand toward the restaurant. "This is what she does. This is her life's work and she's excellent at it. She deserves to be proud of what she's achieved. But I've already 'been there, done that, got kicked out of my house and lost it all' by someone who put their own needs first. I had no place in Chloe's life. I put her first, but she sidelined me for everything and everybody else."

"You think you'd have no place in Takira's life too?"

"I've worked with her and lived with her for three weeks. She's devoted to this restaurant. I deserve better than being an afterthought to someone whose mind is always caught up in their work. And she deserves more than I could give her in return."

And Chloe was quite explicit in naming all my faults. It's better to keep to myself, then nobody gets hurt. Especially me.

Friday nights were always busy. Takira enjoyed the faster pace and the crazy dance everyone performed in the kitchen to get each customer's meal prepared. Friday evening was also when her friends came in to eat and she could show off some of her special meals. They were always open to try something new.

Dante was seating her favorite customer. Dante hadn't been wrong; she *did* attract the little old ladies. Mrs. Daniels was eighty-eight, a fact she regaled to everyone and anyone she met. Takira smiled as Dante pulled out a chair and settled Mrs. Daniels into it. She knew Mrs. Daniels was retelling for the umpteenth time how she had marched with Martin Luther King Jr. Dante nodded and smiled at all the right places, just like she did every time she heard the tale. Takira liked the respect she showed for an old lady whose memory wasn't always working, but her flair for retelling what she did know was.

When Dante brought over Mrs. Daniels's drink order she didn't miss Takira leaning on the bar grinning at her. Dante greeted her with a "don't you dare say a word" look and a nod at Kae who was working behind the bar.

"Do I need to set a place for you at that table?" Takira said, having seen Mrs. Daniels's hand gripped firmly on Dante's arm while she placed her order.

"No, she's still playing hard to get. She hasn't slipped me her number yet." Dante grabbed a cup and saucer to make a cup of coffee exactly how Mrs. Daniels liked it.

Takira liked the personal touch Dante had. She'd noticed it when Dante would bring her a drink it was always exactly how Takira liked it made.

"She's so your favorite." Takira couldn't resist taking another little dig. Dante was immune to it though.

"She says I remind her of her late husband." Dante swirled the milk on top of the cup, creating a fancy pattern. "Except for my being a little too pale. Now, if you're quite finished being amused at my expense, I have a charming older woman to serve coffee to."

Takira tried not to be obvious in her staring after Dante as she went back out among the customers. Dante did cut a fine figure in those tailored trousers and vest. It was hard not to be appreciative.

"She's fantastic with the customers," Kae said, preparing a tray full of drinks. "If I wasn't spoken for…"

Takira eyed her. "You'd what?"

"I'd give her my number without hesitation. I usually like my ladies more femme, but I have to admit, imagining being topped by that kind of butch makes even my little butch heart quiver like a damsel in distress." She moved along the bar to serve a customer.

Takira stared after her, surprised Kae would have fantasies about being with another butch. No, not just any butch...*Dante*. She shook her head to rid it of the thoughts Kae had just conjured in her head. Her gaze slipped back to following Dante as she did the rounds from table to table, checking to make sure the customers were satisfied, greeting the regulars as if they were old friends. *She's perfect in this role.* Claude had always treated it as a job, but Dante lived to serve.

Takira couldn't fault how Dante looked either. She was unashamedly handsome in her black pinstriped suit. The jacket had come off at some point during the day, and Takira had made sure it was safe out of harm's way in the kitchen. The black shirt and black tie made for a wonderful contrast to Dante's stark gray hair. Takira closed her eyes to try to suppress the yearning that bubbled up inside her. She saw Dante every day, sat with her at meals, they talked about business, Finn's improvement, Takira's joy in being back in the kitchen full-time. She learned about Dante's previous jobs, the good and the bad.

Takira had lost count of how many times she'd found Dante and Finn watching cartoons on Dante's lunch break or a movie on the rare time Dante wasn't working. An evening off for Dante usually found Finn fast asleep in her lap while she finished watching what they'd started before putting him to bed. Takira often fought the urge to join them on the sofa to just spend an evening doing something simple. But she always turned around and went back to the restaurant, making sure it was running smoothly as she tried to recoup the money Claude had stolen.

So what do I do? I shut myself away in my office for even more hours at a time and hide behind my own stupid fences. Sulking like a child because Dante says she doesn't date and I don't have enough time in the day to breathe, let alone start a relationship and yet...

She found exactly where Dante stood in the restaurant again. And found Dante looking right back at her. Takira wondered at the small smile that she gave her before Dante turned back to a customer and gathered their plate.

I need to do something to get her out of my head before I drive myself insane.

Takira turned toward the kitchen to pick up the food for Trent and Juliet's table. Takira began gathering the plates. She wanted to be more than friends with Dante. She'd had moments where she'd had to physically stop herself from running her fingers over the shaved sides of Dante's head and through the deliberately tousled hair on top. She wanted to wrap her arms around Dante and breathe in the masculine cologne she wore. She also wanted to wrestle Dante out of her pressed shirts and see just how buttoned up she was when she was naked.

The strangled growl of frustration she gritted out drew Zenya's attention to her.

"You okay there, boss?"

"I'm fine."

"You don't sound fine. Nothing's burning or boiled over so it's not the kitchen making you mad. What's up?"

"I'm..." Takira had no idea what to say. *I'm lusting after my new manager.* She just couldn't explain it without sounding like a lovesick schoolgirl crushing out over her new best friend.

"Do you need to bust loose out of here? Just take off and have a night to yourself away from the pots and pans and people demanding all your time? My cousin owns the new gay bar Dare2BU that's just opened near here. I could get us free drinks all night."

Takira shook her head. "You know full well I'm not the party type, but thank you. Any free time I get I need to spend with Finn now. He's got to be my number one priority." She tried not to grit her teeth saying that out loud. Her number one priority was and always would be the restaurant. But she was learning to let Finn take a bigger role in her days.

"You've got people who would love to look after him if you ever decide to take some 'me' time. One night away won't undo all you've done for him in the last few weeks." Zenya leaned forward conspiratorially. "I know for a fact Dante has missed him desperately since he's started hanging with Kayleigh during the day."

"Really?" Dante had never said a word to Takira about that.

"Face it, you've had it rough lately, what with your sister, your mother, *Claude*." Zenya snarled his name in disgust. "You've got Finn to care for. The stress has got to be piling up around your ears. One night. One night to get your sexiest dress on, tease your hair, go out, and allow yourself to be distracted."

"Any free time I have I'm penciled in for a family night of popcorn, M&M's, and whatever Disney movie Dante has that Finn picks out."

"Dante and Disney?" Zenya snorted, but her demeanor changed dramatically at Takira's severe look. "You're serious? Wow."

"Do not tease her about it," she said. "She's passionate about few things in her life, but when she finds something she likes she's all in."

"Hmm, that's something to remember," Zenya said pointedly.

"And since when did animation become the bastion of children only? It's an art form as expressive as any other artistic medium in film." Takira closed her eyes and groaned silently. She was now quoting Dante's arguments. She cracked an eye open at Zenya's laughter.

"Does she have a favorite character? When it's her birthday I have to get her a Disney related gift instead of some random present. She doesn't exactly strike me as the Disney Princess type."

"Don't judge her by her looks. I know she loves *Frozen*, but I think it's the snowman she loves best in that." She wondered how much she was revealing of the Dante she and Finn got to see. "I know she has a dragon in her bedroom."

"A *real* one?"

Takira huffed at her. "No, not a real one! A stuffed one."

"Like a *Pete's Dragon* kind of thing?"

"Do I honestly look like I know one dragon from another? I am not Daenerys Stormborn of the House Targaryen."

"Well, what color is it, Khaleesi?"

"Red, I think. Kind of skinny with a moustache?" She knew that sounded ridiculous, but she'd only gotten a quick glance of it when she'd helped Dante carry in the TV she'd brought for her room to go with the new PS4 that sat next to it.

"I think that's Mushu, the dragon from *Mulan*." Zenya paused. "Hmm, how ironic. That's a story about a woman who dresses as a man."

"I like how she dresses," Takira said .

"Yeah, I can tell you do." Zenya drew closer to Takira's side. "Maybe you can help her add another thing to be passionate about to her list." Zenya patted Takira's shoulder before she picked up plates to help her serve.

Takira followed her out to Trent's table. She hoped for something, *anything*, to distract her from Dante's unavailability and maybe quell some of her own incessant longings that were chasing after a lost cause.

Where was a fairy godmother when you needed one?

CHAPTER TWELVE

Takira didn't know how she'd managed it, but she eventually found an extra hour in the day. She'd taken a deliberate step back from her workaholic tendencies and, in some much needed one on one time, was now going to be entertaining Finn in the kitchen. She was still prone to moments when his presence surprised her and she guiltily wished things had never changed. But this was how her life was going to be now and she was determined to make the best of it, for both of them.

They were settling in to their new normal. It was hard and tiring and strange at times, but Takira was confident she could make it work. She was also indebted to Juliet who was just a phone call away the second Finn sniffled. Or if she needed a cheering squad to get her past him refusing to eat his sandwich because she'd forgotten to get his particular brand of honey in and only honey in a bottle shaped like a bear would do. There was no point her calling her mother. Her mother was more than happy to talk on the phone to her, but she wasn't interested in visiting or having Takira and Finn go see her. She was always too busy or too tired. Takira couldn't help but wonder if this was the treatment Latitia had gotten once the newness of a baby grandson had worn off.

For a while now Takira had been trying to work out what she and Finn could do as their own special time together. It was Dante who eventually nudged her toward what she knew best.

"Your grandma opened up a whole new world for you being by her side in the kitchen. Share that with Finn. Share *her* with him."

Takira thought that was a great idea. She'd thanked Dante, but she'd just shrugged it off.

"Just teach him how to make those coconut cakes. There's never enough of them so the more hands making them the better."

So today Takira was ignoring the curious stares from her kitchen staff as she guided Finn around them and led him toward a tabletop she'd set up just for them. Finn was a little clingy and visibly nervous in the restaurant's huge kitchen. It was loud and busy, and Takira could see him flinch at every noise. She was beginning to think this was a bad idea when Dante strolled over and asked what they were going to make. Takira was grateful for the distraction, and in her explaining it to Dante she realized that Finn's attention focused more on her too. He visibly relaxed and began to get excited as she pointed out every ingredient.

Dante helped Finn get into his little chef's apron. She took out her phone and gestured for Takira and Finn to huddle in for a photo. "Finn's first cooking lesson. We have to document that."

Takira loved how wide Finn's smile was when Dante showed them the picture she'd captured.

Dante left them to it. "I'll be back when whatever you make comes out of the oven," she told Finn, but her grin was directed at Takira. "You'll need a taste tester."

Takira just shook her head at her, all too used now to Dante and her sweet tooth. Takira had decided on them making cookies, a treat for them to share while watching a movie that evening before Finn's bedtime.

They each had a set of ingredients to work with, all pre-measured before time, and Takira began to help Finn through every step it took to make their cookies. Finn's laughter drew her head up from her own bowl. He held up his hands for her to see. Sticky cookie dough covered every inch of them. There was a tray beside him full of misshapen balls of dough haphazardly lined up that he had made. They weren't going to be the prettiest cookies but he was having fun making them and that was all that mattered.

"Shall I make some extra cookies with chocolate chips?" Takira asked him and got an emphatic nod in reply. They were his favorite, and she'd only just learned that Dante had kept a stash in her office for when Finn was with her. No wonder Finn was never any trouble for her when she babysat him. Takira would have to try that trick herself.

"Grandpa's mommy make cookies?" Finn rolled out another lump of dough and splatted it on the tray.

"Yes, your great-grandma did. She made lots of things and they were all delicious." She watched him pull at the sticky stuff smeared across his palms. "She'd have loved you to pieces."

Finn's head shot up, his eyes sparkling. Not for the first time did she damn her sister for not loving this little boy right. He was desperate to be seen and loved. "I'll do my very best so you never doubt that you're cared for," Takira promised him as she wiped his hands clean. "Hey, Finn, how about we make some special cookies for Dante?" She'd brought a cookie cutter especially with Dante in mind. After all, it paid to keep her manager happy.

"God help me," Takira muttered to herself, "I am such a sucker for that handsome face of hers it's bordering on embarrassing." She reached into a drawer and pulled out the new cookie cutter. She heard Zenya smother a laugh when she walked past and happened to see it.

"Dante's cookies!" Finn cheered then clasped his hand over his mouth to be quiet. "Dante's cookies," he said, whispering it this time.

It was because of Dante's hard work Takira had found time to slow down a little. Takira had no idea what she'd ever done without her. She hoped she never had to find out, both for professional reasons and personal ones. All Takira needed to start her day off with a smile was to see Dante being unguarded and silly with Finn before she got into business mode.

Why couldn't I have fallen for someone more available? Someone less handsome to the eyes and less wearing on my heart? Why am I falling for the only butch I know who doesn't want to date?

Determined to leave those thoughts aside, Takira mixed up some more dough and handed Finn a packet of chocolate chips to tip into a bowl. She knew that wasn't the smartest move, but at least the chips that escaped he quickly picked up and ate. His chocolate covered face made her smile.

"Let's get your cookies in the oven first and then we can mix what chips are left with this dough, cut out the shapes, and bake them."

He nodded at her. She wasn't sure if he totally understood, but he looked so serious at her instructions she could have hugged him. But only after she scrubbed him clean of everything he'd been making that afternoon. She praised herself for the foresight of buying him his own little chef's apron. He looked the part, if a little eccentrically messy. She just hoped it was relatively simple to get cookie mix out of his hair.

Looking at the cookie in her hand, Dante wasn't entirely sure if it was a tease or a treat. The chocolate chip cookie was decidedly *mouse* shaped. Mickey Mouse shaped to be exact. She could easily recognize the three circles that made up his head and very distinct ears. No one had ever made her Mickey Mouse cookies before. Maybe she was reading too much into it. After all, it was just a cookie.

She held it up and inspected it from every angle. Finn was bouncing beside her, waiting for her to say something. Dante deliberately took a bite of an ear. It melted in her mouth. She made the kind of yummy noise Finn recognized.

"Best cookie ever." Dante took another bite to prove it.

Finn let out a cheer and reached for one of his own. Takira just wore a smug look.

"The best kind of cookie that could break your addiction to the coconut cakes?" she asked.

Dante made sure to give her a suitably horrified look. "Nothing is ever going to top those. But if you want to try to beat them, I'm more than willing to taste everything you put before me. For the sake of the restaurant, of course."

Takira picked up a cookie and broke an ear off right in front of Dante's face. "Hmm, for the restaurant she says." She scoffed at Dante and popped the cookie into her mouth.

"Did you have a good day making lots of cookies?" Dante asked Finn.

He began to tell her, in his own inimitable way, all they had done. Dante listened attentively to him explaining about the chocolate chips and how sticky his hands got, and a completely random something about a dinosaur that Dante had no clue how it related to the tale. Then he decided he was done and wanted another cookie.

Takira poured their drinks ready for them to settle in for the movie. It was all very domesticated. Dante found it strangely comforting after being alone for so long. She'd been just as much alone *in* her relationship with Chloe. She just hadn't realized how shut out she'd been until there wasn't even space in her own bed for her.

The heady mix of feelings she got around Takira scared Dante more than she would ever care to admit. She loved spending time with them both, working with Takira, playing with Finn. It was the family dynamic she never expected to want or to enjoy. They were filling a gap she hadn't realized was hanging wide open in her life.

Takira was so easy to be around. She was also beautiful and extremely sexy. Her voice conjured visions of late nights spent tangled between the sheets together, sated and drowsy, whispering secrets to each other. Dante couldn't look at her lips without wanting desperately to taste them.

But Chloe had done her damnedest to leave her feeling unworthy of anyone's touch again.

Dante both cursed and rejoiced at the reemergence of that part of her she'd buried deep. She never thought it would see the light of day again, that she'd ever *feel*. But the pain that accompanied it only served to set alarm bells ringing in her head. She didn't know if she was brave enough to try again.

But maybe Takira might just be the one to make her *want* to try.

They watched the movie in a contented silence, broken only by Finn asking questions before he was engrossed in the story again. Eventually, Finn crawled into Takira's lap and lounged back against her chest. Dante could see his eyes were getting heavy as he fought to stay awake to see the end. He was fast asleep well before Snow White's Prince Charming kissed her awake. The gap between Dante and Takira had lessened without Finn sitting between them. Dante could feel Takira's arm pressed into her own, and she was so tempted to reach out and take Takira's hand in her own. Takira muttered something about Snow White needing a Princess Charming instead before she leaned in even closer and her head dropped on Dante's shoulder.

Dante sat motionless, overwhelmed by Takira's sudden nearness and intoxicated by the smell of vanilla that clung to her hair. She waited a moment, barely daring to breathe.

"Takira?" All she heard was the music playing over the credits and Finn's baby snores rumbling out. Takira let out a sigh and then her breathing grew deep and measured. Dante tried to look at her, but all she could see was a mass of hair hiding Takira's face. She hesitated then strained an arm to reach for the TV remote. She turned down the volume and switched back to the regular channels. She hadn't the heart to wake either one of them yet.

A knock at the door a few minutes later saved Dante from spending the night camped out on the sofa. The rhythmic tapping didn't wake Finn, but it startled Takira out of her light sleep. She jerked upright. Dante got up and gathered Finn.

"Go answer it. It's probably one of the guys from downstairs."
Dante rocked Finn in her arms as Takira hurried to open the door.

It wasn't one of the guys.

"Hi, honey! I'm home!"

Takira was swept up into the arms of a woman who kissed her passionately right there on the doorstep. Takira struggled to break free and pushed back on the woman's chest to separate them.

"You're right, let's take this inside." The woman stepped forward, forcing Takira to take a few hasty steps backward. She didn't miss Dante with Finn fast asleep in her arms. She stared at them, a frown marring her forehead.

"Fuck me, Kira. I didn't think I'd left it *that* long."

Chapter Thirteen

Takira couldn't believe Kelis had just turned up at her door out of the blue and on tonight of all nights.

"Don't you ever think of calling first?"

"You know me, baby. I just go where the spirit and mood takes me. Besides, I sent a text weeks ago that I was going to be in the area." Kelis closed the door behind her. "The girl at the bar said you weren't working tonight. For a moment, I thought maybe you were ill because nothing short of death keeps you from that kitchen of yours. Instead, you're *entertaining*." She looked Dante up and down. "Are you going to introduce us?"

Takira waved a vague hand between them. "Dante, this is a friend of mine." She shot Kelis a hard glare when Kelis scoffed quietly. "Kelis Moore, Dante Groves."

Dante nodded her head at her. "I'll go put Finn to bed."

Takira watched her go, dreading what was going to happen next.

"Well, well, well. Judging by the kid in her arms I'd say it's not hers. I am right in that she's a she? Or am I misgendering him/her/them/they?" Kelis slung an arm around Takira's shoulders. "I know you're partial to butch women, but she out-butches us all. That's serious stud material."

"Don't judge her by looks alone, Kelis. She's so much more than that."

Kelis's arm dropped. "Are you two...?"

"No. She's my new manager."

Kelis tugged on her tie to loosen it. "Then why is she up here with you looking all cozy and domesticated?"

"Because she's sharing the apartment with me." Takira wasn't happy having to explain herself. She wasn't happy with Kelis being there or with her walking around the living room as if she owned it. She didn't, just like she didn't own Takira. But she walked right in, shedding her jacket and tossing it over the arm of the sofa and then flung her tie there too. Takira recognized the pattern. Seduction 101. Take the lead, mark your territory, and seduce your prey. *Well, not tonight, lover girl. Your scene isn't going to play out how you might have planned.*

She couldn't help but compare Dante and Kelis. Kelis's skin was darker than Takira's, and she wore her hair braided in tight rows. She was tall, wiry thin, but muscular due to an excessive amount of time spent in the gym to cut the perfect body. Takira knew that body all too well. Kelis was one of her exes she'd managed to part with on good terms. Any love between them had fizzled fast, but their sex life had never been an issue. They'd fallen into a pattern of meeting occasionally for sex before going their separate ways again.

Takira knew they were using each other, but it was to each's satisfaction. It was like a one-night stand but just happened to be with someone she knew. And she knew Kelis all too well. Kelis was sharp, smart, opinionated, and mostly dismissive of anything that didn't center on her. She had none of Dante's empathy or one iota of Dante's sweet nature and sense of humor. And she was totally devoid of Dante's sense of whimsy that was plain to see when Dante talked about her favorite movies. Or when she mimicked the voices of Finn's favorite characters, much to his amusement. Takira thought it was adorable how much Dante loved her cartoons. It had made her wonder what she had in her own life that garnered the same devotion. All she'd come up with was work. It was a sobering realization.

"So, whose is the kid? Or does your new roomie double as a nanny when she's not working for you? And why have you got a new manager? What happened to that guy who was always by your side? Clint? Craig?"

"The kid is Finn, my sister's son, and I have a new manager because Claude decided to take as much as he could from the restaurant's bank account almost bankrupting me in the process."

Kelis spun around, concern written all over her face. "Have you reported him to the police?"

Takira rolled her eyes. "No, I'm letting him think of it as severance pay." She hated how Kelis could always make her feel incapable of running her own business. She ignored the voice that whispered that she *had* missed seeing what Claude was doing.

"Have they caught him yet?"

"No, so it's business as usual here while I try to recoup the losses."

"He'd better still have your money on him when they get him."

Takira knew he hadn't paid off his debtors so she had no idea what he was doing with her money. Kelis sauntered across the room to her, swaying to an invisible beat. "So, if your buddy Dante is babysitting your nephew, you and I…"

"No one is babysitting Finn. He's mine now." Takira couldn't help but take satisfaction in stopping Kelis in her tracks.

"Excuse me?"

"He's my responsibility now. He lives here. He's mine."

"What kind of crazy shit is that? You're the last person on the face of the planet to have a kid. What asinine thing has your sister done now? Let me guess, she got her butt thrown in jail for partying too hard."

"She was killed in a car accident."

"*What*? When?"

"Weeks ago."

"And you didn't let me know?"

Takira couldn't believe that Kelis could make her sister's death all about her. "We don't share that kind of relationship anymore, Kelis. We're not the sort to text each other with what is happening in our lives. No ties, no entanglements, remember? We're barely friends with benefits. You breeze by here two or three times a year and we…" Takira lowered her voice, "we hook up and then you leave again."

"You've never complained before."

"And I'm not complaining now, but my life has changed, Kelis. And you just waltzing in here tonight isn't a part of what I need at the moment."

Kelis moved a little closer. "It could be. I could help you relax." She brushed her lips over Takira's ear. "You know how good I am at doing that."

The shiver that ran through Takira's body only served to make Kelis bolder. Her lips trailed along Takira's cheek and captured her lips again. For a moment, Takira's body gave in to a touch it recognized. She hadn't had a lover in more months than she could remember, not since Kelis had last stopped by. And Kelis knew how to play her body so well.

The faint sound of footsteps revealed Dante slipping out of Finn's bedroom and unobtrusively trying to leave the apartment. Takira heard the front door open and pulled away from Kelis's bruising kiss.

"Dante?"

"Finn's out for the night. I'll go check on the staff downstairs and lock up when it's closing time." Dante didn't turn around, and her voice sounded oddly strained to Takira's ears. "You have a good night."

Takira watched her leave with a heavy heart. Kelis tried to turn her head back for more kisses, but the moment was lost and Takira pulled back.

"Oh, come on," Kelis whined. "Your roommate has given us the green light to get our freak on." She began unbuttoning her shirt, revealing the taut skin of her chest and a set of abs that looked carved out of stone.

Takira put a hand up to stall her from going any further. "I can't do this tonight."

Kelis's hand paused. "What? You got your period or something? You know there are ways around that and I know them all."

"No, Kelis. I mean *this*." Takira gestured between them both. "*This. Us.* I'm not doing this tonight. I'm sorry."

"If you've got a headache I have the cure for that too. You always told me I had healing hands." She leaned in and Takira pushed her back.

"No. You're not listening to me. Let me spell it out for you. I am *not* having sex with you tonight."

"But that's why I'm here. It's what *we* do."

Kelis looked so perplexed that Takira was turning her down. Takira was torn between laughing at her or screaming.

"Yeah, well, I'm off the menu as of tonight."

Kelis began fastening her shirt back up slowly. "Is it because of this Dante? Are you trading me in for an older, butcher model?"

"I'm not trading you for anything. You're not mine to trade, Kelis. We're fuck buddies. Three, four times a year, you and I just fuck."

"You make it sound sordid."

"It is what it is, Kelis. A no strings arrangement. A butch booty call. But I have Finn now and I can't just mess around."

"You're saying we can't have sex because there's a kid in the apartment?" She edged closer, running her fingers over Takira's chest. "We can be quiet. I only need one hand to get you off while I keep the other across your mouth. Like I did that time in your office. Took you right in your chair and no one in the restaurant had a clue that you were screaming as you came."

"God, you're so arrogant." Takira remembered that day well. Kelis had made a whistle stop at the restaurant before driving on to Kansas City to conduct her marketing business there. She was in the area, had an hour to kill, and Takira had been her pit stop. It had been fast and furious and had quieted some of Takira's pent up needs and desires. Kelis left and Takira went straight back to business. It was always hot and steamy between them, a passionate collision of two bodies desperate for release and then done. Over, finished, spent, until months went by and Kelis found herself in the area again. It was exciting, and for Takira it served as enough to tide her over emotionally because her work always came first.

Until now.

Now she had work, but she also had Finn to care for. Her priorities were shifting and changing. Her heart just wasn't in the mood for a quick bout of sweaty sex with someone who she couldn't hold a conversation with beyond "oh yes, right there" and "harder."

And then there was Dante. No amount of pushing down her attraction would staunch the desperate yearning she had when she was in Dante's company. Takira wanted only her. And sex for sex's sake wasn't on her agenda now.

"But I'm here for the week," Kelis said, throwing herself down on the sofa. She sprawled out with her legs wide open in invitation. Takira didn't take her up on the offer.

"You can sleep on the sofa."

"I'm used to sleeping in your bed. Not that we get much sleeping done." Kelis smiled up at her and patted the cushion beside her, trying to tempt her near.

Takira stood her ground. "You can sleep in the bed then and *I'll* sleep on the sofa. I'm not sleeping with you."

"Why not? Nothing ever stopped you before." Kelis frowned for a moment, then a light of understanding dawned on her face. "Are you worried what the big bad butch will think about her boss getting hot and heavy with me? Don't worry about it." She got a sly look in her eyes. "You could always ask her to join us."

Takira knew Kelis was joking; her ego would never cope with competition in the bedroom. But Takira didn't want to share Dante with anyone, and if Kelis thought she was defusing the tension with that comment she was highly mistaken.

"There's a hotel two blocks over. I'm sure they'll have a room for you tonight."

Kelis's jaw dropped. "That's it? You're kicking me out after I've driven all the way here to be with you?"

"Don't flatter me, Kelis. You're here on *business*. Not once in the three years since we split have you ever just popped by to spend time with me other than to fuck and run."

"Hey, I'm busy too. I'm bucking for a director's chair at my firm."

"That's great news and I hope you get it. But please don't give me the speech about how bad I'm treating you when we're not lovers in the truest sense of the word. We had an arrangement. It suited us both. At this precise moment in time, it doesn't suit me anymore."

Kelis rose and pulled her jacket back on. She stuffed her tie into a pocket. "That butch isn't going to set your sheets on fire like I do for you. She's cut from stone. She'll never let you touch her, and I know you, you like to touch just as much as be touched."

Takira didn't answer her. She wasn't going to presume anything where Dante was concerned. She just knew the more Kelis said, the less Takira wanted to be with her. She didn't want instant gratification and sex without feeling. She wanted to lie in tangled sheets and feel her skin melted into her lover's from the sweat of their passion. To lie there talking about inane things, just winding down and basking in the afterglow. She wanted more than she'd ever wanted before. And she wanted it with Dante. Takira stood in stunned silence as Kelis waited for her to say something. Her head buzzed with a loud white noise that coalesced into one thought.

I'm in love with Dante.

Kelis began jangling her car keys in her pocket. "Can I at least come back in the morning and get breakfast? You serve the best waffles around, and I'm already missing out on this trip. Don't make me miss out on those too."

"Come by in the morning. Maybe we can talk over coffee, like *friends* do. We're long overdue."

"Sure. Maybe then you can tell me how you let your heart be taken by a gray haired butch who makes me look positively feminine."

"I've told you—"

Kelis raised a hand. "I know what you said, but I'm not so stupid that I can't see the look that's blazing in your eyes. You never once looked at me that way, and I'm a catch."

Takira laughed at her and her inflated ego. "We weren't meant to be that way, Kelis."

"And you think you and her could be?"

"Maybe, if I'm lucky."

"You're paying for my breakfast for breaking my heart."

"I never had your heart in the first place. You can buy your own damn waffles. I need your business."

"I hope she knows what she's getting in you. Truth be told, Kira, you're quite a catch too. I was a fool to let you go."

"Thank you, Kelis."

"And if it doesn't work out I'll be more than willing to provide you with pity sex the next time I drive through here." She was totally genuine in her generous offer. Takira was sorely tempted to slap her silly.

"What did I ever see in you, Kelis?"

"Someone who wanted the same as you did. Work first and a little something on the side to relieve the tension now and then. The shared ideals of workaholic lesbians."

"I'm sorry you had a wasted journey." She felt awful, but she'd never had any reason to contact Kelis before. She couldn't remember any text coming through from her either, but Takira had been extremely distracted with the business, her sister, and life in general the past weeks. And really, what could she have texted her? *Hi, just to let you know I'm lusting after another woman so if you happen to be driving by don't drop in expecting sex from me?*

"It's never a waste to see you. Though I wasted money on new underwear for nothing."

"I'm sure whoever you have marked down next on your journey will reap the rewards."

Kelis just shrugged. "Maybe." She checked her watch. "That restaurant of yours still serving?"

Takira nodded.

"Can I at least share a meal with you seeing as there won't be any other eating done here tonight?" She waggled her eyebrows and reluctantly smiled. An honest smile, one that let Takira know she had gotten the message. At least for now.

Takira slapped at her arm hard. "Yes, you can eat here. Let me grab Finn's monitor and we'll go get you some food to hush your foolish mouth."

"You're taking this mothering role seriously."

"I have to, Kelis. I'm all he's got."

"And Dante. He seems to have Dante too from the way she held him in her arms."

Yes, he has Dante. He has her more than I do.

Dante sat in her car outside Trent's home for a long time deliberating what she should do next. She knew she didn't want to go back to the apartment and see Takira with Kelis again. She didn't want to fall back on old habits, drowning herself in alcohol to try to erase the devastating kiss she'd witnessed between them. Dante just needed to be anywhere but where she'd come to consider *home.*

Dante knew there was only one place she could go. One person she could trust with how she felt.

Trent opened her front door to Dante with a smile that faded the longer she looked at her. She ushered Dante in silently.

"I apologize for it being so late. I just didn't know where else to go and you'd given me your address so it was either come here or go to a bar. I can't afford to drink a place dry or deal with the hangover I'd get for trying."

"What's wrong?" She sat beside Dante. "What happened?"

"I think I made a huge mistake coming back here." Dante rubbed a hand over her face roughly. "I should have stayed away and just continued the way I was. I was happy."

Trent grabbed them both a beer from the fridge and handed Dante one. Dante held it between her hands and just stared at it.

"After Chloe, I never dared open my heart to anyone else. I had my chances while I was traveling, but I just couldn't risk it. Besides, they were pretty enough, some were totally hot, but they weren't what I wanted. One-night stands aren't my thing, and I was passing through so many places I just shut that part of my life off. After a while I didn't miss it. You can't miss what you don't have, right?"

Trent just nodded and let Dante talk.

"Then I came home and it's been a challenge. A welcome one but a challenge nonetheless. A new job, new place to live, new colleagues, living with a young child. Do you know Takira asked me one day why I was so kind to him? It's not like I have much experience being around a kid, but I looked into his eyes and saw the man he could be. I don't want him to suffer the kind of upbringing you and I had. I want nothing but positive experiences for him. Happy memories from now on. No one knows how his mother treated him, and his grandmother doesn't sound like the kind of woman to be left to raise a baby. But Takira is trying so hard, even though it wasn't what she wanted at all. And the timing sucked coming so close on the heels of that bastard stealing her money. But she's making sure Finn's cared for and loved." Dante twisted the top off her beer and took a long drink. "I love that kid, Trent. He's a tiny sponge soaking up everything and anything he can acquire. I never thought of kids as something I'd ever want in my life. To be honest, I'm kind of sad I'm not younger to fully appreciate everything he's going to experience because I think he can do great things. He can do anything."

"Kids are fun like that. He's starting to grow in confidence too. His volume's turning up and he's making himself known. Harley loves spending time with him. They'll make quite the team. Maybe she'll be lucky and he'll become her Elton."

Dante smiled. "That would make me so happy."

"But you're not happy, are you? What's happened, Dante? What's brought you here tonight and left you looking lost?"

"I…" Dante hesitated and began picking at the label on her bottle. "I have…feelings for Takira."

"And?"

"And I can't turn them off, shut them up, or squash them down. I've tried. Believe me, I've tried so hard. I thought at first it was because I was living with her and Finn. The familiarity of it all, helping her with him, managing the business. But I find myself gravitating to the kitchen every time she's in there. She's fascinating to watch when she's in her zone. There's a beauty to all she does and it's awe-inspiring. She owns that kitchen in every way. So I allowed myself to wonder and dream a little."

"You deserve to be happy with someone, Dante. You're long overdue."

"I don't always attract the right kind of lesbian. A lot mistake me for stone butch. That isn't my nature. My androgyny didn't favor me with the same handsomeness you got, my friend. I didn't get the lean and mean look that has women falling at my feet. I'm built like a bodyguard."

"Dante…"

"No, I'm very aware that in the butch looks department I'm not exactly the arm candy every pretty young femme wants at her side. I'm short and stocky, Trent, with the strength to pick up a guy by the seat of his pants and toss him out of a bar for harassing the ladies. Chloe made me feel I was desirable, the sexiest butch on the planet, because she chose me out of all the other women in the bar. We'd talk for hours about my family and what I'd been through. She helped me consign it to the past and walk away proud. I moved on. I found a great job when we relocated to Texas. I had a pretty girl on my arm, and I loved her." Dante took another drink and wiped her mouth on the back of her hand. "I loved her so much."

Trent took a drink from her own bottle, then sat back and just let Dante ramble.

"I didn't think I could ever feel like that again. Four long years alone and then I sat in that restaurant and Juliet brought Takira to the table and I felt the world start to revolve again. She's so pretty. I was instantly smitten and she has this wicked sense of humor that I just adore. I want so badly to just reach out and touch her sometimes to prove to myself that she's real. So I began to wonder if I *could* try again. Risk it all despite what Chloe did." Dante looked up at Trent and smiled.

"But I decided, maybe if I took it slowly, I could take a tentative step back into the real world and see if Takira would take a risk on me? I'm rusty as hell, but I'd try my damnedest to make her happy. So tonight was family night, and I'm always included. You know what that feels like. You've made your own family too. She'd baked special cookies in the shape of Mickey Mouse, and I was taking that as a sign from the universe to get my ass in gear and ask her out. We watched a movie and she fell asleep on me. I couldn't move in case it broke the spell. It just felt so right, watching a movie, Finn on her lap, her head on my shoulder. I was happy and was holding that feeling close when the door knocked." Dante took a breath. "Then her girlfriend walked in and kissed her just like the hero waking the princess in all those fucking fairy tales I watch. I missed my chance and she wasn't really free after all."

"But she doesn't have a girlfriend."

"When I left, Takira was kissing her back like a starving woman so I'm guessing there's a big chance it wasn't the wrong door that this Kelis knocked on."

"Holy shit, Dante. That sucks big time."

Dante laughed humorlessly. "Yeah, kid, it does. Feeling like a total loser, I couldn't stay in the apartment with them so I put Finn to bed and got out of there as fast as I could. I was going to stay hiding out in the restaurant until closing up time, but Kae took one look at my face and told me she'd lock up and sent me out to grab some air." She sat back in her seat. "And here I am, regaling you with my pitiful tale of woe."

"Stay here tonight. I can make up the sofa for you. I've slept on it before so it's perfectly long enough for you, short stuff."

"You get sent to sleep on the sofa a lot?"

"No, I don't get kicked out of bed. It was when Harley was teething. I'd bring her down here at night to cry and gnash her gums so Juliet could get some sleep ready to take over the next day. I'd stick a movie on and we'd watch something superhero-y and she'd eventually quiet down. When she fell asleep I would too. This is a comfy sofa."

"I'd like that. I don't think I could face going back to the apartment and risk hearing them continuing what Kelis was intent on starting the second she stepped through the door."

"You're welcome here any time. I can't say we have any clothing that will fit you to sleep in. What with me being so tall and Juliet having all those delicious curves. But if you want to strip down to your skivvies to save your clothes looking slept in, we'll give you a heads-up in the morning so you don't end up flashing Harley your boxer shorts."

"Thank you for listening, Trent."

"You were always there for me, Dante. It's nice to be able to repay the favor. Now, have you eaten tonight? I can heat up a pizza."

"I'm fine. Would you do something else for me?"

"Anything."

"Distract the hell out of me. Tell me about Juliet and Harley. You must have some wonderful stories."

"I have pictures too." Trent reached for her phone.

Dante smiled. "Show me them all."

CHAPTER FOURTEEN

The sound of inconsolable crying woke Takira up before her alarm had the chance to go off. She got out of bed and rushed to Finn's room. It was empty. She could still hear him, his breath hitching as he cried and called out. Takira stopped to work out where in the apartment he was hiding. She finally made out what he was calling between his sobs. He was crying for Dante. She found him in Dante's room, his chest wrenching with the force of his sobbing and the distressing sound of him calling out Dante's name.

Takira called to him carefully, trying not to startle him. He spun around at her voice.

"Dante gone. All gone."

Takira noted Dante's bed showed no signs of been slept in the night before. Finn was trying to clamber up onto it, probably to double-check Dante wasn't hiding under the sheets.

"She's not here, Finn."

Nothing prepared her for the wailing that followed. He sobbed as if his heart was breaking. As he gasped for air, he kept whimpering, "Dante gone." Takira was at a loss how to console him. She had no idea where Dante could be. She and Finn were used to waking up to Dante being in the apartment with them.

"She'll be back," Takira promised. Dante obviously never came back to the apartment after leaving so soon after Kelis's unexpected arrival. Finn didn't care where Dante was, though. All he knew was she wasn't home. And Takira realized she missed her desperately too.

She picked Finn up and took him out of the room, closing the door behind her. Finn buried his face in her neck, his tears scalding her skin as his crying continued unabated.

"Finn, please try and calm down. You'll make yourself sick." She tried to pacify him, but he was beyond being soothed. "Let me make you some breakfast and I bet Dante will be back before you finish it." She had to detach his arms from around her shoulders and set him in his usual chair at the table. He spread his arms out on the tabletop and laid his head on them as he cried.

Takira hurried to prepare his pancakes, but as soon as she started them in the pan Finn's crying got even louder.

"What's wrong, Finn?"

"No clappy song!" He cried so hard he was choking on his tears. He clapped his hands together while crying even more.

Totally at a loss how to calm him down, Takira made his pancakes and laid them before him. He pushed the plate away and laid his head back on the table.

There was a knock at the door, and his head shot up again. He fell down off the chair and rushed toward it.

"Dante, Dante." He hopped in place, anxious for Takira to hurry up and answer the door.

Takira knew it wasn't her. Dante had her own key. This was Kelis making good on her promise to come back for breakfast and expecting it in the apartment and not the restaurant. Takira was not in the mood to deal with her this morning, not with Finn worked up into such a state. She opened the door and Finn pushed past her. He stared up at Kelis, frowned, then shouted "No!" and tried to close the door on her. Takira was tempted to let him do it, but Kelis stuck her foot in the door and looked liable to shove it back at him.

"Good God, is he like this every morning?" Kelis looked unimpressed as she stared down at him.

"No, he's just..." Takira didn't know what he was. She knew he was used to having Dante up and doing something in the apartment when he got up, but this desolate sobbing was something more than that. He was working himself up so much she was worried he'd start hyperventilating. "Finn, breathe, baby, please. Come on, calm down."

Kelis ignored him, walked around him, and took a seat at the table.

"So, any chance of some coffee while I'm waiting for your staff to get the waffles on?"

"You're like two hours early," Takira grumbled. Her nerves were already frayed by Finn's crying without having to play hostess to a woman who was now helping herself to Finn's pancakes. Finn didn't care; he was trying to open the balcony doors in case Dante was out there. Takira knew she wasn't. Dante always left the balcony doors ajar when it was tai chi day so that Finn could slip out and join her. She opened the doors so he could see.

"Dante gone. All gone," he stuttered and gasped for air.

Takira tried to hold him, but he slipped out of her grasp.

"For Christ's sake, leave the damn kid alone, Kira. He'll wear himself out eventually and finally shut up."

"He's never like this, Kelis. He's a calm, placid little boy."

"How lucky am I that I get to meet him when he needs to quit his whining before he gets his butt smacked." Kelis's voice rose over Finn's crying. It didn't help. Finn shot her such a furious glare that at any other time would have made Takira laugh. That look was pure Latitia. Takira had never seen it on Finn's face before. It seemed fitting he directed it at Kelis.

"Stick him in his room if he's going to keep making all this noise. I haven't come here to listen to him carrying on."

Takira resisted the urge to pour Kelis's coffee in her lap. Finn's noise wasn't abating, and Kelis was getting more annoyed. "Are you going to shut him up or what?"

Takira glanced over to where Finn was sobbing into a sofa cushion. "I'm going to let him get it out of his system," she said.

"And you need to tone down the anger around him. He's not used to it."

Kelis stood up and poured herself some more coffee. "I came here to see you, not some whiney ass kid who keeps crying for no reason."

Takira knew Finn had his reasons. Dante wasn't there. His routine had changed. Finn was used to Dante being up before him. Dante made his pancakes. Takira wasn't sure where the "clappy song" came into it, but it was obviously important to him. She fixed herself a bowl of cereal and started her own morning off. She couldn't miss Kelis's pitiful sigh at Takira ignoring her.

"His crying is hurting my ears."

"Then don't listen to it."

"I thought we could talk, but obviously you're busy being mommy to his childish acting out."

"The point being he *is* a child, and children are known to do this kind of thing."

Kelis slammed her cup on the table a little harder than necessary. "I'm going to wait in my damned car until your restaurant opens because I can't put up with his incessant crying. How do you put up with it?"

He hasn't been like this before. Takira realized she'd only ever heard him cry a little when he was tired, but usually he was quiet. She wondered if crying was something else tied into the neglect he'd gotten from his mother. She knew from the few times she'd been with Latitia that if Finn cried Latitia walked off and left whoever was in the room to comfort him. So whatever was making Finn like this was huge in his little head.

Takira was at a loss what to do. Kelis was obviously waiting for Takira to beg her to stay, but Takira just kept eating her breakfast, accompanied by the pitiful shuddering sobs of Finn playing in the background. Kelis stormed out of the kitchen. The door opened and then Takira heard her speak. But it wasn't to her.

"Good luck in there, Mrs. Doubtfire. It's a fucking nightmare."

Takira turned in her seat to see who Kelis was talking to and saw Dante walk in with a puzzled look on her face. Dante noticed Finn straight away.

"Hey, Finn. What's wrong?"

Finn lifted his lead from the sofa and said Dante's name so mournfully it brought tears to Takira's eyes. He ran to Dante and threw himself at her knees, wrapping his arms around them, keeping her firmly in place. She picked him up, and Finn sobbed on her shoulder, clutching her like she would vanish into thin air if he didn't hold on tight.

Dante soothed him and rocked him, murmuring soft words against his head and kissing him. She looked over at Takira.

"How long has he been like this?"

Takira checked the clock. "Well over half an hour. He got up and you weren't here and he just..." She gestured helplessly to how upset Finn obviously was.

"Dante gone. All gone. Don't go. No leave Finn."

"We're all here, Finn. You're okay. Did you have a bad dream?"

Finn nodded. "All gone. No more sleeping. Naughty sleeps."

Dante looked over his shoulder at Takira. "It's okay now. You're awake and we're all here."

"Mommy gone?"

Takira saw Dante freeze for a second. Takira nodded at her. As painful as it was, he had to be reminded.

"Yes, your mommy died. She didn't want to leave you, but she had to go because she was hurt real bad. But she knew you'd be happy with Auntie Kira and here you are. You have Auntie Kira and all the people downstairs who love you. You have Harley and her mommies. Then there's all the other little kids at the play group you hang out and eat sand with."

"And Dante." He rubbed his wet face into her neck, snuggling closer.

"Yes, and you have me. You're not alone, Finn. You just had a naughty dream that frightened you."

Separation anxiety. Takira closed her eyes at the pain that burned its way through her chest at what his desolate cries had been all about. He was frightened of being left alone. She wondered if she should be more jealous of the fact he was crying for Dante and not her. But then Dante *had* been there for him. She couldn't help but wonder how they were going to work around this when Dante inevitably moved out. If she was honest with herself, Takira dreaded that day coming too.

Dante rested her head on top of Finn's and hugged him closer. "I hadn't left you, Finn. I was at a friend's house and had a sleepover. I'm back now."

"No go?"

"I'm not going anywhere, and if I do? I'll be right back. I'm sorry I frightened you. I thought I'd be back before you got up, but you beat me to it. You're an early bird today. Have you had any breakfast yet?"

"I made him pancakes but he wouldn't touch them. "

Dante just nodded. "How about I make you your pancakes, and we'll get you all calmed down because you're making yourself so hot." Dante carried him over to the table, but he refused to let her put him down. "Okay, let's see how well I can make pancakes with you clinging like a koala on me." The pancake necessities were already laid out on the counter from Takira's attempt. Dante wandered off to her room leaving Takira wondering what she was doing until she came back armed with her MP3 player and her speaker. "Let's start this day over, eh, Finn? No more tears now." She kissed his head and he peered up at her. Dante shifted him in her arms so she could wipe his face with a damp paper towel. "That's better. There's the handsome boy I know."

Finn's chest hitched as he slowly worked himself down from his crying fit.

Dante put the music on and bounced Finn in her arms to the rhythm. Takira was fascinated to see Finn relax. How had she not known about this? She'd gotten used to a certain style of music playing in the morning, but she'd paid no heed to it. But for Finn it was obviously a whole other thing. Dante was mixing the batter while Finn still clung to her. Dante was singing along softly. Takira could just make out her voice and was surprised by how well Dante could hold a tune. She also noticed how mindful Dante was to keep Finn angled well away from the heat of the stove. As Dante went about making his breakfast, Finn put his hands up to her face.

"Hi, Finn." Dante smiled at him. "You ready for the best part?" He nodded and Dante put him down. He still kept close to her though. The music tempo changed, and Takira watched in surprise as they both clapped along to a specific piece in the song and stomped their feet like flamenco dancers. Finn laughed and held up his arms to be picked up again once their quick dance was done. Dante lifted him up and went back to the pancakes as if nothing had happened.

"You do this every morning with him, don't you? Play this music, dance with him, make him his pancakes."

Dante nodded. "It's the fun part of that song, and every morning should start off with a bit of fun."

"Where were you last night?" Takira couldn't censor the question before it tumbled from her mouth.

"I visited with Trent and Juliet. I had a couple of beers with Trent, and she invited me to stay so I wouldn't have to drive back. I really thought I'd be back in time before this little guy was up and about."

"He was searching for you. I've never known him to cry so much, Dante. He was inconsolable when he realized you weren't home." She didn't miss the way Dante flinched over the word "home."

"He'll grow out of that eventually as he gets more secure in his place here and the people he's around."

Takira wondered if she'd really heard the underlining jab in those words. She decided to address them anyway. "Kelis didn't stay the night."

"It's not my place to know," Dante said, busying herself with settling Finn down to eat. She took the chair beside him when he fussed over letting her go.

"She turned up again this morning and walked right into this shi—storm," Takira hastily amended her words, but Finn was too busy wolfing down his pancakes like he was starving. "She wasn't very understanding. I have to admit, he shocked me. I've never seen him cry so hard or for so long."

"He was long overdue. He's held back a lot of tears I reckon. It will help him to let them out. He's got all these little emotions inside him he's had to suppress. He's learning he's safe to express them all here. The good ones and the bad."

"God, Dante. How can you be so calm?" Takira felt physically drained from Finn's crying.

"Getting worked up or angry doesn't help calm him down."

"I swear you're some kind of Zen master," Takira muttered.

Dante just smiled at her enigmatically. Takira fell even harder for her in that moment. The attraction was constant now. She wanted to reach over the table and pull Dante in for a kiss. Her eyes must have revealed more than she was willing to admit out loud because Dante's smile faltered a fraction, and her own eyes grew more intent. Takira wondered what was ticking inside that brain of hers. And would Dante be surprised if she realized what was fighting for dominance in Takira's?

"How about I take Finn to the Baydale Babies today seeing as I don't seem to be able to go very far from his side." Dante looked down to where Finn had his hand curled in her shirt while he ate.

"It's your day off though. Don't you have other plans?"

"I'll spend it with Finn. I wasn't going to be doing much anyway. Laundry can wait until later. It's not going anywhere."

"I'll text Kayleigh and let her know she's free for the day. I'll still pay her though for changing her plans last minute." Takira started clearing up her breakfast things. "Dante, about last night..."

"I'm glad you've got someone." Dante's interjection was swift, like she really didn't want this line of conversation to go any further.

Takira wasn't about to be shut down. She shook her head. "I don't. Not really. Not like that. But Kelis and I are...complicated."

"Then I hope you can work it out."

But I don't want to. I need someone I can respect. And I really think that's you for me, Dante Groves.

"I think we're long past that point. I just need to get her to see that I'm not here for her anymore. I've moved on. It's time she did."

"She doesn't strike me as the kind who listens."

"And that's why I need to make it clear to her that this shop," Takira cocked a thumb at herself, "is shut for business." She got up and groaned. "Speaking of which, I have the breakfast crowd to go feed so I need to get ready."

"I'll go grab a quick shower while you get Finn changed, then we can get our day started."

Finn started to fuss when Dante got up, but Dante told him where she was going and what they were doing that day and he eventually calmed down.

Takira needed that kind of stability in her life. Someone who could calm her racing thoughts and let her transfer some of the weight crushing her shoulders over to theirs for a time. Someone to share her life with. Share Finn with. Share her heart. She pursed her lips in thought and Dante caught the look.

"What's that pouty face for?"

"I wish I had the day off to be with you guys." She was heartened by the way Dante's eyes lit up at the thought.

"Maybe some other time," she said. "Just let me know and I'll wrangle the schedule in our favor."

"I'll hold you to that," Takira said.

Soon, her heart replied.

"Remember that one time you actually carried me out of the bar over your shoulder? The night I was so drunk I couldn't see straight, let alone be straight?" Trent had leaned down a little and was keeping her voice low for Dante's ears alone. "I never dreamed that so many years later we'd be standing *here*."

"I can honestly say it never featured in my wildest dreams either."

Dante looked around her at all the little children spread out in the playground pretending to be trees. Finn looked a little perplexed as to why he'd be such a thing. Harley, however, was entertaining the idea with her usual enthusiasm. Trent had said Harley was obviously a Whomping Willow tree from Harry Potter judging by how franticly her "branches" were waving about.

"Speaking of dreams, Finn looks a little better than he did when we met this morning. Poor little guy, he must have given himself quite the scare."

Dante barely took her eyes from him. He'd been clingy all the way to the group but had finally relaxed a little once in the company of so many other children. He kept looking over in her direction to make sure she was still there though.

"He scared the shit out of Takira. She said she'd never seen him cry so much." Dante grinned. "But his hysterics frightened Takira's ex away so that was at least one good thing."

"Takira's got a pushy ex that doesn't understand the *ex* part?"

"I think there's more to it than that, but obviously this Kelis has free rein to come and go in Takira's life. But this time Takira wasn't interested."

Trent smiled but stayed silent.

"What's that enigmatic smile for?"

"I'm just smiling. I mean, you said this Kelis was butch, though not as butch by our standards. And I know from things Takira has said that she might have a particular soft spot for women like us. I'm just smiling because her new manager is any femme's total wet dream."

"Trent!" she hissed. "There are children present!"

Trent just shrugged. "Well, you are. And I think Takira knows that, and why should she settle for a wannabe when she can have you?"

"We're not like that."

"But you could be. You just need a nudge to get back in the dating lane again." She hip checked Dante a little to emphasize her point.

Dante ignored her so Trent changed the subject.

"Are you enjoying your new job?"

Dante nodded. "I love it. It keeps me busy because it's such a big place. I like that though. I'm working on a couple of proposals to see if Takira's agreeable to expanding the business a little. Branching out to get more customers recognizing her brand. Might help restore some of her losses too after that bastard stole from her."

"Do you think he'll try that trick on someone else?"

"I'm banking on it. I might have sent his photo to a few friends in my network. If he steps into any of those businesses they'll let me know."

"And you say I draw people to me. You've got quite a little managerial posse going on."

"Good friends are hard to find. When I find them, I tend to keep them."

Trent nodded. "I live by that mantra."

The voice from one of the teachers rang across the play area, and the children trotted off to get a snack and a drink before their next task. Some of the mothers hovered around their kids, doling out the little juice cartons.

"I'd have thought you'd be in there helping out, Trent."

"I considered it, but I figured Harley spent enough time with me and it would help her branch out a little if I took a step back."

There was some furious whisperings going on from one corner where most of the mothers were congregating. Dante glanced over her shoulder to see what was wrong.

"I'm just saying, what kind of school is this that it lets people like *that* near your children?"

Dante felt her blood run cold when she realized the comment and the looks were being directed at her and Trent. She saw Trent straighten to her full height and look over at the women who were trying to hush the other woman.

"Carrie, shut up," someone said sternly, but Carrie was having none of it.

"Come on. You can't tell me you think looking like that is normal?"

Trent bristled, and Dante tried to ignore them, but the frantic whispering and arguing was distracting. She could see Trent gearing herself up to do something.

"She's not worth it," Dante muttered. Trent shook her head.

"I know she's not, but she's choosing to do this in front of the children and I'm not standing for that."

Trent walked over to the women. Dante wasn't surprised to see some hastily get out of her way. Dante followed behind at a more leisurely pace, ready to back her up.

"Is there a problem here, ladies?" Trent asked politely, smiling at them all, including the one who had started them all off.

Carrie looked Trent up and down. "I was saying that I didn't know why *your* sort would be hanging around here."

"That's because my daughter plays here, and I have every right to be here with her. I pay her fees and I take her home when she's done. Just like any of the other mothers here."

"Well, you're not exactly like the rest of the mothers here, are you? That's painfully obvious to see."

Trent looked around at them all. Some had already moved to stand behind Trent in solidarity. Dante liked them on sight.

"I know I don't look like anyone else except for my friend here who I'm sure you're including in your deliberately loud comments. And I understand that."

Carrie looked around smugly at the other women as if her comments had been justified. Most of the other women just rolled their eyes at her.

"You look at me and you see someone that's not feminine like you. I don't wear makeup or try to get into ridiculously high heels.

Nor do I wear skirts so tight that we can all see the outline of your underwear through them."

Carrie was horrified. "What are you doing looking?"

Another woman spoke up. "Sister, we've all got an eyeful of what you have on display. I've seen more material on a handkerchief than what you're wearing to cover your ass."

Dante bit back a smile while Carrie turned a furious red at having the tables turned on her. She smoothed down her skirt angrily.

Trent waited for everyone to calm down before she continued. "What you're wearing isn't really appropriate Baydale Babies wear in front of impressionable children. But instead you look at me and think you know me and what I am. What you're failing to see is that I'm a woman. I'm just one who looks different from you, but I'm no less a woman than you are. And I wanted a child, a family, so bad. And these looks?" Trent pointed to her face and gestured down her torso. "How I look is exactly how I got blessed with a woman who loves me. And she gifted us both with a beautiful little girl. And what makes that child better and more intelligent than you is that she looks at me and she doesn't see a man, or someone trying to be a man. She doesn't see a lesbian either. She sees the woman who sings her to sleep when she's grumpy. The woman who chases her around the house pretending to be a dinosaur. She sees the woman who kisses her when she falls and helps her stand back up again. The woman who plans on telling her every day that she can be whatever or whoever she wants to be because she's perfect just the way she is just by being herself." Trent took a step closer to Carrie who took a step back. "So you can be as opinionated as you like about me. I've been insulted by better people than you about my looks, and you know what? None of your judgment matters one iota because that little girl loves me and I love her. When we walk away from here once class is over, my daughter and I will leave to go about our lives together. We're happy. Are *you* happy?"

Carrie blinked stupidly at her. Dante wondered if Trent's impassioned speech had broken her.

"Of...of course I'm happy," Carrie stuttered.

"Good, because that's all I want people to be. Life's too short to worry if someone isn't your idea of normal. I'm normal in my world."

"You're normal in mine too," a woman said and patted Trent's arm. Others joined in with her.

"Your daughter's a credit to you. She's such a friendly little girl," another commented.

"Where's your child?" Trent asked Carrie.

"I don't have one. I'm here with a...friend." She looked around, but her friend had stepped away from her and had joined the throng around Trent and Dante.

"I see. Well, that makes me wonder what kind of school they run here that allows people like *you* near these children. What with your loud voice and bigoted views." Trent leaned forward and Dante bit the inside of her cheek to stop her laughter from escaping at how Carrie cowered at Trent towering over her.

"Mama!" Harley came bounding over. She held something up in her hand. "Look! Found a wiggly!"

As usual, Finn followed behind, his hands clasped behind his back as if he was just out for a stroll.

Trent knelt down to look at what Harley had found. "That's a caterpillar. He's going to need to be put back carefully on a leaf so when he's ready he can become a...?" She posed the question and looked at Harley for the answer.

Harley chewed at her lip as she thought it over. "I don't know."

"He'll get big wings..."

Harley's eyes lit up with wonder. "A dragon!" She looked at the caterpillar with awe. "Can we keep him?"

"No," Trent said calmly. Dante could see she was trying not to laugh along with the other mothers at Harley's fertile imagination and hopes. "He'll become a butterfly, not a dragon."

Harley breathed out a soft "ooh" and held her palm out for Finn to look at. "Gonna be a butterfly."

Finn looked at the caterpillar curled up in Harley's hand. They both stared at it as if expecting it to magically explode with wings right that second.

"Now?" Finn asked Trent.

"One day, when he's ready. Then he can become everything he's meant to be."

Harley handed him to Trent. "Mama, put him safe, please. Needs a good place to change. Mama find it."

Trent took the caterpillar from her gently. Trent looked up at Carrie who was watching them silently. "Harley, say hi to this lady. I've been telling her what a good girl you are."

Harley preened at the praise. She smiled and leaned into Trent. "Hi, lady." She patted Trent's arm. "Is my mama."

Finn came over and tugged at Dante's pant leg. She picked him up, and Carrie's eyes grew wider still at the picture *they* made. Dante smiled at her.

"I'm guessing there's nothing more to be said here, is there?" Dante was satisfied when Carrie shook her head.

Carrie looked around, found her friend, and muttered, "I'll go wait in the car." She walked off trying to keep her head high and her handbag tucked against her backside so that no one could see her through her skirt. Peals of laughter followed after her.

A woman stepped forward. "I'm Janet, and I'm so sorry about her. She's my brother's girlfriend, and I could just slap her silly for some of the stupid things that come out of her mouth."

"That's okay," Trent said. "I've heard worse."

"That doesn't make it right, though. You don't deserve that judgment, for any reason." Janet included Dante in her gaze. "Either of you."

"Families come in all shapes and colors. As long as there's love nothing else matters," another said and everyone agreed.

These weren't the usual women Dante associated with, but she liked them and respected them. She made a quick decision.

"Ladies, if any of you have time to spare after the group I'd like to invite you to Takira's restaurant on the main road just before the Baydale Mall. I'm the new manager there, and your first drink is on me. The restaurant is child friendly. Just ask Finn here. It's his home." Finn hid his face in her neck as all eyes turned to him. Dante grinned at Trent's surprised face. Most of the women took her up on the offer straight away.

Janet started laughing. "Carrie loves eating at Takira's. She's going to s-h-i-t a brick when she walks in and finds you there. God, I hope I'm with her when she does."

Dante gave the women directions to the restaurant. When they drifted off to watch their children for the last playtime of the morning, Trent leaned in to Dante.

"Why did you do that?"

"Because good friends are hard to find," Dante said.

"And when you find them..."

"*We* keep them."

CHAPTER FIFTEEN

The apartment seemed unusually quiet without Finn. Dante's absence was hard to get used to as well. Takira missed the sound of her singing under her breath to her music playing softly in the background. It was nearly time for dinner, and they'd promised to be back in time to eat with her. Takira had prepared something in the restaurant earlier in the day and brought it back up to the apartment so she and Dante could talk.

She'd been dying to get the story behind Dante coming back from the Baydale Babies group with most of the mothers and their children in tow earlier. She hadn't said a word when Dante paid for all their drinks, but she'd been too busy serving everyone and greeting those who knew her. A lot of the mothers stayed for something to eat or to book a table for later in the week, and Takira began to wonder if Dante had invited everyone back to garner them new customers. Whatever Dante's motives, it had proved to be quite lucrative.

She heard footsteps by the door and hurried to open it. Kelis stood on the other side. Takira didn't hide her disappointment in time.

"Wow. Again not the welcome I was expecting."

"I wasn't expecting you at all."

"After this morning I wanted to make sure we were still okay. I mean, it's not like we got a chance to talk what with the kid and his crazy meltdown."

Takira bristled at Kelis's description of Finn being upset.

"I can conduct this on the doorstep if that's what you want…"

Knowing she was going to regret it, Takira stepped back and ushered Kelis inside.

"Are you alone?" Kelis looked around and then smiled. "Finally." She reached out to pull Takira to her, but Takira slapped her hands away.

"For the last time, Kelis, *no*. I've told you I'm not interested."

"You were always interested before. You used to be as invested as I was in this."

"But I don't want us to continue like this. I'm sorry, but I can't do this anymore. I have other things to deal with."

"Other women to fuck?" Kelis said harshly, throwing herself down on the sofa and slamming her briefcase beside her.

"If I do that's really no concern of yours, is it? We were never exclusive." Takira paused. "Well, I may have been, but I know you weren't." The guilty look on Kelis's face finally answered that for her.

"You've always been special though."

"And you were to me."

"Then why? Because of this Dante you're living with?"

"Because of too many reasons to even begin to explain. But I can't keep doing this when I want someone else. I don't work like that."

"So that's it? You just throw away everything we had for some unknown woman who's built like a brick shit house when I look like *this*?" Kelis gestured to herself grandly.

Takira fought not to roll her eyes at Kelis's conceit. "Be honest, we never really had each other to start with, Kelis. We dated for a few months, we split, then we fell into this once in a blue moon meet and have sex routine. It suited me at the time. You're an excellent lover, but I need more than that."

"I could give you more."

"I'm sorry, but I don't want more from you." Takira grimaced at how stark her words sounded, but she couldn't hold back anymore. Kelis wasn't getting the message, and Takira was losing her patience.

"So we're done?"

"Yes." She watched a frown darken Kelis's face. This wasn't going to be pretty. Kelis's temper was one of the reasons why Takira had called it quits on their romance in the first place. Kelis had a nasty manipulative streak that never came into play while they just met for sex, but as a partner she was controlling and not above using tears as a ploy to make Takira capitulate.

The apartment door opened, and Finn burst in all smiles and excited chatter, with a new train held proudly in his hand. Takira felt her heart lift at how happy he sounded. He was like a totally different child from the one who had been so grief-stricken that morning. He was also carrying a little bag of groceries. It consisted of a bottle of syrup and a bag of M&M's which Takira hoped was for her. Dante didn't eat them and Finn wasn't big on candy. Takira smiled as Dante followed him in, and Dante smiled back until she noticed Kelis sitting on the sofa with a face like a thunder cloud.

Finn bounded over to Takira, showing her what he'd helped to bring in. "We got stuff for pancakes," he said and hopped over to Dante to "help" her unpack.

"Quite the family," Kelis said, spite hardening her tone.

"Don't do this, Kelis. We weren't going to last forever."

"I always figured we'd get back together."

Takira shook her head. "No, there was never any chance of that, and I'm sorry if I ever gave you that impression. We burned those bridges long ago. We just kept getting back together to pick through the ashes."

She had to move away from her. Takira stood back and her attention shifted to Dante as always who was putting things away with a quiet efficiency. Takira wanted to go to her and ask her about their day. Judging by how Finn was bouncing like Tigger, he'd had the best day ever in Dante's company. She drifted toward the kitchen as Finn galloped past her. He was as happy as he could be. He wasn't watching where he was going though and tripped over Kelis's briefcase that was lying on the floor as he rounded the sofa. Kelis reacted in anger and raised her hand to lash out at him.

Her hand never touched a hair on his head. She cried out in pain as Dante's tightening grip on her wrist stopped her from moving. Dante pinned Kelis's arm behind her back, immobilizing her.

"Hey!" Kelis struggled to break free.

"Tell me you weren't going to strike that child."

Dante's voice was colder than Takira had ever heard it before. It sent a shiver of apprehension trembling through her. Not for herself but for Kelis. Takira helped Finn up. He was no worse for wear, but he had quieted. Takira kept her body shielding him from seeing Dante holding Kelis's arm in a death grip.

"Finn, go play in your room until dinner, please." Takira handed him the train he'd dropped and pushed him a little toward his room. He gave her a curious look and looked around her at Dante who nodded and he wandered off without a grumble.

"Let go of me." Kelis fought against her, but Dante wasn't letting up.

"You were going to hit Finn. You're lucky I'm not breaking your wrist in two for daring to raise a hand to him." Dante applied more pressure, and Kelis yelped and twisted in her seat.

"My laptop is in there. He could have broken it."

"You weren't worried about your laptop when you threw it on the floor when you came in," Takira said. "He's two and a half years old, for fuck's sake. What were you thinking?"

Kelis grimaced as the pain obviously intensified. "I'm sorry?"

"You asking or telling her, girl?" Dante squeezed tighter.

"Okay, okay. I was just going to help him up."

"Oh God, Kelis, now isn't the time to start lying." Takira had had enough. "Dante, let her go."

Dante looked like she wanted to drag Kelis out by her hair and beat her senseless. There was a part of Takira that wished she could let her do that. Dante let her go. Kelis whined and cradled her wrist to her chest.

"Yeah, you should be letting go of me you fucking—"

"Kelis, get the hell out of here and don't come back."

Kelis's mouth dropped open. "What?"

"I've put up with you not taking no for an answer. But that stops now. You were going to hit Finn, and I don't want you anywhere near him ever again. I told you, he's my main priority now and you crossed the line. I don't want you to come here again. Not now, not in a few months' time when your schedule has me penciled in. This is over. We're done. Get out."

Tears began to fall as Kelis tried to apologize. For Takira, it was all too late. She should never have let them go on as long as they had.

Dante stood by watching Kelis's theatrics with an uncaring eye. She began to undo her shirtsleeves and roll them up. Takira was distracted by how sexy it looked when Dante exposed her arms and there was Mickey Mouse's yellow shoes peeking out to entice her. It was when she took off her tie that Kelis started to look a little more alarmed.

"You going to have your freak wo-*man* here throw me out?" Kelis stood up and began picking up her briefcase.

"She was a bouncer at a few places, I'm told. If you don't leave of your own accord I'm sure she'll be happy to show you off the premises."

"I wouldn't have hit him, Kira. You know that."

"I saw differently. I know you're angry with me, but to take it out on an innocent child is low."

"Well, he's not your child. You'll never be his mother," Kelis spat out. "You never even wanted kids. Your damn restaurant is your baby, and nothing else ever comes first for you."

"I won't be his mother because I'm his aunt. I don't intend on taking Latitia's place. But he's my responsibility and part of that responsibility is to keep him safe. And he's not safe around you."

Dante had removed her vest and was tugging her shirt free from her trousers. Takira was enjoying how mesmerizing Dante made the simple task of undressing look. But she looked like she was gearing herself up for a fight and Kelis knew it. She finally held up her hands.

"Okay. I'm sorry, truly I am. I'm sorry for what I nearly did, and I'm sorry for not listening to you when you said we were done, and I'm sorry it's ending this way."

"So am I, but it's still over. Please don't bother me again, Kelis. You're not welcome here anymore."

Kelis nodded and cast a look at Dante. "Would you really have broken my wrist?" She fingered her bruised skin gingerly.

"I'd have started there," Dante said with enough menace that Kelis swallowed hard.

"Just look after her, okay?" Kelis muttered to her.

"*Both* of them will be safe with me," Dante replied and pointedly opened the door.

With one last look at Dante, Kelis turned back to Takira. "I really am sorry. I screwed up big time."

"Good-bye, Kelis."

Kelis left without another word. Takira shut the door behind her, and for a moment rested her head against it to take a breath. Then she turned and threw her arms around a startled Dante, hugging her tightly.

"Thank you. I wouldn't have been quick enough to stop her from hitting him."

"I read her intention before she even lifted her hand. You gain a second sense when you work in bars. The more brooding the drunk the more likely they are to go off."

Takira tucked her head onto Dante's shoulder, thrilling when Dante's arms came up to encircle her. The feeling was everything she'd dreamed of and more. Dante's body was solid, warm, and strong. Takira felt safe in the circle of her arms.

"I'm sorry it ended like that for you."

Takira pulled back a little to see her face. "Are you really?"

"I'm not sorry to see her go," Dante said. "She didn't seem to make you happy."

"No, she never really did. I'm embarrassed by the fact we just used each other in the end."

"You shouldn't be. There's no shame in seeking comfort."

"I was having hook-up sex with my ex. Please don't make it sound altruistic." She felt Dante's silent laughter shaking her shoulders.

"Was she always so quick to anger?"

"Yes, but it's easy to turn a blind eye to that behavior when you only see someone at the most three times a year and then for maybe just an hour."

"She was very possessive for someone who clearly had no ties to you."

"Well, she was under the impression she was claiming territory. I kept telling her I wasn't interested in her anymore, but she wouldn't take no for an answer. My rejection was never going to sit well." Dante's head rested against hers a little and her arms tightened a fraction more. All she could hear in her head was Juliet urging her to seize the moment. Takira decided to throw all caution to the wind. The timing was terrible, but she might never get another chance.

"I'd told her there was someone else I'm more interested in," Takira said, leaning back in Dante's arms to watch her face. She was surprised to see the light in Dante's eyes fade.

"Oh."

Takira raised an eyebrow at Dante's flat response. She took a deep breath. *It's now or never. If I don't try I'll never know.* "I have a feeling she doesn't know because I've tried so hard to respect her boundaries. But I'm going to explode if I don't tell her how I feel and how much she means to me."

Dante looked crestfallen, and the sight tore at Takira's heart. She groaned inwardly as another thought struck her. "And there's no other way to get Juliet's damn singing out of my head unless I do this."

She took Dante's face in her hands and kissed her. Dante stiffened with surprise, then her arms tightened around Takira's waist and she kissed her back. The kiss turned hot and heavy quickly then deepened as Dante took control, rendering Takira almost boneless in her arms. Takira ran her fingers over the soft bristles of Dante's shaved hair, cupping the back of her head to pull her closer still. She couldn't get close enough. The feel of Dante's body pressed into hers was intoxicating. They gasped for air when it became a dire necessity and only then did their fervent kissing slow down and finally stop. Takira's lips felt bruised, but she didn't care. She touched her fingers to Dante's mouth and smiled when Dante pressed a kiss to them.

"Wow," Dante said, breathless and her eyes a little glazed. "That was like adding gasoline to a flame."

Takira agreed. She couldn't stop looking at Dante's lips. She pressed forward with a series of soft, tender kisses, Dante's smile blooming under her own.

"So what was this song Juliet spurred you on with?" Dante asked as she caressed Takira's face and threaded her fingers into her wayward curls.

"Something only you could appreciate." Takira ran a finger over Dante's tattoo, the muscle twitching under Dante's soft skin. "She's been teasing me with it ever since I mentioned how you make me feel. It's from *The Little Mermaid*."

A frown creased Dante's forehead before she let out a laugh. "She told you to *kiss the girl?*" Her laughter grew louder. "I haven't been called a girl in forever." Dante quieted and pulled Takira closer, burying her head in Takira's hair and whispering, "Wow."

Takira held her close. Tremors ran through Dante's body and her hands were shaking as she ran her fingers through Takira's hair.

"Wow what?" she asked softly.

Dante smiled at her. "Fairy tales *can* come true."

Takira wondered why Dante didn't sound entirely happy about that fact.

Tempted to go down into the restaurant and hide out there, Dante instead made herself sit on the sofa and watch as Takira tried to corral a hyper Finn and get him in bed. He smiled as he playfully eluded Takira and continued "choo-choo-ing" his new train around the room as he dodged out of her reach. He had no idea what had nearly happened earlier; he was just a bright and happy boy who had spent dinner time regaling Takira with everything he had done and seen that day. Everything from the "nearly butterfly" to the shopping trip Dante had taken him on.

Dante listened to the sound of bath time and gently ran her fingertips over her lips. Takira had kissed her and, God, Dante had kissed her back. It had been like bursting a dam wide open. She'd been starving, and one touch of Takira's lips on her own was all it took to expose every want and need that clambered inside Dante, all desperate to get out and *feel*. She was still a little shell-shocked by it all, how desperately she'd wanted to devour Takira, just take her and lose herself in her.

I am so screwed.

It changed nothing. Exchanging passionate kisses couldn't mean anything. Dante's heart yearned to go further, strip Takira down and learn her scent and her soft spots and her taste. But her head was flashing out alarm bells, warning her that she was heading into dangerous territory. It had been so long since she'd let someone in, let someone hold her. But she couldn't get the feeling of Takira in her arms out of her head. They'd fit together so perfectly. Takira, being that bit taller, had molded herself into Dante, tucking her head into Dante's shoulder. It had left them both the protector and the protected. Dante had felt unprotected for a long time.

The scent from Takira's hair lingered in Dante's memory, and it was a comfort to her. It smelled of home, and Dante hadn't had a home in more years than she could recall.

God, I am beyond screwed. I feel like every nerve in my body is exposed and she's a live wire zapping me back to life.

Dante was terrified. She wanted so much and felt undeserving of any of it.

"I know we have a lot to talk about." Takira came back into the room. "But I really want to know how you and Trent ended up bringing all those mothers back with you to the restaurant this morning."

Dante felt the pressure lift off her chest at the innocuous query. She knew Takira was letting her off light and they'd get around to other things soon enough. For now, Dante relaxed a little and told Takira all about the eventful morning she'd had and how Trent had made her point so eloquently.

Dante was so proud of Trent, how she owned the woman she had become. Dante had felt like that once, before Chloe tore her down and left her feeling worthless. She'd felt something inside her stir at Trent's words, making her take back the remnants of her pride and her self-worth. It had made Dante stand just that little bit taller when she'd walked out of the school surrounded by a gaggle of women who would never see how broken she had been.

"Juliet would have called that woman out if she'd have been there. She's very protective of her girl." Takira settled herself on the sofa beside Dante, twisting in her seat so she could face her. "And you can't miss how much Harley loves her mama."

"Harley is so good with Finn. She's so patient and calm including him in everything she's doing."

"Juliet firmly believes in nurture over nature. Harley might not have Trent's DNA, but her personality is undoubtedly her mama's. She has Juliet's smarts. And *that* look."

Dante knew exactly which one Takira meant. She'd seen Juliet give Trent a look at the party. A blink that lasted just a heartbeat longer than usual, and then those eyes had pierced through Trent and she'd been a goner. Whatever superpower Juliet employed in that look, it was obviously Trent's weakness and she gave herself up to it willingly.

"So today you fought off a bigot, you braved the stores with Finn in tow…"

"He's really no hassle. You just have to talk to him the whole time, telling him exactly what you're there for, and what you have to do. He's desperate to be involved and to do something. He's got a big world to explore."

"He fell asleep with his new train in his hand."

"He deserved it. He was such a good boy today. Besides, he needed a red one to go with his set."

"You don't miss anything do you?"

"Not where some things are concerned," Dante admitted, her nerves starting to jangle as Takira's gaze grew intent.

"Kelis saw you as a threat."

"I'm no one's threat."

"You are to me. A threat to my sanity for a start. From the moment I laid eyes on you, Dante, you've fascinated me."

"From the start?"

Takira nodded. "I turned around to greet you, and I'm still surprised I managed to get more than a few words out. You're way too handsome for your own good. My inner femme swooned on the spot."

Dante had to smile. "You're too kind."

"Were you ever going to tell me you found me equally as enticing?"

Dante shook her head. "No," she replied honestly.

Takira rested her head against the sofa cushion and studied her. "Are you going to give me a reason why?"

Because you deserve better than me. You deserve more than I can give you. You need someone who's not broken and battered.

"Okay, I can see you running through a list in your head of reasons why we shouldn't be together, and I'm going to stop you right there before you get lost in excuses. I kissed you and you kissed me back." Takira's smile grew. "Oh my God, you kissed me back. I'm not prepared to let that feeling go, Dante. I promise you, we can take things slow. Real slow. Baby steps all the way if that's what you need. But I've seen you watching me when I'm cooking, and I'm pretty damn sure it's not always the food you're drooling over."

Dante's laughter broke free. *Busted.* She knew her face was flaming at being caught out staring. She couldn't help it. Takira was beautiful and Dante wanted her so desperately. "You're the first woman I have met in years that has made me *feel*." Dante took a deep breath. She felt it shake in her chest as her need to protect herself warred with her need to be touched and *seen*. "You need someone younger than me, someone less prone to the middle-aged spread going on here." Dante poked herself in the stomach. "I'm skirting round the edge of menopause, Takira. You really don't need the madness that could entail."

Takira stared at her for so long Dante started to get nervous.

"You're seriously saying I need to find a cute skinny young thing? Been there, done that, honey. Kelis had abs for miles. She was my age. We had nothing in common and rarely talked about anything except to give directions in the bedroom to get each other off. You and I *talk*, Dante. And it's not just familiarity because we share this apartment together. I'm not drawn to you because I happen to see that face of yours every day. I see Zenya every day, I see Kae every day. I have a plethora of other lesbians in my midst. I'm interested in *you*. And yes, you can play the *older woman* card, but really, that means nothing to me. You're older than me. So what? You have gray hair. I don't care." Takira reached out to run her hand through the longer hair that topped Dante's head. "I love it. It suits you. And I like knowing you and Finn can get your hair shaved at the same place and save on a trip." She edged closer along the sofa. "As for you not having rock solid abs, I'll need to look more closely into that." She grinned as she ran a hand down Dante's arm and along the edge of her trousers to rest upon Dante's belt buckle.

Dante sucked a breath in when Takira's fingers brushed against her T-shirt and left a trail of fire in their wake.

"You have a Mickey Mouse belt buckle. I've never noticed that before." Takira traced the picture cut into the metal. "What is it about the mouse you like, Dante?"

"When I was growing up I wasn't allowed to watch much TV. My father thought it was the tool of the devil and would hypnotize the masses. Which, looking back, he wasn't entirely wrong about. He allowed me one show to watch and I watched *The Wonderful*

World of Disney, as it was as educational as it was entertaining. My parents left me alone a lot while they worked so I pretty much lived in the local movie theater. I'd wander from screen to screen and spend hours watching every Disney movie I could." She remembered how alone she'd been even before her parents had cut her off.

"People always look at the animations and think how cute they are and childish, but there's a whole lot more going on in them. An undercurrent of menace that I caught on to at a very young age. I could see the true story *behind* the bright colors and the songs that distracted you away from the hidden messages. I didn't watch the horror movies my classmates were sneaking in to see. I had Disney. Right there amid the animation, I learned about child abduction, child abandonment, child exploitation, child endangerment. Then there was animal cruelty in many forms, and let's not forget the cheery fact your parents will die and leave you all alone in a cold, harsh world. All this education came wrapped up with a cheery sing-along song sheet and an eventual happy ending. Believe me, you learn more than you think when you really watch them. My father never had a clue what he was letting me see."

Takira's fingers stilled on Dante's belt. "You're kidding, right?"

"They are violent little stories that would need a higher parental rating if they were done in live action. Funny how drawings or the computer generated graphics they use now makes the violence more acceptable, isn't it?"

"I'm not going to ever watch one again in the same light."

"I love them because, despite it all, they always let the hero come out on top. Those movies were my escape. Each cartoon ingrained in my memory cementing my happy place. I just never stopped watching them when I grew up. They're still important to me and they're entertaining. When life got really sour at home I dreamed of running away to Disneyland and working there." She made a face. "But I'm not exactly princess material, and I think I'd have been claustrophobic in the mouse suit."

"I don't need you to be a princess or a prince. I just need you to be *you*."

Dante covered Takira's hand with her own. "I can't promise you a happy ending. I don't know how those work in real life."

"I'll settle for the story never ending then. I know you said you didn't date and that's why I tried so hard to step back and not let myself get involved with you, but I can't do it anymore. I think we could be more than just roommates, Dante. I think you could be so much more for me if we gave it a chance."

"I didn't fare too well in the last relationship I tried. The words 'crashed and burned' spring to mind."

"Honey, I've just spent the last few years having intermittent sex with an ex who should have stayed that way. It's embarrassing to admit it. I work so much that I had to have someone literally come to me, having warned me to schedule some time in my day for us to...do whatever and then both go back to work. I didn't even get a meal or a bunch of flowers. It was clinical and soulless and nothing more than a brief release of tension before I buried myself back in the kitchen. I was so wrapped up in myself I missed my last manager stealing from me. It's taken Finn and you coming into my life to make me ease back a bit and realize there's more that I want out of life."

"And you want me?" Why would someone as amazing as Takira want *her*?

Takira sprang forward and kissed her. Their lips clung and Takira took another kiss from her before nodding. "Yeah, I want you, Dante Groves. You made me slow down and see outside of my kitchen. I see *you*. And having you and Kelis in the same room only pointed out what I needed, and she came up sorely lacking in every department." She kissed Dante again. "I want to get to know you and all the silly things about you that no one else knows."

"Like what?"

"Like, what's your favorite movie of all?"

Dante didn't hesitate. "*Wonder Woman*."

Takira frowned. "That's not a Disney movie. It's not even animation."

"I'm a huge fan of Disney, but I do watch other movies too. And Gal Gadot as Diana Prince? That's my kind of heroine."

"I haven't seen it."

"You haven't seen *Wonder Woman?*"

"I was busy. I have a restaurant to run."

"For fuck's sake, I got here just in time to save you from yourself. The next free night after Finn has gone to bed we're watching *Wonder Woman.*"

"Will that be a date night instead of a family night?" Takira asked slyly, giving Dante a look that was full of so much promise she felt her cheeks get hot under Takira's scrutiny.

"I guess. But I'd rather take you out on a date, a proper date. And not here in your own restaurant because that would just be tacky."

"The staff would love it. They'd hover like flies around us," Takira said. "I'm sure some of them have bets on us."

"Really?" Had she been that obvious in her longing that everyone around her knew?

"I think our ease around each other and the fact you are a Finn magnet has made them hopeful for us to get together."

"But you're the boss and I'm under you."

"Not yet you're not," Takira said, laughing at Dante's inelegant spluttering at her quick wit.

"You know what I mean."

"They don't care about the boss/worker dynamic. We don't have that in this restaurant. We're a family and they want to see me happy. And they're starting to love you so they want to see you happy too."

"They love me? I wouldn't go that far."

"What can I say? You're easy to love." Takira shrugged and gave her a shy smile, one at odds with her earlier sassy comments.

Dante wished she could believe her, but she couldn't. Everyone that should have loved her let her down and left her feeling worthless.

Takira cupped Dante's face in her hands. Dante lost herself in Takira's dark eyes.

"Leave the past in the past, Dante. Let yourself feel *now*. You, me, and Finn? We're all 'nearly butterflies' just waiting for that moment we get to break free and fly." She nuzzled at Dante's cheek, leaving tiny kisses there. "Care to fly with me?"

Dante saw the hope in Takira's eyes. Could she really take a brave step forward to try again, to open herself up to all the hurts that feeling could bring? Finally, she nodded, and Takira kissed her with purpose and passion. Dante let herself get lost in the joy of it.

She let herself take a step into the flames of need and desire, daring them to engulf her and sear her soul.

A muffled cry from Finn's bedroom broke them apart like guilty teenagers. Dante bit back a disappointed groan at the intrusion while Takira looked horrified.

"Oh my God, I forgot all about him!" Takira quickly stood up. "His first memory of us together is not going to be him walking in on us butt naked on this sofa!" She made a move toward Finn's room but turned back to give Dante one last kiss. "We'll revisit this moment another time. For now, hold that thought."

Dante watched her go check on Finn. She did as she was told. She held on to every thought she had of Takira and let them spark hope in her heart.

CHAPTER SIXTEEN

They'd been very careful with the PDAs around Finn the next morning, but Dante soon realized Takira was very tactile and would reach out often to touch now that she knew she could. After spending so many years without any form of physical contact, having someone touch her intimately made Dante flinch. It was in reaction to her being startled every time Takira wrapped her arms around Dante's waist or leaned in to plant a kiss on her cheek. It only served to make Dante realize how starved for affection she had been, especially in her last relationship. Dante had spent most of breakfast apologizing for jumping or stiffening until even she got sick of her body's shock at being touched. Takira had just laughed it off.

"You'll get used to me soon enough. I'm just making the most of the fact that after you jump you melt into my arms. *That's* never going to grow old."

Dante had been unsure how they were going to proceed now. Everything had changed, and Dante was still unsure about it all. But she was sure she wanted to be with Takira and just had to start breaking the barriers down she'd built up so high to guard her heart.

She found Kayleigh and Finn in residence when she came back to the apartment from her lunch break. Finn jumped up and ran to Dante's side.

"Hey, Finn. Are you being a good boy for Kayleigh?"

"He's always a good boy," Kayleigh said, getting up from the floor to join them at the kitchen table where Finn was watching everything Dante was removing from her bags. "That's a beautiful bouquet, Dante. Monica could probably tell you every single flower that's in it, but all I see is lots of yellows and pinks. But they are pretty yellow and pinks." She stuck her head in the bouquet and took a deep sniff. "Wow, they smell nice too."

Dante removed the most fragile item she'd been carrying in the bag. She placed it on the table, and Finn and Kayleigh crowded in closer. Finn scrunched up his face in curiosity at it.

"What's that?"

Dante turned the rectangular shaped tray around so they could view it from all angles. "It's a bonsai tree." She hunkered down at the table to see it from straight on. "I've always wanted one, and the florist had this one on display. I couldn't resist it."

"Will it grow into a real tree?" Kayleigh asked, copying Dante and crouching to get a different view.

"No, the bonsai is deliberately cultivated to be a smaller version of the bigger tree it resembles. It's a Japanese art form to tend these little trees, one that's thousands of years old. I've got to get special tools to prune the leaves just right to look after it. But I've always wanted one, and now that I have a permanent job, this was a present to myself." She ran her finger gently around the edge of the ceramic pot. "Because I'm setting down roots of my own now."

Kayleigh smiled. "That's really neat. What are you going to call it?"

Dante raised an eyebrow at her. "Excuse me?"

"You have to name it. Monica says that talking to plants is very therapeutic and there's no point having a conversation with your bonsai unless you're going to name it so you can address it properly."

Dante hummed and eyed the bonsai critically. "I have no idea what to call it. It doesn't look like a Billy Bonsai."

Finn didn't offer anything more than, "Pretty baby tree."

"Groot," Kayleigh announced decisively.

"Really?" Dante grinned at the thought.

"It's a baby tree, and the way the branches are shaped they look like arms dancing just like baby Groot did when he was boogying to the Jackson 5."

"I like the way you think, Kayleigh. What do you think, Finn? Shall we call this bonsai Groot?"

Finn nodded. "I am Groot!"

"Thank you, Kayleigh, Groot it is. Hopefully, it won't dance." She laughed when Finn let out a disappointed sound. "Okay, now that Groot has been introduced to you both I need to gather some of the things I've brought and get ready. I have a meeting with the boss at two, and I dare not be late." She shook the bag of M&M's and made Finn laugh. "Whose favorites are these?"

"Aunt Kira's!" Finn shouted.

Dante reached in the bag for something else. She handed a gingerbread man over to Finn who gasped and began gnawing on it. Dante got him a glass of milk to accompany it. She then pulled out a tray of doughnuts for Kayleigh.

"I don't expect you to eat the whole lot now. I thought you could maybe take them with you and share them with your friend Sam tonight."

"Thank you. How did you know these were my favorites?"

Dante smiled. "Because you never turn down a glazed doughnut. I pay attention to what the people I care about like the most." She gathered up the rest of her groceries and put them away. "And I care about this little guy." She kissed Finn on top of his head. He smiled up at her with a mouthful of gingerbread. "And I care about you because you work so hard to look after Finn. I appreciate that and I know Takira does too." Then, after hesitating just a fraction, Dante kissed Kayleigh on her forehead. Kayleigh's eyes widened.

"That's what Trent does."

"She used to do that to me when she was younger. She said because I was shorter than her it was the easiest place to reach."

"I always feel special when she does it to me because she doesn't do it to everyone."

"She always made me feel special too. You're going to grow up just like her. You care, Kayleigh, and that makes you special in your own right. Your Sam's a lucky girl."

Kayleigh opened her mouth to argue then closed it at the look Dante gave her. "I want what Trent and Juliet have. I think, maybe one day, Sam might be my Player 2."

Dante laughed. "Yeah, I was right. You're going to grow up *exactly* like Trent. Okay, you two, I'm going back to work so no loud parties up here."

"We'll be good," Kayleigh said. "Good luck with your meeting. Though I'm not sure what kind of meeting requires M&M's and a bunch of flowers." Her eyes sparkled with mischief. "I may be just a kid, but I'm thinking Takira is a lucky girl too."

Dante wagged her finger at Kayleigh playfully. "Now *that* look was all Juliet. You're dangerous. Between their influences and your own smarts, you are going to be formidable."

"Thank you for the doughnuts, Dante."

"They're payment for the fact you're going to have to clean up after Finn has finished demolishing his gingerbread. Sorry!" Dante ducked out the door after remembering to pick up the vase she'd brought and had filled with water.

Time to get down to business.

CHAPTER SEVENTEEN

A knock on the door brought Takira's head up from where she'd had it buried in paperwork. Slowly but surely, she was clawing back money to replace what Claude had stolen, but it still chafed that she was having to start all over again to save it. She looked at the time and smiled. *Dante*. Because unlike the rest of her staff, Dante didn't just knock and immediately enter.

"Come in, Dante." She couldn't hide her joy when Dante walked in. Her smile grew even wider when she saw what Dante was carrying in with her. "You brought me flowers?" Such a simple gesture, but it meant the world to Takira. The vibrant colors lifted her spirits, and the smell from them was divine.

Dante's hands were full, but she still managed to lean in to kiss Takira sweetly. Then she busied herself searching for a space on Takira's desk to put everything down and arrange the flowers for her.

"I've just had a few minutes upstairs with the kids. I treated them so," she pulled out the bag of M&M's from her pocket, "I thought you might like these."

"Are you trying to sweeten the deal, Dante?" Takira said, gravitating closer to her because she just couldn't stand not being close.

"You're already sweet." Dante finished arranging the vase and brushed off her hands. She pulled out the file she had tucked under her arm and brandished it. "I have some supplier updates and a proposal for you."

Takira put a hand over her heart, feigning surprise. "Oh my, so soon? Are you going to go down on one knee?" She tried desperately not to laugh at Dante's confused look that quickly turned into understanding. Dante's cheeks flamed red. Takira thought it was the cutest thing ever.

"A business proposal," Dante said, shaking her head at Takira's theatrics. "We're taking baby steps, remember? You might come to decide I'm not worth the hassle."

Takira reached for Dante's chin and tilted her head up so they could lock eyes. "You are worth more than you realize. I'll spend every hour of every day proving that to you if I have to."

Dante stared deep into Takira's eyes as if searching them for the truth behind her words. She relaxed, and Takira stole a kiss before stepping back so as not to push any further. Baby steps, slow and steady to win Dante's trust and her heart.

"So, flowers, candy, and work proposals. I like the way you conduct business, Ms. Groves." Takira sat back behind her desk. She pulled the vase a little closer so she could make the most of the pretty bouquet. "Thank you for these. They are beautiful."

"I thought they'd cheer up the office and you. I know you're looking through the finances today. And that's why I asked for a moment of your time." Dante sat and opened up her file. "Firstly, can I mention that I went to school with many of your suppliers?"

"No kidding?"

"I've been going through them all and recognized a lot of names. So I've been doing a little calling around and reacquainting myself with some of my old cohorts." She grinned. "I chatted with Charlie, you'd know her as Charlotte Smith. She supplies a great deal of your produce. When we were barely teenagers, she and I got shit-faced drunk on wine her father was making from fermented fruit. We were found singing awful eighties tunes at the top of our lungs while lying precariously on the roof of their barn."

"I can't imagine you so drunk that your music standards slipped."

"It wasn't the first time, and it wouldn't be my last until Germany when I realized that being drunk wasn't the best state to find myself in. Took me a lot of years to finally come to that conclusion." She shook her head." Anyway, Charlie and I were reminiscing and we've come to an agreement concerning her prices for what you buy from her. I know she was due to raise them?"

Takira nodded. She'd been worrying about the extra cost the produce would add to her bills for weeks now.

"Well, she's freezing them for you for now. I didn't give her any details of what's happened here, that business is *your* business. I merely asked for a favor and she agreed to it. But she's not doing it out of the kindness of her heart. We're talking quid pro quo. What she proposed got me thinking, which leads me into the proposal I have for you."

Dante grinned. "Charlie is getting married next year to Orson Weller. As you can imagine, we teased the hell out of him in school with that name. Anyway, he supplies your seafood, and through Charlie, I've managed to get him to keep his prices down too. In exchange, they'd like to have you cater their wedding."

Takira's mouth dropped open. "We do party bookings but not weddings."

"I know, but this is the third time I've had someone ask me if you cater bigger events. There's an opportunity there just waiting for you to exploit it, Takira. I believe if you remove the breakfast bar from that one side of the restaurant you can free up space for more tables and designate it specifically for parties, be they birthday or wedding ones."

Takira mulled it over for a moment. She could picture it and began calculating what they'd need and what they could do with the freed up space.

"Charlie and Orson would be bringing a sizeable party into the restaurant, both have been married before so there's extended family added into the mix. They wouldn't expect the food for free, but seeing as they are helping you, you'd be repaying the favor by catering their shindig with a sizeable reduction in costs. This could be a lucrative addition to the restaurant. Yes, it would be extra work, but in the long run it would garner more business, bring in more customers, and spread the word that Takira's isn't just for mealtimes but also caters for special occasions. We could hit the local business areas with a leaflet campaign. They could come and hold business meals here, expanding your clientele. Bringing more money into the business and bringing in customers." Dante closed her file. "And that's just from me talking to Charlie and Orson. Some of the other suppliers are cutting their prices for you when I looked around and found we could source it cheaper elsewhere. I gave them the option of keeping your very regular business over you going somewhere else for a cheaper price. You're very well respected, Takira. These suppliers like doing business with you. I have a list here of the new costs and who we know are reliable and ones to keep on our side. Maybe Christmas time you can invite them in for a meal and show them how much appreciation there is for their hard work. Everyone likes to be appreciated. It makes them work harder."

"You never cease to amaze me." Takira's head was spinning with what Dante was proposing. It would mean more work, but the restaurant could manage it. It would be great for business, and keeping clients and suppliers happy would be an added bonus.

"Well, if that's something you'll consider, I have something else. You need a bigger parking lot. I noticed that the first time I drove in. That lot next to you is neglected and overgrown. If you can set aside the funds for it, I'd recommend you buy the adjacent lot and extend your parking. More parking spaces, more customers." Dante put her file on Takira's desk. "Everything I'm proposing is in here. I have itemized costs and also quotes for removing the breakfast bar and for purchasing the lot and clearing it for resurfacing."

Takira reached for the file and skimmed through it. The blueprints for her expanding her business and serving a larger customer base were right before her eyes. "I'll show this to Juliet and get her thoughts on it." She eyed Dante. "You have fantastic managerial skills and such a head for business. Why aren't you running your own place?"

"Because I have no yearning to do that. I like helping others get their business running at peak efficiency. That's where my satisfaction in my abilities lies."

"You realize I'm not ever letting you leave Takira's, don't you? You're too valuable an asset."

"There's nowhere else I'd rather be."

"I'm talking on both a business and personal level here."

"So am I. Which leads me to my other proposal." Dante took a deep breath, seeming to calm herself. "I'd like to ask you out on a date."

"Yes. Yes and yes. To whatever you're proposing, yes."

Dante laughed. "Okay, that was the easy part. Let me get back to you on a date and time."

"Bully my manager into giving us both the time off for an evening," Takira said. "That's if we're doing an evening date?"

"Yes, I think an evening date would be perfect." Dante stood. "My business is concluded here and my shift is about to start so I'll let you get back to your work. Enjoy your flowers. Oh, and if you manage to go upstairs be sure to say hello to Groot."

Takira frowned. "Who is Groot?"

"Finn will show you."

"You'd better not have bought a puppy!"

Dante laughed. "No, no fur balls in the restaurant. But it is something you can talk to and not worry you have to take it for walks."

"Has anyone ever told you you're insane, Dante Groves?"

"I'm crazy about you, Takira Lathan."

"Then it's a good thing I feel the exact same way about you, isn't it?"

"It's the best thing," Dante said and opened the door. "I'll get someone to bring you a snack because I know you skipped out on lunch again."

"What would I do without you?"

"Eat M&M's and argue that you were still eating healthily because you eat the green ones first." Dante tossed her a wink and closed the door behind her.

"Damn, she knows me way too well." Takira reached for the bag and ripped it open. She automatically began searching out the green ones. She popped one into her mouth and grinned. *I'm going on a date with Dante.* She ignored her screen and just sat back in her chair and let that thought sink in. She told herself it was no big deal. It was just a date. With Dante.

Date night found Dante standing before her bathroom mirror rubbing her hands over her newly shaved hair. She and Finn had gotten their hair cut earlier that day, and then she'd dropped Finn off for his first sleepover with Harley. He'd been a little clingy once he realized Dante was leaving, but she'd assured him she'd be back for him the next morning and she'd show Trent how to make her special pancakes. Suitably eased by that promise, he'd soon gotten distracted by Harley and was off playing.

Now Dante was making sure her "dress casual" missive she'd given Takira also applied to what she was wearing. She couldn't help but miss the vest and tie that were her trademark style, but she gave herself a satisfied once-over. She wore her black jeans cuffed just right over her boots and a soft black denim shirt that sported Mickey Mouse shaped studs that she knew Takira would get a kick out of. She fastened on her limited edition Invicta Mickey Mouse watch that only saw the light of day on special occasions. Dante felt this was definitely one of them.

There was something a little strange about getting ready for a date when your partner was getting ready on just the other side of the apartment. Dante wiped her palms on her jeans and willed herself not to screw this up for what felt like the thousandth time in an hour. She grabbed her wallet, fastened its chain to a belt loop, and gave herself one last critical look.

She could hear Takira singing along with the radio. Dante took a moment to enjoy the sound before she hastened to gather things they would need for their date. Dante had chosen to do something different.

"Oh my," Takira said, walking into the living room and devouring Dante with her eyes. "You rock black denim so well. A stud in studs, my kind of aesthetic." She moved closer and trailed her fingers over the bright silver studs down Dante's shirt. "These are subtle." She popped one open and smiled. "Yet easy to open. That's good to know."

Dante laughed at her and brushed her hand away. She fastened the stud back up. "There's no messing with the Mouse before date night."

Takira hooked her arm through Dante's as she led her out the door. "That implies there might be messing allowed afterward." She squeezed Dante's bicep. "I love a slow burn."

"Between me being celibate for four years and how your last romance was conducted, I'd say we're not so much slow burn as sedentary."

"Well, maybe we can change that." Takira leaned in and kissed Dante's cheek.

"Maybe." Dante smiled, enjoying the feel of Takira's lips lingering. She couldn't resist letting her gaze travel over Takira's tight blue jeans teamed with a flowery feminine shirt that was open to display more than a hint of cleavage. A body full of curves and a bright smile that warmed her heart.

"So where are you taking me?" Takira had been trying all week to get Dante to spill her surprise.

"I'm still not telling you. You'll find out soon enough."

"You'll find I'm not big on patience."

"Then it's a good thing you don't have long to wait." Dante picked up her bag from beside the door. "Eric is closing up tonight if we're not back in time, so forget about the restaurant for an evening and let's just go out and relax."

Dante led Takira out the back of the restaurant and got her settled in her car. Takira was looking around it when Dante got in.

"This is my first time in your car. This isn't what I'd expect you to drive."

"It was all I could afford by the time I got back from Europe. It's clean, gets good mileage, and serves my purpose. Finn likes it, though I think he sees it as one of the old clunkers from *Cars*. One day I'll trade it for a more Lightning McQueen model."

"Something tells me you're not big on status symbols."

"I don't think my midlife crisis will be triggered by my not driving a slinky sports car that I'd need to limbo to get out of."

Dante drove out of the parking lot and headed into town. Minutes later, she pulled into a space at a local bar. Takira let Dante help her from the car.

"I used to work here, years ago. Back when Trent was just a young pup and Elton couldn't grow a beard to save his life. We can grab a drink from the bar if you wish, but I haven't brought you here to reminisce." She led the way into the crowded bar and caught the eye of the bartender who hollered out Dante's name and pushed her way through the patrons to hug her tight.

"I can't believe you're back! Roller said you'd popped in." The geeky looking woman eyed Takira. "And in such fine company too."

Dante introduced them. "Takira Lathan, this is Petra Marston. She was just a young thing when I worked here."

"She taught me everything I know," Petra said. "God, we've all missed you. I'm glad to see you're not with that nurse anymore. We heard bad things about her once you left."

"Yeah, I kind of had to learn about those bad things firsthand."

"Bummer, dude. But you're back now? Are you coming back here? Roller would move heaven and earth for that to happen."

Dante felt Takira's hold on her hand tighten just a fraction. "No, I've already got a job at Takira's. I'm the manager there now."

Petra's eyes widened. "Shit, you're *that* Takira? I've heard great things about your place."

"You'll have to come pay us a visit one day," Takira said.

"I'd love that." Petra tugged at Dante's arm. "Come on back, everything has been set up for you. Roller got it all cleaned just for you."

Dante grinned at her exuberance. Nothing had changed except her hair seemed to be a shade more…blue? Dante squinted a little in the defused colored lights of the bar.

"Your hair is blue," she remarked.

"Yeah, I change it every Pride. Yours is even whiter now. I could see you coming a mile off. It's so shiny!"

Dante looked over her shoulder at Takira's laughter. "I get no respect."

Petra led them behind the bar and through a door into a hallway. She opened up another door marked No Entry and gestured for them to go down the set of steps leading to a basement. "While you get settled I'll get your drinks. What are you having?" Dante and Takira gave their orders and Petra scampered off.

Dante led Takira down the small staircase into a large room decked out with theater seats. Takira's mouth dropped open in surprise.

"I was not expecting *this*." She gestured around the tiny theater hidden under the bar. The screen wasn't huge, but it was big enough and the seats were clean. "I'll be honest, for a moment as we descended I was fearing some bizarre little S&M setup."

"I hate to disappoint you but I'm really not into that kind of sex. I'm not completely vanilla, but all those leather straps would chafe like a bitch on a body like mine." Dante felt seared by Takira's scrutiny as she ran her eyes over her.

"Well, I'm hoping you're open to taking the lead, but I would have drawn the line at calling you *mistress*. I love Rihanna to bits but, to be honest, chains and whips *don't* excite me."

Dante gestured for Takira to pick out a seat. "This little theater used to be where they'd show the rare gay movies that never made it to the regular theater way back in the sixties and seventies. Back then they'd 'borrow' movies from the theater that used to be just up the road from here before it got torn down and the multiplex took its place. It's all working and set up to show movies on a big screen and even in a crude version of surround sound now. Roller got a friend to acquire the projection equipment from the old theater. It was all going to be trashed anyway. It's not a proper theater experience with all the bells and whistles, but it's an experience in itself."

"It's a secret theater. I've heard about those. I never expected one in Columbia." Takira sat them right in the middle of the seats and pushed down the chair next to her for Dante.

"We have the place to ourselves tonight." Dante rummaged in her bag and pulled out a bucket of popcorn and a big bag of M&M's. "I came prepared."

Petra came back with their drinks, then she disappeared to the back of the room. The lights dimmed then turned off completely as the screen lit up the room. The movie started without the annoyance of endless commercials or pointless trailers.

"*Wonder Woman.*" Takira leaned in to kiss Dante before fixing her eyes firmly on the screen.

Dante opened the M&M's and placed them on Takira's lap. She positioned the popcorn between them. Before even the opening scene had made its way on the screen, Takira reached for Dante's hand and never let go.

Dante had seen the movie numerous times. Sitting there in the darkness of the basement, on old theater seats that were comfortable if a little shabby, Dante was at her happiest. She had Gal Gadot about to light up the screen before her and her own woman who filled her with wonder sitting beside her. In that moment her life was perfect and she wished she could stay in it forever, holding Takira's hand in her own, and surrounded by Amazons. Wrestling one-handedly, she managed to pull out a little box Zenya had filled with her favorite treats. Takira risked a look away from the screen to shake her head at her when she'd obviously caught the smell of coconut. Dante offered her a bite, and Takira took a generous one with a smile. She then kissed Dante's lips, leaving the rich taste of raspberry jam clinging to them. Dante licked her lips and enjoyed the treat even more.

CHAPTER EIGHTEEN

I still can't believe Princess Buttercup was General Antiope!" Takira was buzzing from the joy of the movie. It had been a fantastic story, she'd loved all the action, and she'd fallen in love with the leading lady. She knew Dante understood; she had admitted to the same affliction.

They were back at the apartment well before midnight after sharing an after movie drink with Petra and Roller.

Dante grabbed them both a bottle of water and joined Takira on the sofa. Takira reached for Dante's hand and ran her fingertips over her palm. "I had a terrific night tonight. I can't believe you managed to score a copy of *Wonder Woman* for us to watch in that little place. It was magical. So much better than being in a proper theater. Especially as we got to make out during the credits and not have to worry about being kicked out."

"It's an experience, that's for sure. Roller said they hadn't used it in a while. I'm just glad it was okay for a first date. I was so worried I'd screw up and you'd hate it."

"Honey, you didn't screw anything up. I got to eat popcorn and M&M's watching so many wonderful women kick ass on the screen. And I got to hold your hand the whole time. It was perfect. Hands down, my best date ever."

Dante leaned her head back against the sofa. "I had fun too. It's been a long time since I did anything like that. And I enjoyed spending time with you and having you meet some of my old colleagues."

"Am I going to have to worry Roller is going to try to sneak you back to working with her? She seemed hell-bent on that idea no matter how many times I told her to forget it."

"No, I'm perfectly happy where I am, working here with you. I can't think of anywhere else I'd rather be." She placed her water aside and reached for Takira.

Her kiss was soft, and Takira opened up to her without hesitation. She loved the feel of Dante's lips as they brushed over hers gently. That first kiss was tentative, feather soft. Dante's tongue teased her, and Takira willingly allowed her entrance. A shiver ran through her, igniting all her nerve endings until her whole body screamed out for more. More Dante, more kisses, more of her touch. Takira willingly let Dante set the pace. She clung to Dante's arms and reveled at the strength she could feel. Dante wasn't pure muscle, but she was solid, so strong, and yet so gentle. Takira couldn't resist any longer. She held on tight with one hand while she ran her fingers through Dante's newly shorn hair. The bristles tickled her fingertips and the softness of the longer hair on top just begged for Takira to thread her fingers through it to pull Dante closer.

"My God, you are so sexy," Takira said, cupping Dante's face in her hands when they finally broke their kiss. She saw something, a brief flash that darkened Dante's face and dimmed some of the light in her eyes. Takira stilled. "Dante, I find you incredibly attractive. You know that, right? I mean, I know it's our first date, but I'm ready to let you run around all my bases and hit a home run."

Dante shook her head at her, a reluctant smile on her face. "What am I going to do with you?"

"Anything you want," Takira said seriously. "I mean it, Dante. I want you. I always have. You're everything I could wish for. You're beautiful and you drive me totally crazy in those suits you wear. You're kind, you're funny, and you're great with people.

Finn loves you to pieces." Takira didn't care if it was too soon. She had to tell her. "I love you too."

Dante stared at her for the longest moment, disbelief warring with an intense look of hope that shone so clearly from her eyes. Takira gently brushed her fingers over Dante's cheek as she waited for her to speak.

"You can do so much better than me," Dante said finally.

Takira shook her head. "No, I don't believe I can. Nor would I want to." She pulled Dante down for another kiss and poured all her feelings into it. "I want *you*."

"I want this *so* much. I want *you* so much." Her chest started to heave as her emotions took over.

Takira lowered her hand. She could feel Dante's heart pounding beneath her palm. She could almost feel Dante warring with herself.

"I feel like I'm going crazy. I've walled up my emotions and needs and wants for so long, and you come along and, like a wrecking ball, just smashed right through. I have no defenses with you, Takira. No defense *against* you."

"What are you so afraid of, Dante?"

"You. And me. Mostly me. I'm afraid that I can't be what you want and it would kill me to watch the light die in your eyes like it did with Chloe."

"I'm *not* her."

"No. That's why I'm still here." Dante clung to Takira. "I never used to be like this," she finally admitted. "I used to stand tall and stare people down, and I owned my life." She slipped out of Takira's arms and pulled away. She ran a hand through her hair and sighed. "I've put up with a lot of dismissive looks from people throughout my life. I was the kid that people would tell my parents that hopefully I'd change as I grew older and I'd grow into my looks. Well, I did, but my face still wasn't what my parents wanted to see."

Dante started to pace. "I've never been one to give my heart easily, and dates were few and far between and I was okay with that. But Chloe was different. Chloe led me to believe that I was her girl. Emphasis on the girl, because for all of this," Dante gestured to herself, "I'm still very much a woman. I may dress like a man, but I am not one and I don't want to be one. I just want to be *me*."

Takira nodded but stayed silent. She could tell Dante needed to get this off her chest and Takira wanted to hear it.

Dante took in a shaky breath. "It means the whole world to me that you love me, Takira, because I know I feel the same way about you."

Takira's heart leapt in her chest. She started to rise, but Dante put out a hand.

"But I don't know if I can ever shake the damage Chloe did to me. She took a very proud and strong butch woman and made me feel unacceptable all over again. She did it so insidiously that I didn't even realize my pride had been stripped from me until I walked out of that house with what little stuff I had and she had the last word."

Dante lowered her eyes and wouldn't look at Takira.

"She told me I wasn't woman enough to be a lesbian. That I certainly wasn't woman enough for *her*. That my looks had turned her off in the end and she couldn't bear me to touch her. So she'd had to take comfort from other women. *Real* women. Not ones who dressed like men." Dante's hands shook as she rolled up her sleeves, obviously using the familiar routine to distract herself. "I was just an experiment for her amusement. How truly masculine am I underneath my shirt and tie? Am I secretly hiding a dick in my boxer shorts? And Chloe's favorite brand of pillow talk, just what did my brain tell me I was when I looked in the mirror and saw *this* face looking back?"

Dante's shaking worsened, and Takira gathered her into her arms. Dante clung to her like a woman drowning at sea.

"I just saw me, Takira. I only ever saw me. A woman who is attracted to other women. A woman who feels more comfortable wearing men's clothing rather than a dress. But for all I look and act masculine…I'm still a *woman*. Just a different one." Dante buried her face into Takira's hair and slumped into her arms. "I'm just *different*. I'm just *me*."

Takira smoothed her hands over Dante's broad shoulders. She whispered soft, soothing sounds in Dante's ear and laid gentle kisses on the side of her head.

"And that's what I love about you the most," Takira said and held on tighter as she felt and heard the heart wrenching sob break free from Dante's chest. She never let go. Takira just held on and lent Dante her strength.

❖

The sound of the kettle boiling sounded shrill in the quiet of the kitchen. Dante sat at the kitchen table watching Takira mixing up mugs of hot chocolate. Takira measured out marshmallows to melt onto the top and sprinkled cocoa powder over them. Then she gathered a plate covered in Dante's favorite cakes. She sat as close as she could to Dante without physically being in her lap.

"Of course, you've already had some of these tonight seeing as they were your movie treat. Let me guess, Zenya?"

Dante nodded, already reaching out for one.

"You know I'm going to be suspicious of any raise that woman gets now. I'll always wonder is it because of her work or because she's sneaking you cakes."

"She does work very hard, and her salary will be up for review at some point. Once the business has settled back down you'll need to make a decision about upping her wages. She deserves it."

Takira hummed. "Before that, I need to have words with her about sneaking out *my* treats for *my* girl. She's got her own woman to spoil."

"I've been meaning to ask. Is there a reason why she keeps engaging me in Disney specific discussions?"

"She's trying to guess who your all-time favorite character is."

Dante looked at her watch. "I wear him all the time."

Takira punched at the air. "Yes! I guessed right. You're all about the Mouse."

"I like so many of the others too, but Mickey is ingrained on my soul. Especially from *The Sorcerer's Apprentice*. I love him in his wizard's hat and gown." Dante took a long drink from her mug and licked at the frothy mallow moustache it made. Takira chuckled at her predicament, then leaned in and licked the moustache off. "We'd better not be visiting Starbucks soon if that's how you're going to warn me I have a little something on my face."

Takira gave her one last kiss and drank from her own mug.

Dante couldn't believe that after the tears she'd just shed, Takira's response was to cuddle her close and then make her hot chocolate. With coconut cakes. She couldn't tear her eyes from Takira as she drank. Takira was amazing. Dante was totally smitten by her. She couldn't honestly remember the last time she had cried in the presence of someone else.

Her parents had always frowned upon any kind of emotion being displayed so Dante had learned very early on to keep it bottled up inside. That was why she understood Finn so well and encouraged him to *feel*. If he was frustrated, she let him grumble, if he was sad, she let him cry. If he was happy and louder than usual, she took him to the park to yell it all out in freedom. She didn't want him to ever feel that he couldn't express his emotions.

Takira hadn't judged her or told her to be quiet or to stop. She'd just held her and let all the sadness and disappointment and sheer heartache pour out.

"I can't believe you made me Finn's Magic Mallow drink, the one he gets when he needs cheering up."

"It was what Grandma used to make for me when my mother or Latitia were dragging me down. She always knew when I needed it. I thought you needed it too." Takira rested a hand on Dante's arm and rubbed gently. "You okay, honey?"

"Better than I've felt in years. Though a little embarrassed you had to be witness to it all. I'm sorry."

"Let me tell you something." Takira reached for Dante's free hand and held it tight. "I fell for you on sight. I took one look at your face and was captivated by your looks." She shushed Dante when Dante tried to interrupt. "I think you're gorgeous. I love how your eyes get this look of sheer joy when you and Finn are dancing to Kate Bush in your pajamas first thing in the morning. *Every* morning. It never gets old. I love the spark of mischief your eyes get when you think you are sneaking those damned coconut cakes past me in the kitchen. I swear you and Zenya could be baton carrying Olympians with how smoothly you pass them to each other behind my back." She traced a finger along Dante's eyebrow. "I love how these are as gray as your hair, and how this one," she rubbed over the right one, "quirks up like Spock's when you're confronted with something that intrigues you. I love these lines on your face that show how much you smile. And I love your smile. It warms my heart and turns my legs to Jell-O when you direct it my way."

Dante was stunned into silence as she listened to Takira list her favorite things about her. No one had ever done that. And Dante knew she meant it. That was what kept her quiet. Her soul soaked every word in and sparked hope in a heart that had long lay barren.

"I especially like the look of pride you get when Finn does something successfully, no matter how small it is. The corner of your mouth lifts just here." Takira touched Dante's mouth. "I never saw that look on Latitia's face once. Not when he started to crawl or learned to walk or even when he said his first word."

"I love that kid." Dante's smile grew under Takira's hand.

"I know you do and he knows it too."

"I didn't expect to. I didn't realize he'd burrow inside my heart just like his aunt did until there was nothing I could do anymore to try to keep you both out. I have no defenses against either of you."

"Are you afraid of me?"

"I'm more afraid of how hard I've fallen for you in such a short space of time. I have been so careful not to let anyone close. And I'm frightened that I'll eventually disappoint you too."

"You couldn't do that, Dante. I see you through different eyes than Chloe did."

"I'm not like Kelis though. She's butch, but she's not this butch." Dante ran her hand over her face. "She is also way younger than I am. I'm going to guess I'm the oldest woman you've... known."

"I'm not comparing you with Kelis because there's no competition. You win hands down on every level. And I don't care that you're older. Age is all relative. I just know I look at you and my heart skips a beat and I want to be with you all the time. And I really want to kiss you a lot." She grinned at Dante. "*Really* a lot. And I don't want to stop at just kissing. I want all of you, Dante. Every gorgeous butch inch of you that is strong and solid and the woman you are."

Dante unintentionally blurted out the thoughts that were growing louder by the second in her head. It was like she was trying to get everything out in the open so it didn't come back to haunt her later. "I don't like penetration." She cringed at Takira's blink of surprise. "I mean, I don't mind fingers, but I just can't... with a strap-on." She shook her head at the nervous rambling that tumbled from her mouth. *God, I used to be so smooth once. Where the hell did that Dante go?* "I can pack. I don't unless it's expected though. I mean, it's not something I'd wear to work because that wouldn't be the kind of hospitality I'd really want to convey to the customers." Dante grimaced as the words just kept falling from her mouth. Takira was smiling at her though so Dante rolled with it. "I'd happily use a strap-on with you...for you. If you like that kind of thing?" Takira nodded and Dante couldn't help herself smiling at the thought of doing that. "Cool. Yeah, I can do that for you. I just don't get any pleasure from it for myself." She shut up and shrugged.

Takira smiled at her faltering words. "I would never ask you to do anything you weren't comfortable with. I don't like being bitten. I am not a chew toy. You want something to bite, I can prepare you a steak. Do not come chewing on me and leaving hickeys all over me. They hurt and they are *not* attractive."

Dante nodded. "I'm not keen with biting either. This is good. Us, talking about this. It's usually some awful trial and error situation that just makes me uncomfortable not being able to express how I feel." She couldn't believe how easy it was to talk like this. To list sexual preferences as if they were just discussing their favorite flavor of ice cream. She nudged Takira gently. "What do you like most of all?"

"I like to be touched, stroked, and kissed all over. And I like to do the same in return. I'm so glad you're not stone because I want to map out your body with my hands and my lips and learn all the places that make you gasp out loud."

Dante swallowed hard at the images that conjured up. "We might want to use my bedroom seeing as it's the one farthest away from Finn's."

Takira chuckled softly. "Are you a screamer, Dante?"

"I'm just worried we'll disturb him." She gave Takira a look. "Are *you* a screamer, Takira?"

"I'm a moaner. If you get my engine running I'll purr all night for you."

Dante felt her insides clench at the thought of having Takira naked, under her, *all* night. She shifted in her seat so she could face her. "I like the sound of that."

"What's your favorite thing?" Takira shifted in her seat too. They were mere inches apart.

"Soft kisses on my neck, someone taking the time to get me excited and not just grabbing me and rubbing hard in the hopes it gets me off."

"I like to cuddle after. Sometimes I think that's my favorite thing of all. To be held and stroked, lavished with lots of butterfly kisses on my face as I fall asleep in your arms."

Dante didn't miss the use of a personal pronoun. *Your* arms. She felt her skin prickle, and the need to touch became harder to ignore. She watched Takira's mouth form her words as she continued. She couldn't stop her mind from wandering to where she'd like that mouth to be.

"I missed out on that with Kelis. When you fuck and run there's not much time for the niceties of savoring the moment after and holding someone near so you can hear their heartbeat. And we weren't like that, even when we were together. There was no romance at all. It makes me sad that's all I thought I deserved."

"Chloe pretty much put the Berlin Wall between us in bed. We had designated areas, complete with exclusion zones. I didn't get held much, and whenever I tried to hold her she'd brush me aside and cite one of the tens of reasons why I couldn't touch her at that precise moment in time. I got the message fast and yet still stayed. I guess that's all I thought I deserved too." Dante leaned forward just a fraction and pressed a soft kiss on Takira's nose. "But I like to cuddle too," she admitted quietly. "I've missed that simple intimacy."

"We're perfect for each other."

"I hope so."

"I *know* so."

"You know, I don't usually sleep with someone on a first date, but you're making it very hard for me to stick to my usual code of conduct."

"Can you make an exception? Just this once? Because I think we both need each other, and I'm fighting the urge here to pop every mouse stud on your shirt in quick succession and show you exactly how much I want you."

"Only you could make that sound sexy."

"What, popping your mouse eared buttons? Only you, my love, could wear them with such style." She leaned in for a tantalizingly brief kiss. "I like that you're not afraid to show what you love."

Dante made a self-deprecating sound. She was afraid of *everything*. Takira caught Dante's face in her hands and made her look at her.

"I know you're afraid of this, of *us*. I'm going to work very hard to prove to you that I love you for exactly who you are. Mickey Mouse ears and all." Takira tweaked one of Dante's studs. "We're going to be so good for each other."

"I promise that I'll always do my very best for you and Finn," Dante said.

"Oh, honey." Takira drew closer and rested their foreheads together. "You've done that from the very start."

CHAPTER NINETEEN

Takira had seen Dante's bedroom numerous times before. She'd never been inside it possessed with such urgency like what consumed her now. She tried desperately to temper the need to rip Dante's shirt off her. Dante gave her a knowing smirk.

"Don't even think about scattering these studs all across the room," she said, stepping back out of her reach. Dante started to pop each one open slowly and deliberately.

Takira stepped out of her heels, never taking her eyes off Dante as she rolled down her sleeves. It was maddening but totally turning her on. The shirt hung loose, tantalizing Takira with the brief flashes of flesh underneath.

Dante beckoned Takira forward and wrapped her arms around her. Takira felt safe and warm and loved. Her ardor calmed a little, and she relished the strength of Dante's arms around her, anchoring them together. Soft kisses rained down on Takira's face making her smile. Dante never forgot a thing.

"It's been a while since I've done this," Dante said, unfastening the buttons on Takira's shirt and letting it slip from her shoulders onto the floor. "Forgive me if I'm a little rusty."

"I'll nudge you in the right direction, never fear." She ran her fingers through Dante's short hair, tugging her down for a kiss. Dante tasted of chocolate and raspberries. Her mouth was soft at first, letting Takira take what she wanted. Then Dante's arms tightened around Takira's waist as she pulled her in closer. Their bare skin touched and Takira hummed her approval. She wanted more than just the brief touch of flesh; she wanted all of Dante all over her. They traded languid kisses while Takira pushed Dante's shirt down. It pooled around Dante's biceps until she reluctantly loosened her grip on Takira and shrugged the shirt off. Takira ran her hands over every inch of Dante's shoulders. She worshipped their breadth and squeezed Dante's muscles.

"God, why do you keep all this goodness hidden beneath your shirt and tie?" She couldn't touch her enough. Takira started undoing Dante's bra. She wanted more skin *now*.

"Because you run Takira's and not Hooters."

Takira snorted softly. She continued undressing her, desperate to rid them both of their clothes. Dante let her bra fall away and moaned as Takira's hands caressed her. She shuddered under Takira's ministrations, grabbing hold of Takira's waist tightly when Takira brushed her thumbs over Dante's taut nipples.

"So beautiful." Takira kissed her way down Dante's neck. She felt Dante's trembling intensify when Takira sucked a plump nipple into her mouth and ran her tongue over it roughly. She couldn't stop tasting her, Dante's scent was a heady aphrodisiac, and Takira was already addicted. She drew Dante's breast deeper into her mouth while she began slipping free the fastenings of Dante's button-fly jeans. As soon as she could get them off Dante's hips, she had a hand cupping one of Dante's butt cheeks. She squeezed the firm flesh.

Dante gasped. "Fuck, you're going to give me a heart attack." She lifted Takira's head away from her nipples and roughly kissed her. She fumbled with the front clasp on Takira's bra and snapped it open. Then she cupped Takira's breasts, rubbing her palms over her nipples until they firmed.

Takira's head rolled back as every brush of Dante's hand shot bolts of arousal straight through to her core. She loved how Dante held her firmly in her grasp, caressing just hard enough to be exciting but not hard enough to hurt. Takira knew how strong Dante was but loved how gentle she could be. Her nipples were tight and aching from Dante's attention. Dante lowered her head and flicked her tongue over the hard tips before sucking on one in a rhythm that made Takira moan out loud. She began unzipping her own jeans, desperate to be free of the constricting fabric.

"Get me out of these," she begged and Dante hastened to help. They both took off their jeans. Takira tugged on the waistband of Dante's boxer shorts. "What, no Mickey Mouse theme on these?"

"Having Mickey Mouse on your shorts isn't usually conducive to getting you laid." Dante gave her a wry look. Takira just smiled at her, looking her up and down in appreciation. Dante was all woman and she was about to be all *hers*.

"My sweet Dante, in or out of Mickey Mouse shorts, you are getting laid tonight and any other day or night you desire."

"I can change. I do happen to own a pair…"

"Another time, darling. Let's get you out of this charming basic black pair because they are in my way of you being totally naked, and I need some skin on skin action."

Dante stepped out of them.

Takira's eyes swept over her hungrily. "Oh yeah, you are *so* getting laid."

❖

Dante loved how sure of herself Takira was. There was no hesitation in her needs or wants. Dante found that refreshing. Her blatant appreciation of Dante, something she couldn't miss *or* dismiss, made Dante's heart lighten considerably. Her confidence boosted, Dante scooped Takira up into her arms bridal style. She loved the squeal that escaped Takira's lips and relished how Takira clung to her, eyes alight with happiness and arousal. Dante couldn't hold back any longer. She laid Takira down on her bed and crawled on top of her. Resting up on her elbows, she gently lowered herself so they were face-to-face. Her thigh slipped between Takira's. She shifted deliberately so it pressed against where Takira was the most swollen, hot, and wet.

"Do you know how beautiful you are?" Mesmerized by how pretty Takira looked with her eyes darkened with desire and her hair spread out across the pillow, Dante started to move. She pressed a kiss on Takira's parted lips. "Together this first time, watching each other's faces. Then I want to taste you." She ran her tongue around Takira's lips as Takira gasped and her hips rocked up to press against Dante's thigh.

They easily established a rhythm. Takira's thigh became slick with Dante's arousal, and Dante could feel how wet and needy Takira was. They clung together, both reluctant to separate their steadily growing hot and sweaty skin. Takira's blunt nails dug into Dante's back, her soft moans interspersed with words of encouragement and love. Dante felt like she was making love for the first time. It had never felt so right. She could feel Takira start to shake beneath her; her grip tightened as her breath began to catch.

"Oh God, you're making me come." Takira kept her eyes firmly on Dante. "Come with me."

"I'm right behind you," Dante said, feeling the pressure building on her clit as she rocked harder on Takira's thigh. "Let go, I've got you."

Takira's head dug into the pillow and her eyes closed. She let out a loud cry as she came. Her body jerked in Dante's tight hold as Dante pushed her through the aftershocks that wracked her body. The sight of Takira coming in her arms pushed Dante over the edge. She buried her face in Takira's neck and rode her roughly as her orgasm ripped through her. She swore she saw stars. She felt Takira kissing her, murmuring soft words as she eased Dante down to lie on top of her.

"I'm too heavy for you," Dante said, trying to move, but Takira wouldn't let her shift.

"No, I need you on me. You ground me. You make me feel safe." Takira wrapped her arms and legs around Dante and clung to her.

Dante snuggled in. She luxuriated in the softness of Takira's body beneath hers, and at the strength in Takira's hold as she cuddled Dante close. Dante breathed Takira's scent in. She ran her hand lazily down Takira's body and slipped in between her legs. She was soaked. Takira opened up even farther for her as Dante trailed her fingers through her slick folds and gathered up her wetness. In a moment of whimsy, Dante painted the shape of a heart on Takira's belly. She lazily traced every ruffle and tender spot while she wrote out words of love on Takira's flesh.

"I love you, Dante." Takira squeezed her tight in her arms. "I love you so damn much."

"I love you too. Can I show you?"

Takira spread her legs wider. "You can show me anything."

Dante slipped two fingers inside her gently and felt Takira welcome her in. She eased her way down Takira's body, intent on feasting on her. With her free hand, Dante stroked Takira's belly and tugged gently on her tight curls framing her sex. She pressed deeper inside Takira with her fingers while her thumb rubbed circles around Takira's clit. She felt Takira clench around her as she grew even more aroused. Takira had been right; she *did* purr when stroked the right way. Dante shifted even lower to run her tongue firmly over Takira's sex. Takira grabbed Dante's head and pressed her in closer.

Surrounded by Takira's scent, her arousal, and her swollen sex, Dante pressed her lips to Takira's clit and sucked on it gently, all the time pumping in and out and drawing soft cries from Takira. She quickened her pace and sucked a little harder and thrilled in the bucking of Takira's hips as she chased the orgasm Dante was determined to bring her. She lashed at Takira's clit with her tongue and heard Takira's voice break as she went still and then exploded. Takira rode her orgasm out on Dante's fingers, dancing to an unknown tune while Dante rested the flat of her tongue on Takira's clit and felt the pulsating climax ripple through her.

Takira fell back on the bed with a cry and shivered. She lifted her head up and shot Dante an accusing look.

"Rusty, my ass!" she said and lay back down with a huge smile.

Dante grinned, feeling pretty damn good about herself. She eased her fingers out of Takira carefully and laid kisses on Takira's quivering sex. Then she ran her tongue over the heart she'd drawn, tickling around Takira's belly button for good measure as she made her way back up to pull Takira into her arms. Takira draped herself all over Dante, still spasming and shaking.

"I knew you'd be able to fuck me senseless," Takira muttered into Dante's breast as she tried to catch her breath.

Dante stiffened as she felt Takira's fingers move between her legs and brush against her clit. It had been so long since someone had touched her. She closed her eyes and concentrated on every soft touch Takira made.

"When I can see again I want you to sit on my face," Takira said.

Dante knew Takira couldn't miss the way her body reacted to those words.

"You like the sound of that, eh?" Takira's fingers swirled through the moisture that gathered at Dante's core.

"I've had lovers sit on me, but I've never been the one to actually do it myself," Dante admitted.

Takira lifted her head up to stare at her. "*Really?*"

Dante nodded.

"Well, I guess you can teach an old dog new tricks." Her saucy smile made Dante laugh out loud, and she willingly gave herself over to anything Takira's heart desired.

CHAPTER TWENTY

It was barely six o'clock when Takira woke and had a moment of panic when she wasn't in her own room. She calmed down when she realized she was in Dante's bed with Dante sprawled out beside her. Takira remembered falling asleep with Dante spooning her from behind, her large hand against Takira's belly, holding her close. At some point during the night after they had worn themselves out, they had separated but still lay as close as they could be to each other. Takira leaned herself up on her elbow and stared at Dante's nakedness. She could feel her anger rise at how Chloe had disparaged Dante's looks. She was the epitome of a butch woman, built strong and square, with masculine features but an undeniable female form. Takira had kissed every inch of her last night, loving everything from the bluntness of her fingers to the added weight around her hips. Dante's shape turned Takira on like no other. She was strong, not from endless hours in the gym to sculpt the perfect body, but from experience.

Takira shuffled a little closer and studied Dante sleeping. Her face was relaxed and calm, her breathing slow and measured. In the morning light coming through a gap in the curtains, Dante's hair shone like silver. The same light cut a bright strip across Dante's chest, and Takira watched her breasts rise and fall with her slumber. She had to steel herself from touching Dante's belly, fear of waking her warred with the ache she had to just touch her again and never stop. Dante's legs were solid. Takira smiled as she remembered Dante's thighs wrapped around her head. A heated burst of desire melted her insides at the memory of Dante's arousal smearing her face as Dante had rode her lips and tongue. Her strong hands had gripped the headboard as Takira had taken her, wrenching noises from Dante that even she looked surprised at. So many years of abstinence. Takira was willing to help Dante consign them all to the past. She was too excellent a lover to waste, and Takira was not letting her go. Dante was hers, heart and soul, just as Takira was Dante's.

"What are you thinking about, sweetheart?" Dante's voice was rough with sleep. She stretched and shifted. Takira was entranced by how her body moved.

"How much I love you."

Dante opened her eyes and gave her a beautiful smile. "Wow, now that's the best way to wake up and greet the day."

Takira snuggled into Dante's chest and kissed her. "Good morning, sunshine."

"Good morning, love."

"I wish we could stay like this all day." Takira burrowed deeper into Dante's arms.

Dante shifted to look at the time. "We have an hour or so before I need to go get Finn since we're both working today."

"I need to have words with my manager about this poor state of events. I should have today off to lie around naked with my lover and make love to her until neither one of us can walk."

Dante grinned. She rubbed at her eyes and yawned. "Yeah, you already did that. I'll be lucky if I can get myself up off the mattress, let alone walk straight."

"Did I fuck you senseless, baby?" Takira crooned at her.

"Totally, but it was worth every minute. You're not just a master chef, you're hot stuff in the sheets too." Dante laughed when Takira swatted at her playfully.

"Well, you know the old saying, if you can't stand the heat…"

"Stay out of the kitchen," Dante dutifully finished. "No way, not now that I've found you."

"You must like playing with fire, Dante." Takira brushed her fingers through Dante's tousled hair.

"Like a moth to your flame, sweetheart. Speaking of fires, you need to douse that look in your eye because I need to be reasonably respectable when I go get Finn from his sleepover. I am not walking into Trent's house reeking of sex."

Takira made a big deal of getting off Dante and getting off the bed. "Come on then, let's go wash away the evidence of a night spent tangled among the sheets. My shower is bigger. We can save time and share." She wiggled her fingers to Dante to entice her up. "Want to test your Bambi legs in there, see if they can hold you up while I eat you out?"

"I can't be late and you're opening up today," Dante warned her.

"I'm a chef. I know all about preparation and timing." She pulled Dante to her feet. "Get moving before I phone Juliet to keep Finn, and then Eric to say we're sick."

"Don't make me have to dock your wages for skipping out on work." Dante followed Takira through the apartment, holding on to her hand.

"You're a hard taskmaster," Takira grumbled.

"I learned from the best." Dante pulled her to a halt and kissed her. "Now let me show you something I learned last night. Something about you and a particular spot I found that makes you purr like a pussy cat."

"I can't be late!" Takira mimicked her saucily.

"I'm a manager. Time management is my bitch."

Takira's heart soared at the newfound confidence in Dante's demeanor. A loved up Dante was a sight to behold. Happiness shone from her like rays off the sun. In quieter moments, though, Takira couldn't miss the unmistakable shadows of doubt and caution that still clouded Dante's features. Takira promised to not let those take hold. She'd never give Dante cause to doubt herself again. She was beautiful in her own magnificent way and Takira would spend a lifetime showing her that.

❖

After arriving at Trent's home a little later than planned, Dante bowed to Finn and Harley as they finished her impromptu tai chi lesson with them. Finn had been adamant they were doing their regular set and Harley was more than eager to have a go. Dante shooed them off to go play while she wandered back to join Trent who was sitting on the step of her back door.

"You do realize I'm probably going to have to take that up myself now to keep Harley entertained with it?" Trent said.

"She's really good. She learns incredibly quickly." Dante stretched and lifted her face toward the sun with a smile.

"There's something different about you today and I don't think it's the tai chi." Trent stared at her then exclaimed, "Oh my God, did you sleep with Takira?"

Dante's smile grew bigger when Trent held up her fist for a congratulatory fist bump.

"Way to go, Dante. I'm guessing by the self-satisfied look in your eye you smashed that long streak of celibacy to smithereens."

Dante nodded. "Smashed it and ground it to dust beneath my heel."

"Sooooo?" Trent asked. "Was it worth the wait?"

"God, yes." Dante kept her gaze out over the yard, watching the children playing in their pajamas.

"So, what happens now? Are we talking about a quick soaking to break your drought or are we talking something more serious here?"

Dante was quiet for a moment. "Something much more serious than I could have imagined. And it's pretty much been leading up to this from the moment I stepped into the restaurant and saw her. That damn ex of hers just made me realize how much I wanted Takira to be mine."

"The bitch who was going to hit Finn? She's fucking lucky she had you to deal with. I wouldn't have stopped at restraining her."

"She was fortunate that she left under her own steam because I would have cheerfully grabbed her by the seat of her pants and tossed her from the restaurant."

"So are you and Takira just going to date for now or what? Takira has a child. It's not just her you're taking on."

Dante nodded. "I know. But I kind of took him on the second he walked into that apartment looking so lost and scared." She nodded toward Finn as he spun himself around and around until he made himself dizzy and sat with a thump on the ground. Harley joined him, laughing at him. "Look at how he's grown. He's exploring every happy possibility he can grab. It's a joy to see."

"How do you feel about raising a child? Making him *yours*?"

Dante shook her head. "I could run through all the same excuses I have for why Takira and I shouldn't be together. I'm too old, I'm still sorting out my own life, he deserves better than me."

"Those excuses would mean nothing to him, even before you fell for Takira and there was a chance you two could be together. He's been yours from the start, Dante. You didn't have to look after him while Takira was sorting out childcare, but you did. You spend quality time with him. Just look at him."

Dante looked over to where Finn and Harley lay on a play mat pointing up at the clouds.

"He's yours whether or not you and Takira make a go of what's between you. He's already found a place in your heart. I know that heart, Dante. It's been hurt and battered, but it's still beating and it still knows how to love. He's proof of that."

"Having children never featured in my hopes and dreams, Trent. How can I raise a child?"

Trent leaned into her. "Well, you helped raise me and Elton when we needed guidance. You watched over me when I was hurting so much I thought alcohol was the only thing to ease the pain. You guided me, gave me pride in myself and how I look and act. You helped make me the butch I am today. You weren't my parent, but you treated me better than both of mine ever did. You're doing the same for Finn. And he doesn't care how old you are. You feed him, he gets to watch cartoons with you. He does tai chi with you in the morning before the world he lives in is awake. He's given unconditional love from you to be exactly who he is."

Trent rested her head against Dante's. "Yeah, I think you can raise a child just fine. He loves you, Dante."

"His aunt does too."

"Wow! Why the hell didn't you lead with that?" Trent threw her hand around Dante's shoulder and hugged her tight. "And you?"

"I told her I loved her too."

Trent's cheer rang out across the yard, and Harley's and Finn's heads turned to see what the noise was all about. Harley came running, Finn right on her heels. Trent caught Harley as she ran into her arms and onto her lap. Finn did the same to Dante.

"See? You've got this."

Dante kissed Finn's head and cuddled him close.

"Family," Trent said. "It's the only thing that matters and those of us who got dealt a crappy hand get to choose our own. You're a fan of fairy tales, Dante. Don't lose your happy ending just because you don't think you deserve one. You do. So just live it."

CHAPTER TWENTY-ONE

Body straining, heart pounding, Dante clung to the bed sheets in a desperate attempt to keep herself grounded. Having her hands occupied meant she couldn't pull on Takira's hair to guide her where she needed her to concentrate her sucking or press Takira's head more tightly between her legs. Takira had been very specific in saying she was in charge and Dante was just to lie back and enjoy it.

"Oh God," Dante moaned. She fought to catch her breath, but instead she let out a whine as Takira changed the direction of her tongue. Bursts of electricity shot to Dante's core, liquefying her. Takira deliberately ran her tongue over and around Dante's clit slower. It drove Dante insane. "There, like that, just like that. Harder, please."

She felt Takira's smile against her swollen flesh. Takira had two fingers slowly and gently stretching Dante open. No one had ever taken time to linger over foreplay with her before. Takira wasn't in any hurry; she was slow and meticulous, and she had built up Dante's need like a spark ready to ignite dry tinder into an inferno. The analogy fit all too well but Dante was too busy feeling Takira's fingers pressing inside her, sliding through her arousal and setting up a rhythm that bowed Dante's body to Takira's will. Her stomach clenched as she felt the pressure mounting inside her. With her free hand, Takira rolled Dante's nipple between her fingers, pulling and tugging.

Dante was nearing a sensory overload. Eyes shut tight, Dante let out a desperate plea, "Don't stop." Her body tensed, then exploded in pleasure. Dante was aware of Takira grabbing her thighs to keep her down on the bed. Her hold kept Dante at the mercy of her mouth, and Dante's second orgasm was sharper, harder and almost painful. She called out Takira's name harshly then collapsed, shaking. She managed to lift a shaky hand to gently tug at Takira's hair. "No more. I can already see fireworks."

White flashes met Dante's sight when she opened her eyes. She blinked rapidly, but the lights kept illuminating the room. The sound of thunder rumbled in the distance.

"When did it start thundering and lightning?" she asked, feeling boneless and wrecked. Dante felt Takira slip her fingers out from inside her, and she moaned at the loss. Takira licked random patterns through the juices that soaked Dante's thighs. She shifted from between Dante's legs and moved up the bed to pull Dante into her arms and hold her tight.

"We were preoccupied, but I think it's been going for a while. Sounds like it's getting closer."

Dante snuggled into Takira's breasts. "Where have you been all my life? If I'd have known making love with you could feel like this I'd never have left Columbia. I'd have sat on this empty lot waiting for you."

Takira kissed her. "You're such a romantic."

"You're a fantastic lover. Is there nothing you don't excel at?"

"Basketball."

Dante looked up at her. "That's oddly specific and decidedly random."

"I suck at sports. Latitia was a cheerleader though for the school's football team."

"Why doesn't that surprise me?"

"She was cozying up to all the football players and never found out I was under the bleachers with one of her fellow cheerleaders. I scored more than the team did."

Dante laughed. "I try not to remember school. It was a nightmare from beginning to end for me. Puberty hit and all the girls started wearing makeup, high heels, and short skirts. I, however, looked like a man in drag in the dresses my mother forced me to wear. You couldn't pay me enough to go back to that period in my life again."

Takira hugged her closer. "Dante?"

"Hmm?" Dante was starting to feel drowsy. Takira was tracing a finger over her Mickey Mouse tattoo, and it was strangely hypnotic. They'd been making love for hours, making the most of their uninterrupted time found only in the dead of night.

"Tell me something no one else knows about you."

"Like secret things?"

"Anything. Give me three things about you that you'd only share with me that I can keep safe in my heart."

Dante considered that for a moment. She rubbed her face against Takira's skin. Its softness soothed her. "I've never seen *Dumbo* the whole way through twice."

Takira looked down at her. "Really?"

Dante shrugged, a little embarrassed. "I can't get past the scene where they take him away from his mother as a baby and she cradles him through the bars of her cage in her trunk. It breaks my heart and I just can't watch it. I know the movie ends well, but it's that scene. It cuts my heart open."

She waited for the ridicule but none was forthcoming. Instead Takira kissed her sweetly.

"You're a tender hearted woman, Dante. I love that about you."

"Let's see what else." She grinned sheepishly. "I have a guilty pleasure no one knows about."

"I know full well about you and my coconut cakes."

"No, not those. The whole restaurant staff knows about me and those." She rolled her eyes at Takira. "I love watching those dance movies, the *Step Up* ones? I love the whole rags to riches, overcoming adversity stories they tell. I can't dance much myself, but I wish I could move like those kids. They're cheesy movies, but if there's one on TV I will usually stop and watch it. Besides, the first one had Jenna Dewan in it and she's a total babe."

"You've got some smooth moves all of your own, my love." Takira kissed her long and lingering. Dante almost forgot what they were talking about. She lost herself in the feel of each kiss as Takira tasted her.

"What's number three?" Takira whispered against Dante's lips.

She hesitated. Should she reveal this? Did she dare? She looked directly into Takira's eyes and saw no deception, just love shining back. *No turning back now, no more secrets. Time to trust again.* "When Kelis was here? Touching you, demanding your attention, commanding the room? All I could think was 'stay away from my family.'" She was tempted to close her eyes, to not see Takira's reaction to her admission.

The bright smile that blossomed on Takira's face made Dante's heart calm its frantic beat.

"Oh, my sweetheart. *Thank you.* Thank you for feeling that way even then." Takira's arms tightened around her. "That's when I had my epiphany too. I stood watching her laying down the law to me, and I wondered what I ever saw in her. I knew then and there I was in love with *you.*"

Dante held on to her tightly. She lifted Takira up and over onto her back. Takira laughed.

"I'm never going to get tired of how strong you are. The way you carried me in here earlier? Just swooped me up off the sofa into your arms, came and laid me on your bed and then fucked me senseless? Totally swoon worthy."

"I live to serve."

"Well, you'd better not be gearing up to start another round because—"

Another flash of lightning struck and lit up the room. The thunder followed right on its tail.

"That's right over us," Dante said.

They both heard Finn calling out for them. Dante scrambled for the T-shirt that Takira had ripped off her earlier. She was thankful it sounded like Finn was searching Takira's room first.

"You need to get dressed!" She tossed her T-shirt to Takira and almost fell out of bed trying to snag a hold of one that was waiting to go into the laundry. They both hurried to get decent.

Finn came running down the hallway to Dante's room. "Dante! Sky go boom!"

"That's thunder, Finn. You're okay. It's just a storm. It will go soon."

Finn rushed to her side of the bed and leaned against it, his arms up. Dante lifted him onto the bed, thankful Takira had seen fit to pull the sheet up over them.

"Aunt Kira?" Finn looked at her with a curious face at the sight of her in Dante's bed. "You frightened too?"

Takira nodded and pinched Dante under the sheet when Dante almost laughed. "Yes, the thunder was *very* loud."

Dante grinned at her. How the hell were they going to get out of this mess now? Thank God she had remembered Trent's teasing parting comment to her about always having clothes on hand because of little children having no compunction about running into a bedroom when folks were busy getting down and dirty.

Finn clambered over Dante's legs and settled in between them. They all sat leaning against the headboard in silence. Dante leaned forward a little to see Takira. "We look like the three wise monkeys sitting here."

Takira snorted and covered her eyes with her hands. Finn slid down the bed and rested his head on Dante's pillow.

"Go to sleep, Finn. Auntie Kira and I will keep you safe from the storm." He snuggled on top of the sheet and closed his eyes.

He held out a hand to Takira and one to Dante. They both held him safely between them.

"How do we explain it the next time he comes to find me in your bed?" Takira whispered.

"Bed bugs, a nightmare, maybe you needed a snuggle buddy?" Dante said. "How about you tell him the truth? That Dante loves Auntie Kira so very much and when you love someone like that you get to share a bed and steal sheets off them."

"Do you think he'll be all right with that?"

"Darling, he's two and a half years old. He'll just look at us and ask for a cookie."

Takira looked down at Finn already asleep between them. "So this is what family looks like."

Dante only had eyes for Takira. "Yeah, I think it is. How lucky are we?"

"Well, I would have gotten luckier if he hadn't come in right when you were ready to top me."

"*Top* you?"

Takira kept her face deliberately bland. Dante could see she was fighting not to smile.

"I may or may not have been listening to a few of the staff who think you are every lesbian's dreamboat."

Dante snorted, then checked that she hadn't disturbed Finn. "You're teasing me."

"No, there are a few women, gay and straight alike in that kitchen, who would kill to have even a fraction of the heady delights I have savored in your arms."

Dante stared at her. Takira wasn't kidding. "How am I supposed to work with them now knowing that?"

"By remembering that you're *my* dreamboat." Takira pulled Dante in for a kiss above Finn's head. "And you can top me anytime you wish…when I'm not topping *you*."

Dante whined a little when they pulled apart. "I hate storms," she said, listening to the thunder rumble above. Finn slept blissfully unaware of it all. "Think I can get him back in his bed?"

"Do you want to risk it?"

A particularly loud clap of thunder made Finn move in agitation. Resigned that the night was over, Dante shifted under the sheet to sleep.

"Stupid weather," she grumbled, but her heart wasn't in it.

Everything she loved was beside her safe and sound. She could hear Trent saying, "*See?*"

"If he starts snoring I'm going back to my room," Takira said, lying down too.

"Don't even think about it. If he stays, you stay."

"I'd take you with me."

"You've got yourself a deal."

CHAPTER TWENTY-TWO

Takira's was abuzz with people dressed in their party clothes, coming together to celebrate the arrival of little Natasha Juliet Simons and also the engagement of Scarlet and Bryce. Elton and Monica's daughter had entered the world a little earlier than expected but she was a beautiful baby sporting a fine wisp of jet black hair just like Monica's.

Takira was busy making sure everyone had drinks while also taking a moment to enjoy the party. She had been thrilled when Elton and Monica had asked to hire the new designated party area in the restaurant and then Scarlet and Bryce had booked the same to make it one big party with dual celebrations. It brought in extra money, and although it created extra work, Takira was proud of the long line of bookings the restaurant now garnered for celebrations. Especially among the gay community. She had Dante to thank for that. She had networks of old friends who spread the news like wildfire around Columbia.

Slowly but surely, Takira was rebuilding the cornerstone back under her business. It was going to take time, but she had a strong foundation in her staff, her reputation, her determination, and in a manager who excelled at her job.

Takira looked around the room and spotted Scarlet and Bryce. Scarlet was showing off her ring for the umpteenth time and they both looked so joyful and content. Takira's gaze unerringly found Dante next. She was talking with Elton and Monica and had Natasha cradled in her arms. The sight melted Takira's heart.

"Wow, tone down the heart eyes, boss," Zenya said, coming up behind her and following her gaze. "Man, she looks good holding a baby, doesn't she?"

Takira glared at her. "Do not get any ideas. We have Finn. He's more than enough to handle."

"But she looks so cute holding an itty bitty baby in her arms." Zenya bumped her gently. "Just sayin'."

"She looks even better holding me in her arms, just sayin'," Takira shot back.

Zenya burst out laughing and conceded the win to Takira. She looked around the busy restaurant. "We should have catered for parties before. They are a blast and the customers never stop drinking."

"We had to wait for Dante to come and use her organizational skills to pull them off without it affecting the rest of the restaurant."

"I hate to say it, but there's a part of me that's kind of glad Claude did what he did. We'd have never had Dante without his thieving ways and I think we're much better with her."

"Business has been booming with her managing. I don't know what I'd do without her."

"In or out of business."

Takira nodded. "In everything. God, how did I get so lucky, Zenya? I've managed to keep my business afloat after the debacle with Claude. Then Dante appears, and she just shoulders the whole lot as if she's Atlas holding up the world. And she just scooped me up into her arms too. *And* Finn. She's amazing."

"And sexy too in that new vest you had Monica sneakily make."

Takira loved how the new vest fit Dante's form. It was black with the familiar three circles mouse head dotted everywhere in white. Monica had done a tie out of the extra fabric, and Dante had been thrilled to pieces when Takira had handed it over. Today was its first outing, and Takira thought Dante cut quite the dashing figure in it. She'd expected Dante to consign it to date wear, but it was designated work attire the second Dante laid eyes on it.

"You love her, don't you?" Zenya said.

"With all I am."

Zenya went still beside her. "Hmm, Takira?"

"What?" Takira was too busy planning the undoing of Dante's tie nice and slow and putting it to much better uses.

"Is that your *mother* who's just walked through the door?"

Takira nearly gave herself whiplash turning so quickly. "Fuck! What is she doing here?"

"I don't know, but her face doesn't exactly look like it's here to make merry." Zenya took a step back to beat a hasty retreat. "I'll leave you to her."

"Coward!" Takira hissed after her. For a brief moment, Takira considered doing the same thing and just hiding. She hadn't seen her mother in months. She'd been busy with the restaurant, then busy carving out a life with Finn and Dante. Her mother had constantly come up with excuses for them not to go see her, and Takira had eventually taken the hint and stopped phoning. If her mother wasn't interested in either her or Finn, then Takira wasn't going to put herself in the position of not being welcome on her doorstep.

Takira took a deep breath and prepared herself for whatever had brought her mother to *her* doorstep.

Her mother looked less than happy that she had to work her way through a very busy restaurant. Takira met her halfway.

"Mother, what are you doing here?" She steered her out of the path of a server who was laden with plates. "Why didn't you call me? I could have come and picked you up."

"It was a spur-of-the-moment thing. I haven't seen you in months."

The accusatory tone was front and center. Takira decided to ignore it, as usual. "I've called you plenty of times, Mother. As you can see, I've been rather busy." She gestured around the restaurant.

"Is it always like this?" Her mother wasn't impressed.

Takira smiled. "Yes, thank goodness. This means business is going well."

"There's a lot of noise from over there." Her mother directed a censorious eye over to where Takira's friends were celebrating.

"I have two parties combined. One celebrating the arrival of a new baby into the family, and the other is an engagement party. They're not noisy at all."

"Well, I'm glad to see you're making a success at this."

Takira knew she didn't mean it but smiled all the same. She spotted Dante heading her way, unaware who she was with. Takira had no way of warning her.

"Hey, I've told Monica she can use the apartment for feeds. That's okay, isn't it?" Dante said, slipping behind the bar to set up some more drinks.

"That's no problem at all. Give her your key and then she can come and go when she pleases."

Her mother stared at Dante, looking her up and down with sharp eyes, judging her. "Do you work here, young man?"

Dante stiffened slightly but soon recovered. "I'm the manager of Takira's, ma'am." She shot a look in Takira's direction before asking, "May I get you a drink?"

"No. It doesn't look like I'm staying, not while Takira is obviously too busy to visit with me."

"I can make time for you, Mother." Takira saw Dante's eyebrows raise at that. "After all, it's been a while since we last caught up. But I am helping host two parties and run the restaurant so you'll have to forgive me for my divided attention. I wish you'd have called."

"Well, I have a life too. Not everything is done for *your* convenience."

Takira took a deep breath and tried to channel all the calmness she had seen Dante embody. It didn't help when her mother was still staring at Dante like she was something under a microscope.

Takira decided there was never going to be a better time to introduce them. She stilled Dante's movements and turned her around.

"Simone Lathan, I'd like you to meet Dante Groves."

"Yes, yes, your manager," her mother said.

"Also my partner."

Her mother frowned. "You sold half the business to him?"

"No, partner as in my *girlfriend.*" Takira watched her mother's face change as she digested that information.

"*This* is your girlfriend?" She shook her head and ignored the hand that Dante held out to her. "Are you serious?"

"*We* are. *Very* serious." Takira said, gearing herself up for a fight. She felt Dante shift beside her ready to shield her should the need arise.

"You might want to take this off the restaurant floor. Your office, perhaps?" Dante muttered.

Her mother wasn't budging. "You're with this *woman*? She looks a lot older than you and she has more gray hair than I do. What little hair she does have. She doesn't even look like a woman. She looks like a man dressed like that." She gave Dante a pitying look. "Do you want to be a man, is that it? I just don't understand it. I mean, I can see you're not pretty—"

"Mother, that's enough. Don't you dare speak to Dante like that." The sharpness in her voice startled her mother for a moment and she stared at Takira in surprise. Takira could see her friends looking over at them.

"I'm just saying, you could do better. Surely there are tons of pretty lesbians out there for you to choose from," her mother said dismissively, as always desperate for the last word.

Takira clung to Dante's arm, hoping that all she had fought back from to feel good about herself wasn't about to be ripped apart by her mother's comments. Dante didn't need someone else trying to break her down when she'd been working so hard to rebuild her confidence again. Takira hadn't missed the minute flinches Dante had tried so hard to suppress as every barb from Takira's mother hit home.

"Dante, is it? And what kind of odd name is that? I suppose it fits you."

Takira felt Dante's muscles tense beneath her hand. Dante's hand covered her own to stop her from lashing out as well.

"Hey! No! Grandma, play fair!" Finn's loud and clear voice startled them all. He pushed his way past her to stand in front of her, his finger pointing at her in admonishment. He looked furious.

"Phineas, don't you use that tone with me, young man." Her mother looked suitably shook at being chastised by one so small. "Is this how you're bringing him up? To shout at people?"

"Only when those he loves are threatened," Takira said.

Finn put his arms up so that Dante could lift him up into hers. He put his arm around Dante's neck and glared at his grandmother. "My Dante! You, stop being mean!"

Her mother huffed. "He's too young to understand. He thinks she's a man, some kind of bizarre father figure."

"No! Is my *mama*, not a daddy!"

The whole of the restaurant fell silent at Finn's voice. Takira saw Trent move away from the others, Elton following her as always and Bryce was right beside him. Backup was on its way. Dante would never be alone again.

Her mother's mouth hung open. Finn clung to Dante's neck and Takira clung to Dante's arm. She felt Dante steel herself as if preparing for battle. Before she did anything, Dante kissed Finn's head and whispered, "Thank you." Then she turned to Takira's mother.

"I understand I don't look like you expect a woman to look. I know that. I see myself in the mirror every day, and I know I'm not pretty and I know my girly curves got lost along the way somewhere." She looked over to where Trent stood. "A wise woman once said 'you look at me and think you know me and what I am. What you fail to see is I'm still a woman, one that looks different to you, but a woman nevertheless.' You may not approve of how I look, and that's okay. But I love your daughter and I love your grandson, and nothing you can say will change that. And how you *feel* about that won't change it. It will just change how we deal with *you*. We bring love and laughter and happiness into our family. I'd love to share that, share this family with you because Takira and Finn are all you have left now. You've already lost a daughter. Don't lose the other by dismissing her and her feelings and the family she has built for herself."

"How dare—"

"I dare because I have been dismissed all my life. By my own family and by people I thought cared for me. It took your daughter and your grandson to make me feel normal again. Because I am normal, as normal as you are. I just come differently packaged."

"You'll never be his mother," she blustered. "Neither of you will."

"I won't replace his mother. Latitia won't ever lose that distinction," Takira said. "I will always be his aunt by blood but a mother by my love for him. And he's already chosen Dante as his own. She's not taking Latitia's place either; she's created one all of her own. And if you see them together you'll see no amount of bigotry or ignorance will tear them apart. You gave me Finn to raise, Mother. *We're* doing that. He's legally mine now and maybe, one day," Takira looked at Dante with a hopeful heart, "maybe one day Dante will become legally *his*." She saw the joy of that sparkle in Dante's eyes. "So, how about we start this over again and you meet my girlfriend and kickass manager of this place and get to know her properly? Or you can leave. The choice is yours."

Her mother suddenly became aware she had a lot of accusatory eyes directed her way.

"Take the blinders off your eyes, lady," Mrs. Daniels said from a table nearby. "That Dante is a gorgeous hunk of woman, and your daughter is damn lucky to have her. She's hardworking, always polite, and she listens to an old lady ramble without rolling her eyes. She's a sweetheart. And if you don't want her, I'll snap her up in a heartbeat."

Takira fixed Mrs. Daniels with a look. "Am I going to have to keep an eye on you?"

Mrs. Daniels puffed out her chest and smoothed down her collar. "You'd better believe it, girl. You landed yourself a good one."

Holding tighter to Dante's arm, Takira nodded. "I know." She watched her mother trying to decide how best to get herself out of the predicament she found herself in.

"Phineas, come give your grandma a hug." She held out her arms to him.

Finn burrowed deeper into Dante's hold and ignored her. "Dante, go see the baby again? Natasha blows bubbles!"

Takira loved how many s's Finn managed to fit in Natasha's name. Takira rubbed at Dante's arm. "Why don't you two go back to the party and play with the baby some more. I'll get Mother a drink and we'll move our conversation somewhere a little less public." She could see everyone's eyes were still on them. Takira took Dante's face in her hands and kissed her, right there in the restaurant in front of staff and customers alike. She heard the cheers ring through the building.

"Welcome to Takira's," Dante said, grinning from ear to ear. "Where the food is amazing and the welcome is always hot!" She winked at the customers and laughed when Takira swatted at her and shooed her away. Finn was laughing too, and it made Takira's heart sing. If her mother wanted no part of this, then it was her loss. She watched Dante get pulled into the welcoming arms of Trent, then Elton got a hold of her, and one by one, their friends came and gathered Dante in among them. Finn was back with Harley whose little voice rang out with "Look! Is my Tasha!" as they clustered around Natasha who gurgled and blew raspberries at them, much to their squealing pleasure.

This is my family, Takira acknowledged, watching them all celebrating life.

"You've changed," her mother said quietly. "I supposed that's her fault too."

"No, Mother, this is who I've always been. You just never paid enough attention to me to see."

"I had to look after your sister."

"And I looked after myself. Now Dante looks after us all and I'm happy." *So happy.* She couldn't tear her eyes away from Dante who was now helping Zenya. They were making sure everyone got a slice of the special cake decorated in pink and black to celebrate Natasha's arrival. Another cake was on hand that was the engagement cake for Scarlet and Bryce.

"Yes, I can see you are."

Takira turned her attention back to her mother. She hadn't heard that tone from her for a long time. She sounded surprised. Takira decided to give her one last chance.

"Would you like a piece of cake?" She was amazed how polite she could be after what her mother had just done.

"Is it a slice of that peach thing your grandmother used to make with you?"

"It's one of my best sellers here, done to her exact recipe."

"Then yes. Thank you."

Takira slipped into the kitchen and cut two generous slices of the cake and gathered up forks. She wandered back into the restaurant and placed a plate in front of Mrs. Daniels, leaning down and giving her a kiss on the cheek. "Thank you."

"Don't you let Dante ever feel she's not worth it, child."

"I don't intend to. She means the world to me."

"And don't let your mother make you feel the same way either." Mrs. Daniels patted Takira's hand. "Go shake some manners into that woman. Get the stick out of her butt too while you're at it."

Takira laughed at the look of pure devilment in Mrs. Daniels's eyes as she dug into her cake with gusto.

"Hmm, just like my mama used to make. You do your grandma proud, Takira."

That praise gave Takira the courage to face her mother.

"You've got quite the business going on here," her mother said, looking around her and studiously ignoring the looks of distaste she was garnering.

"Yes, I do. And the best staff to help me run it." Takira caught Dante's ever watchful eye keeping track of her. She mouthed "I love you" to her and was thrilled how Dante's face creased into smiles and looked almost bashful. Dante mouthed back "I love you too" and then was laughing as Scarlet leaned into her, teasing her by making kissy faces.

Takira was proud to have the best staff and such marvelous friends in her life. She led her mother upstairs. She couldn't help but wonder what her mother would make of the fact that Dante's presence was now visible all over the apartment.

❖

Takira's mother looked around the apartment she'd only been in twice before. She drifted over to the large painting hung on the wall. It was Dante's prized limited edition piece *Fantasia* by Thomas Kinkade. The reprinted canvas re-created every brush stroke and bright color of the much more expensive original painting. Finn loved it and often sat looking at it as if it were a TV screen. Takira had begged Dante to hang it in the living room so they could all share it.

"I like this."

"It's Dante's." Her mother's astonished look didn't surprise Takira.

"She's got a good eye for artwork," she said begrudgingly.

"She loves her Disney." Takira caught her mother's gaze and held it. "She is the most beautiful woman I have ever laid eyes on. Inside and out. Don't judge her by what your eyes *tell* you to see, Mother. Her heart is full of wonders, just like this painting."

"Finn calls her mama."

"Apparently so." Takira had never heard him call Dante that before and had been as stunned as Dante had looked. It made Takira feel almost giddy that Dante was such a strong force in Finn's life that he saw her as a parent now.

"And she likes Disney, you say?"

"Yes, Mother."

"Your father loved those kind of movies too. I told him he was far too old for them, but he kept going with you girls anyway. I think he used you two as an excuse so he could see them. When you got older, he just took himself off to watch them. It kept him out of my hair while I did the housework." She gave Takira a pointed look. "He and this Dante of yours would probably have gotten along. In any case, he'd have liked to see you this happy."

Takira realized that was probably the closest her mother was going to get to apologizing or saying something remotely nice. "Eat your cake, then you and I will go back downstairs and we'll try again with the introductions. Dante deserves an apology, don't you think?"

"That woman of yours probably hates me already."

"Mother, if she hated you she'd have picked you up and tossed you out the door without breaking a sweat." Takira got a strange kind of satisfaction watching her mother pause in her eating when she realized Takira wasn't joking.

"She takes care of you?"

"In more ways than I ever knew I needed. I love her. She's the other half of my heart."

"Your father always said that family was what you made it."

"Well, we're making ours a good one the best way we can."

"I'm proud of you, Takira."

Takira reeled back at the softly spoken words. They shook her to her very core.

"What? I've said that before," her mother said brusquely.

"No, not ever. You've never said that to me for anything. Not even when I was a child and got straight As." Takira could only stare at her. She'd never expected to hear those words come from her mother's mouth.

Her mother looked suitably chagrined. "It's about time I said it then, isn't it?"

Takira nodded dumbly. "Why are you here, Mother? I've asked to see you for weeks now and you've brushed me off. What's made you come to me?"

She hesitated. "I realized that my grieving for Latitia was driving an even bigger wedge between us. I couldn't seem to stop it. I just wanted to be alone and let my anger grow. I came here and expected to see you grieving too, but instead I find you happy and smiling and Finn is doing perfectly well without me."

"I'm feeling her loss too, but I have a life of my own that doesn't just stop. I can't put everything on pause while I mourn. I have this business to run, I have Finn to raise, and I have a new woman in my life I want to be happy with. It sounds callous, but life goes on regardless. She was my twin. We didn't have the best relationship in the world, but I do miss her. But her son needs me to care for him, and my anger and sadness at her death won't help him heal." Takira looked her mother directly in the eye. "And he has his own problems."

She nodded. "I know. I couldn't tell your sister how to raise her own child. She wouldn't listen. You know what she was like."

Like mother like daughter. Takira pushed her anger at them both aside for her own peace of mind.

"Dante and I are making our own family with Finn. It's probably not what you want either, but he's happy and I won't let anyone take that away from him."

Her mother bristled for a moment at Takira's tone, but she didn't bite. Takira watched as her mother seemed to weigh her options.

"You are all I have left now, and I realize I have a lot to make up for. How about you give me a proper tour of this restaurant of yours? I'll see if Finn will even speak to me, and maybe I can redeem myself a little in your Dante's eyes."

"Why, Mother?" Takira just couldn't believe her mother would even care enough to bother. She never had before.

"Because that woman of yours is right. Life is too short and I've already lost so much. I can't lose you too. Or Finn. Besides, your father would be so disappointed in us if we didn't try."

"*I* tried, Mother."

"Now it's my turn. Be patient with me, I'm old and cranky." She gave Takira a tiny smile.

"You've always been cranky," Takira said bluntly. "It's your default setting."

"I'll admit it's not one of my better qualities."

"It's about your only quality," Takira muttered under her breath.

"Just sit me at a table and let me watch you in action. I've never done that before."

Takira eyed her skeptically but nodded. "Sure. I need to get back down there anyway. I'll find you the perfect spot to see Takira's in action."

She couldn't help but smirk to herself. She wondered if she could get away with seating her at Mrs. Daniels's table and letting Dante's "other woman" give her mother some long overdue home truths. It would be worth supplying Mrs. Daniels with free coffee for a month for that.

CHAPTER TWENTY-THREE

The familiar pattern of knocks on the door brought Takira's attention away from her monitor. Dante had made an appointment with her, and she was right on time as always. It still tickled Takira that Dante felt the need to schedule specific times for them to talk. She knew it was Dante being professional, but Takira was not above grabbing Dante by her tie some days and leading her into the office for a "discussion" when the need arose. Schedules and professionalism be damned.

"Come in, Dante." She couldn't hide her happiness when Dante walked in. Her smile grew even wider when she saw what Dante was carrying in with her. "Flowers usually mean date night. I love flowers with a promise." She waited while Dante placed the vase on her desk, then unwrapped the flowers and arranged them to look their best. Their subtle fragrance started to permeate the room. "How do you always manage to find flowers with the richest scents?" She inhaled deeper. "Beautiful, but nowhere near as intoxicating as the scent that drives me crazy." She gravitated closer because she just couldn't resist the pull Dante had on her. She rested her head on Dante's shoulder and breathed in the scent of her cologne. It was so uniquely Dante.

Dante turned the vase this way and that so that Takira would get the best effect of the flowers from her seat. Takira waited for her to finish and then slipped into Dante's arms and kissed her. Gentle at first then with increasing hunger because she'd missed her, missed doing *this*. Dante was addictive, and Takira wasn't about to let her go.

Dante held Takira closer still. "You know I'm actually here for a legitimate reason and haven't just come by to steal kisses from you."

"I can combine business and pleasure." Takira cupped the back of Dante's head to draw her back again. She loved the feel of the bristly hair against her palms. Their kisses were slow and drawn out. Dante nipped at Takira's bottom lip and then soothed it with her tongue. The moan that shuddered out of Takira caused them both to pause.

"Oh my God." Takira's breath caught. She could feel her insides turning molten. "I have never wished I had a sofa in here so damn much."

Dante chuckled. "As much as I would like to continue doing this, I do need to bring up some business with you."

Takira whined. She wasn't even ashamed of the pitiful sound that escaped her. "But business is so boring. This is so much more productive."

"Okay, who are you and where's the workaholic Takira I know and love?"

"You corrupted her. You and Finn with all your movie nights and play dates and making me enjoy time spent with you. I could have been a lonely workaholic, but no. You had to come along and save me from myself and show me a brighter future." She kissed Dante again. "A life with you and Finn and the endless catalogue of Disney/Pixar movies. Who knew they had so many?"

"Well, it looks good on you." Dante stepped out of Takira's arms and led her back behind her desk. She pulled out her chair for her. "Please, I need the desk between us. You're way too tempting when you're in reach."

"God, the things I could do to you on this desk." Takira licked her lips and thrilled to see Dante's gaze drawn to her every movement with an undisguised hunger in her eyes. "The things you could do to *me*."

Dante sat down with a thump on the seat opposite her. "Now I'm never going to be able to come in here and not see that." She rubbed at her eyes. "Nope, still there."

Takira laughed at her and sat back in her chair, enjoying the power she had over her. "So what's so important that you sent me an email again to set this time aside for a meeting?"

Dante took her phone out of her pocket and began scrolling after something. "I needed to show this to you in private."

Takira couldn't help herself. "You know the whole idea of sexting is that you have to send me the photos, not bring them to me?"

Dante's face reddened. "Will you please just…you drive me crazy, you know that, right?"

"Good. You could do with some crazy in your life."

Dante handed over her phone. "Recognize this person?"

Takira looked at the screen. "That's Claude. How did you get this?" It was a picture of Claude in handcuffs escorted by police. "What is this?"

"I may have contacted some of my friends in the business about his sticky fingers, and they may have passed the word on through the grapevine. I put out a tentative search in case this guy decided to try his luck again and took a job in another restaurant or bar. Zenya got me a photo of him to send out so I could warn my friends in as many places as I could reach."

"So *this* is what you've been conspiring about every time I saw you with your heads together and baked goods being exchanged?" Dante nodded with a sheepish look on her face. "And here I thought you were making sure I was making coconut cakes on a more regular basis because she's always adding the damn things to my list of to-dos every other day."

"Guilty as charged, I might have had a hand in that too," Dante said. "But this," she gestured to the phone, "this was a chance I took in case he surfaced in the waters I swim in. This photo was taken a few hours ago in Chicago. He handed in a résumé earlier this week, and someone who had his picture recognized him straight away. They took this shot of him leaving after his interview where he was met by Chicago's finest. They'll be in touch with the police here who have your case so you should probably expect a call from them."

Takira couldn't believe her eyes. Yes, it was Claude. His hair was a little longer, but she'd worked with him closely and knew him too well. She stared at the screen. "I can't believe that's him. I never thought I'd see him again."

Dante handed her a phone number. "If you want to call the Chicago police first then call them on this number. That's the guy who'll probably be handling your case. I can't guarantee you'll get the money back Claude took, but he's been stopped from doing it to someone else's business."

"You set all this up?" Takira kept staring at the phone in disbelief.

"I told you, I take my job seriously. He gives managers a bad name and...he hurt you and I couldn't stand for that. I had to do something. I had to at least try."

"How long has this been going on?"

"Pretty much from my first week here. He screwed you over and you didn't deserve that. I wasn't expecting anything to come of it, but I took the chance anyway. And it paid off."

"You really are something else, Dante Groves. You're nigh on indispensable."

"Just doing my job, Ms. Lathan." Dante held up a hand to stop Takira from getting up.

"What? You'd better believe I'm going to kiss the hell out of you for this." Takira brandished the phone. She sat down with a frown when Dante pointed her back to her seat.

"Just wait. You can ravish me in a moment."

"Don't think I won't hold you to that," Takira muttered.

"Before I leave you to make the call, I also want to give you this." Dante handed over a file.

Takira opened it. Her eyes widened in shock. "Fuck me!"

"Ohh, I really hope none of the staff chose that exact moment to pass by your door."

"You have a draft of a proposal here for a partnership between me and Mr. Tim York? Zoe's dad?"

"He'd like his name to be forever linked to the barbecue sauce, but he's more than happy to come and share the recipe with you. I didn't presume to work out a price. I figured you and Juliet could hash that out. The funny thing is, he's proud as hell to have his sauce in your restaurant. You two have a mutual admiration thing going on. You could have had his recipe sooner if you'd just asked him."

"I can't believe you did this." Takira read and reread the document that was a promise she could use York's sauce in the restaurant. She was stunned into silence.

"And I didn't have to sleep with him either." Dante gave her a smug smile. "I know it's spending out initially to buy his rights, but I believe this could build on your sales and you'd soon make back what you pay out for the recipe. Then maybe you'd consider having a barbecue weekend or a designated evening here at the restaurant? You could open up the garden area at the back of the building that's doing nothing, set up a barbecue pit, and make the most of the sunshine and your excellent food. Not everyone wants to sit inside when the weather is nice, and Tim's sauce on *your* spareribs would pull in a crowd."

Takira bit her lip to stop it from trembling. She was so close to bursting into tears at everything Dante had done for her and the business. "When did you talk to him about this?"

"I had a word one evening when he came to pick up Sam and Kayleigh after they babysat Finn. We talked over coffee and a piece of blackberry cheesecake while the girls bonded over sundaes and tried to stay relatively clean while Finn had one with them. Blackberry cheesecake is Tim's favorite too, by the way. It would be a nice gesture to have one on hand should you want to invite him here to discuss terms and treat him to something you do so well."

Takira let out a laugh through her tears. "You are something else, Dante. Whatever did I do without you?"

Dante just shrugged. "I told you I'd do my best for your business. Whatever you want, I'll do my damnedest to get it for you."

"And if I want you most of all?"

"You've already got me, babe. I'll just ask for your patience with me while I try my best to be worthy of you."

"Honey, you're already worthy and more besides." She skirted around her desk and sat in Dante's lap. "Thank you. Thank you for looking out for me and going above and beyond what I expect from you in your work." She cuddled in close and just held Dante tight. No one had ever worked so hard to do something solely for her benefit. It moved her beyond words.

"You're worth it," Dante said.

"So, any more surprises tucked away up your perfectly rolled up sleeves? Good news usually comes in threes." Takira wiped at her eyes, laughing at how happy she felt and how overwhelmed she was by all Dante had done for her.

"Well, the flowers do have an ulterior motive. I'm asking you for a date."

"Yes." Takira didn't hesitate for even a second.

Dante laughed. "Trent and Juliet have already said they'll babysit. Something about them having a 'threesome'? Which, once they'd stopped laughing at my face, turns out they are babysitting Natasha too so they figure the more the merrier."

"They are crazy tackling three children."

"Trent's in seventh heaven over it. Though she did ask for tai chi lessons from me in case it's more nerve-wracking than she expects."

"So, where are you taking me?"

"I'll see what I can come up with. It's hard when the best restaurant in town is out of bounds."

"I could—"

"You are not cooking for our date." Dante was firm. Takira found she really liked that tone from her. In the right setting, with low lighting, it made her *crave*. She saw the gleam in Dante's eye; she knew exactly how that tone turned Takira on.

"Okay. So you pick the place, and I'll just make sure that for the end of the evening you have some coconut cakes waiting for you back home." Her heart began to race at the light that lit up Dante's eyes.

"We could just stay home and indulge in my favorite treat."

"Am I going to always come in second to those damned things?" She pretended to pout.

"No, I think you have first place pretty much sewn up in my heart." Dante kissed her firmly and with a promise.

Takira could feel herself shaking. It made her hold on to Dante all the tighter. "You've carved that space out in my heart too."

"So yes to a date night and I'll still get cakes?" Dante yelped when Takira pinched her side. "Just checking." She rubbed her face against Takira's hair and sighed. "I need to get back. But first I need to go make myself presentable because I can't go out there looking like a love-sick puppy. I'll never hear the end of it. I don't anyway, but I don't want to give Zenya and Kae any more ammunition in their incessant teasing of me."

Takira cupped Dante's face in her hands. "You are a wonder, Dante Groves. And I am so glad you're mine."

"Heart and soul, always and forever."

"Unless Mrs. Daniels brings in her A-game and steals you from me." Takira eased herself out of Dante's lap, bopping Dante's nose at her daring to laugh. "I guess I'm going to call the police. God, what do I even say to them?"

"They'll know what to do. If you need me I'm just out in the restaurant."

"And if I always need you?" Takira made her voice drop a little. She smiled when Dante shivered.

"Then I'm right here for you." Dante stood. "Make the call. They got your guy. Help them screw his ass to the wall." Dante shut the door behind her.

Takira looked at the two pieces of paper in her possession. A police number and a partnership pending. "Dante, you always continue to surprise me." She picked up the phone and began dialing. "God, I love that woman."

❖

A few weeks later, blindfolded and steered by Takira's steady hands and Finn's infectious giggling, Dante let them lead the way. She'd had one of Takira's scarves wrapped around her face since she'd gotten in the car, so she had no idea where she was or what they intended to do with her.

"You were awfully amicable to the blindfold, honey. I'll have to remember that."

Takira's amused voice sounded close to Dante's ear. Dante tried to get some idea of where she was by sniffing at the air, but she got no hint of food so they weren't anywhere near a restaurant. They were still outside, but she could hear muffled music, and there were voices around her. Takira warned her of a step and then a door opened and the sound of voices assailed her ears. Dante could hear the clink of glasses and the music from a jukebox playing.

"Are we in a bar?" she asked.

"No peeking," Takira said.

"I can't see a thing through this scarf, I promise." And she couldn't. She'd been effectively blind to everything on the drive to wherever Takira had planned as their destination. All she knew was Takira had her hand on Dante's back and another on her arm as she guided her around obstacles and Finn had a tight grip on her other hand.

"Okay, now we're going down some steps. Count them out, Finn," Takira said.

They walked down them slowly.

"One, two, five, nine..." Finn sounded out.

Dante laughed. "How many steps we talking here?"

"Just a few more, "Takira promised.

Dante took a few more steps then stopped. There was a strange silence. It was almost *too* quiet. Takira slipped the scarf from her eyes, and Dante blinked in the bright lights.

"Happy birthday!"

She jumped at the loud voices as her vision cleared and she recognized she was in the not so secret anymore theater under Roller's bar. It was full of familiar faces who started up a loud and cheery rendition of "Happy Birthday to You" and then sent up three cheers for her. Dante couldn't believe her eyes.

"I thought I said no party," Dante whispered to Takira.

"This isn't a party. This is a trip to a movie and, oh look, so many of your friends just happen to be here too." Takira pretended to look surprised.

"You're incorrigible."

"It's your birthday. We are celebrating it because you are loved. Besides, I'm saving the trip to Disneyland for your fiftieth." She kissed Dante's cheek and pushed her forward. "Go say hi to your guests."

Finn's hand slipped from her grasp as he spotted where Harley was hanging with her mommies. Dante made her way through the crowd, saying hi to the staff of Gamerz Paradise that she'd gotten to know through Trent and Elton. Zoe, she knew through her father who was also in attendance with his wife. Dante was still riding high on the acquisition of his barbecue sauce. Takira had been *very* appreciative of Dante's dedication to the business. Dante's mind wandered just a fraction at the memory of just how well Takira had thanked her. She was so busy trying to remember just how many orgasms Takira had wrung from her before she'd cried uncle that she almost didn't hear Simone's birthday wishes. Dante dragged her mind back from being naked between the sheets with this woman's daughter.

Three seats stood empty in the middle of the rows designated for Dante, Takira, and Finn. Dante knew Finn would end up on a lap before long. Everyone settled into their seats once Dante had done the rounds.

"Are these the same seats we sat in when I brought you here for our date?" Dante asked Takira when she took her seat by her side.

"Yes, they are our seats now."

Finn sat on the other side of Takira and was trying to get into the bag he'd found on his seat. Everyone's seat had a goodie bag. He finally opened it and brought out a familiar Mouse shaped cookie. "I got treats!"

Dante held up her own bag. "I do too!"

Takira laughed at them both. "God, you two couldn't be more alike if you tried."

"We love the treats you make for us, don't we, Finn?

Finn nodded and took a bite. "Mommy makes the best treats."

Takira stiffened fractionally at the title she was still getting used to answering to. Finn had just started using it one day, the same as him calling Dante Mama. Dante believed he was marking out his family like he'd watched Harley do with hers. Harley had two mommies, and Finn knew he did too. Calling them by the new designations solidified their roles in his world. It would never take Latitia's place in his life away, but Takira had taken the role on and he recognized her for it.

Dante nudged Takira out of her musing. "Should I be worried your mother is here and sitting in the back row with Mrs. Daniels and Mama Simons?"

Takira snuck a peek over her shoulder in their vicinity. "Maybe their sweetness will rub off on her. I live in hope."

"She's been nice to me," Dante said, knowing that their introduction probably hadn't been the best of starts, but Simone had been trying to be more polite and understanding of Dante's place in her family.

"That's because you're just a big teddy bear and everyone loves you. Especially me." She leaned in to kiss Dante.

"Hey, if you're going to be doing that all through the movie you should be sitting on the back row." Scarlet leaned forward, her arms on the back of their seats.

"Like you and Bryce won't be sneaking kisses, Little Miss Engaged." Takira rubbed her finger over Scarlet's ornate engagement ring. "You need to finalize your wedding feast with me. I have it on good authority from my manager that you'll lead the way in setting a trend of brides-to-be having a wedding party at Takira's."

Scarlet nodded. "I've been handing out your leaflets in my gallery. And the fact you catered my last show gave us both a boost."

"That was a great experience, and I got a lot of new customers from it so thank you."

"That was a fun night," Dante said. "I love that photo of Finn, Harley, and Natasha you had displayed as soon as everyone walked in. And thank you again for letting us all have copies."

"That was a blast. Three little kids let loose in a photo studio, but they were fantastic letting me pose them and set the scene. And then we had ice cream afterward. I wish all my models were that easy to manage."

Roller and Petra served everyone drinks while they waited for the movie to start. Takira leaned into Dante who was looking around the small room at all the people who were there to celebrate her day.

"What are you thinking, honey? I can hear your brain ticking over, thinking deep thoughts."

"I was thinking that when I walked into your restaurant all I wanted was a meal and to stop still for a moment. I never expected to find love and a family on the menu. And all this." Dante gestured to all the people happily chatting among themselves. "Hands down, this has to be the best birthday I have ever had, and I can't wait to see what movie you've chosen for us to see."

"I think you'll like it."

"I'm sure I will." Dante settled into her seat, and Finn scrambled up onto her lap.

The lights flickered to warn everyone the movie was ready and then they went down. Dante squeezed Takira's hand. She grinned as soon as the movie started. *Mulan.* Dante kissed Takira in gratitude.

"I know how much you love that dragon," Takira said, snuggling in with her head on Dante's shoulder as they all settled in to watch.

Part way through the movie, Dante's eyes drifted to the people on her row. She could see Monica had lifted up the armrest and sprawled out on Elton's lap, fast asleep. No doubt catching up after dealing with a tiny baby all day. Elton was running his hand gently through her long hair while he chewed on three Twizzlers dangling from his mouth like spaghetti. Juliet was beside him. She held Natasha who was sporting a tiny set of baby headphones so that the noise from the movie didn't bother her. She was sucking greedily from her baby bottle. Harley sat on Trent's lap, totally engrossed in the movie, but her hand held on to Natasha's tiny foot. Trent's arm was around Juliet's shoulders, and she divided her time between watching the movie, making sure Harley was okay, and watching Juliet with the baby. Dante wondered if the smile Trent wore was her remembering Harley like that.

Finn was leaning back against Dante's chest, and they were trading bites from their respective cookies back and forth. Takira still held Dante's hand as she leaned into her, always close.

Dante had never expected this. She hadn't expected to wake up on her forty-eighth birthday to all of this. She wondered what would have happened if she hadn't returned to Columbia. If she'd never met her old friend who'd repaid the kindness Dante had shown her threefold. Dante had received a job, a love, and a family.

She looked down at Takira's hand in hers. They were so alike. Both had a strong work ethic. Both loved fiercely, deeply, and when it was right, with their whole hearts. Both had been hurt by past partners and uncaring parents. Dante knew most people looked at them and saw only their differences—color, age, physical appearance. She knew none of that mattered because their love grew *because* of all that. She looked at Takira and saw the woman she loved. She looked at Finn and saw a future. She looked at her friends, old and new, and saw family. Family that were sitting in a tiny little room watching a cartoon with her. It didn't get much better than this.

"I made you two birthday cakes," Takira whispered in Dante's ear. "One we're going to share with everyone here, but the other is at home. You have a very large coconut cake that has your name alone all over it."

Dante took it back. It *could* get better. She grinned at Takira and kissed her with all the love she could express considering where they were.

"I knew you loved me for my baking," Takira said, squeezing Dante's hand.

"For that and more, my love. I love you so much that I'll even share my cake with you."

"Now I know it's true love." She snuggled in closer to Dante's side.

"With every heartbeat, Takira."

She wrapped her free arm around Finn a little more and took a bite from the cookie he held over his shoulder to her. He had their goodie bags on each side of him and was helping himself from both while also feeding Dante. Crumbs were all over them, but Dante didn't care in the least. She had excellent food, a great movie, the best of company surrounding her, and the loves of her life cuddling her close.

For Dante, who'd felt out of place for so much of her life, that was just the icing on the cake.

The End

About the Author

Lesley Davis lives in the West Midlands of England. She is a die-hard science-fiction/fantasy fan in all its forms and an extremely passionate gamer. When her games controller is out of her grasp, Lesley can be found seated at her laptop, writing.

Her book *Dark Wings Descending* was a Lambda Literary award finalist for Best Lesbian Romance.

Visit her online at www.lesleydavisauthor.co.uk or on Twitter @author_lesley

Books Available from Bold Strokes Books

Accidental Prophet by Bud Gundy. Days after his grandmother dies, Drew Morten learns his true identity and finds himself racing against time to save civilization from the apocalypse. (978-1-63555-452-6)

Create a Life to Love by Erin Zak. When sixteen-year-old Beth shows up at her birth mother's door, three lives will change forever. (978-1-63555-425-0)

Daughter of No One by Sam Ledel. When their worlds are threatened, a princess and a village outcast must overcome their differences and embrace a budding attraction if they want to survive. (978-1-63555-427-4)

Fear of Falling by Georgia Beers. Singer Sophie James is ready to shake up her career, but her new manager, the gorgeous Dana Landon, has other ideas. (978-1-63555-443-4)

In Case You Forgot by Fredrick Smith and Chaz Lamar. Zaire and Kenny, two newly single, Black, queer, and socially aware men, start again—in love, career, and life—in the West Hollywood neighborhood of LA. (978-1-63555-493-9)

Playing with Fire by Lesley Davis. When Takira Lathan and Dante Groves meet at Takira's restaurant, love may find its way onto the menu. (978-1-63555-433-5)

Practice Makes Perfect by Carsen Taite. Meet law school friends Campbell, Abby, and Grace, law partners at Austin's premier boutique legal firm for young, hip entrepreneurs. Legal Affairs: one law firm, three best friends, three chances to fall in love. (978-1-63555-357-4)

The Last Seduction by Ronica Black. When you allow true love to elude you once and you desperately regret it, are you brave enough to grab it when it comes around again? (978-1-63555-211-9)

Wavering Convictions by Erin Dutton. After a traumatic event, Maggie has vowed to regain her strength and independence. So how can Ally be both the woman who makes her feel safe and a constant reminder of the person who took her security away? (978-1-63555-403-8)

A Bird of Sorrow by Shea Godfrey. As Darrius and her lover, Princess Jessa, gather their strength for the coming war, a mysterious spell will reveal the truth of an ancient love. (978-1-63555-009-2)

All the Worlds Between Us by Morgan Lee Miller. High school senior Quinn Hughes discovers that a broken friendship is actually a door propped open for an unexpected romance. (978-1-63555-457-1)

An Intimate Deception by CJ Birch. Flynn County Sheriff Elle Ashley has spent her adult life atoning for her wild youth, but when she finds her ex, Jessie, murdered two weeks before the small town's biggest social event, she comes face-to-face with her past and all her well-kept secrets. (978-1-63555-417-5)

Cash and the Sorority Girl by Ashley Bartlett. Cash Braddock doesn't want to deal with morality, drugs, or people. Unfortunately, she's going to have to. (978-1-63555-310-9)

Counting for Thunder by Phillip Irwin Cooper. A struggling actor returns to the Deep South to manage a family crisis, finds love, and ultimately his own voice as his mother is regaining hers for possibly the last time. (978-1-63555-450-2)

Falling by Kris Bryant. Falling in love isn't part of the plan, but will Shaylie Beck put her heart first and stick around, or tell the damaging truth? (978-1-63555-373-4)

Secrets in a Small Town by Nicole Stiling. Deputy Chief Mackenzie Blake has one mission: find the person harassing Savannah Castillo and her daughter before they cause real harm. (978-1-63555-436-6)

Stormy Seas by Ali Vali. The high-octane follow-up to the best-selling action-romance, *Blue Skies*. (978-1-63555-299-7)

The Road to Madison by Elle Spencer. Can two women who fell in love as girls overcome the hurt caused by the father who tore them apart? (978-1-63555-421-2)

Dangerous Curves by Larkin Rose. When love waits at the finish line, dangerous curves are a risk worth taking. (978-1-63555-353-6)

Love to the Rescue by Radclyffe. Can two people who share a past really be strangers? (978-1-62639-973-0)

Love's Portrait by Anna Larner. When museum curator Molly Goode and benefactor Georgina Wright uncover a portrait's secret, public and private truths are exposed, and their deepening love hangs in the balance. (978-1-63555-057-3)

Model Behavior by MJ Williamz. Can one woman's instability shatter a new couple's dreams of happiness? (978-1-63555-379-6)

Pretending in Paradise by M. Ullrich. When travelwisdom.com assigns PR specialist Caroline Beckett and travel blogger Emma Morgan to cover a hot new couples retreat, they're forced to fake a relationship to secure a reservation. (978-1-63555-399-4)

Recipe for Love by Aurora Rey. Hannah Little doesn't have much use for fancy chefs or fancy restaurants, but when New York City chef Drew Davis comes to town, their attraction just might be a recipe for love. (978-1-63555-367-3)

Survivor's Guilt and Other Stories by Greg Herren. Award-winning author Greg Herren's short stories are finally pulled together into a single collection, including the Macavity Award nominated title story and the first-ever Chanse MacLeod short story. (978-1-63555-413-7)

The House by Eden Darry. After a vicious assault, Sadie, Fin, and their family retreat to a house they think is the perfect place to start over, until they realize not all is as it seems. (978-1-63555-395-6)

Uninvited by Jane C. Esther. When Aerin McLeary's body becomes host for an alien intent on invading Earth, she must work with researcher Olivia Ando to uncover the truth and save humankind. (978-1-63555-282-9)

Comrade Cowgirl by Yolanda Wallace. When cattle rancher Laramie Bowman accepts a lucrative job offer far from home, will her heart end up getting lost in translation? (978-1-63555-375-8)

Double Vision by Ellie Hart. When her cell phone rings, Giselle Cutler answers it—and finds herself speaking to a dead woman. (978-1-63555-385-7)

Inheritors of Chaos by Barbara Ann Wright. As factions splinter and reunite, will anyone survive the final showdown between gods and mortals on an alien world? (978-1-63555-294-2)

Love on Lavender Lane by Karis Walsh. Accompanied by the buzz of honeybees and the scent of lavender, Paige and Kassidy must find a way to compromise on their approach to business if they want to save Lavender Lane Farm—and find a way to make room for love along the way. (978-1-63555-286-7)

Spinning Tales by Brey Willows. When the fairy tale begins to unravel and villains are on the loose, will Maggie and Kody be able to spin a new tale? (978-1-63555-314-7)

The Do-Over by Georgia Beers. Bella Hunt has made a good life for herself and put the past behind her. But when the bane of her high school existence shows up for Bella's class on conflict resolution, the last thing they expect is to fall in love. (978-1-63555-393-2)

What Happens When by Samantha Boyette. For Molly Kennan, senior year is already an epic disaster, and falling for mysterious waitress Zia is about to make life a whole lot worse. (978-1-63555-408-3)

Wooing the Farmer by Jenny Frame. When fiercely independent modern socialite Penelope Huntingdon-Stewart and traditional country farmer Sam McQuade meet, trusting their hearts is harder than it looks. (978-1-63555-381-9)

A Chapter on Love by Laney Webber. When Jannika and Lee reunite, their instant connection feels like a gift, but neither is ready for a second chance at love. Will they finally get on the same page when it comes to love? (978-1-63555-366-6)

Drawing Down the Mist by Sheri Lewis Wohl. Everyone thinks Grand Duchess Maria Romanova died in 1918. They were almost right. (978-1-63555-341-3)

Listen by Kris Bryant. Lily Croft is inexplicably drawn to Hope D'Marco but will she have the courage to confront the consequences of her past and present colliding? (978-1-63555-318-5)

Perfect Partners by Maggie Cummings. Elite police dog trainer Sara Wright has no intention of falling in love with a coworker, until Isabel Marquez arrives at Homeland Security's Northeast Regional Training facility and Sara's good intentions start to falter. (978-1-63555-363-5)

Shut Up and Kiss Me by Julie Cannon. What better way to spend two weeks of hell in paradise than in the company of a hot, sexy woman? (978-1-63555-343-7)

Spencer's Cove by Missouri Vaun. When Foster Owen and Abigail Spencer meet they uncover a story of lives adrift, loves lost, and true love found. (978-1-63555-171-6)

Without Pretense by TJ Thomas. After living for decades hiding from the truth, can Ava learn to trust Bianca with her secrets and her heart? (978-1-63555-173-0)

Unexpected Lightning by Cass Sellars. Lightning strikes once more when Sydney and Parker fight a dangerous stranger who threatens the peace they both desperately want. (978-1-163555-276-8)

9 781635 554335